Praise for *War with the Newts* and Karel Čapek:

A bracing parody of totalitarianism and technological overkill, one of the most amusing and provocative books in its genre.

—Philadelphia Inquirer

[This] depiction of man's propensity to bring environmental disaster on himself through pure technological hubris . . . brilliantly illustrates the danger of our untempered search for "solutions" to nature.

—Chicago Tribune

A sendup of multiple early-20th-century isms.

—Washington Post Bk. World

Issued in a new, vibrant translation, this immensely entertaining novel has lost none of its relevance and spark.

—Library Journal

Karel Čapek (1890-1938; CHOP-ek) was Czechoslovakia's leading novelist, playwright, story writer, columnist, and critic during the first twenty years after the founding of the nation in 1918. He was the inventor of the literary robot in *R.U.R. (Rossum's Universal Robots),* as well as a writer of delightful detective stories, humorous columns, and a great philosophical trilogy of novels *(Three Novels).* But of all his work, *War with the Newts* has continued to warn and entertain the most readers around the world.

Other Books by Karel Čapek
from Catbird Press

Toward the Radical Center: A Karel Čapek Reader
edited by Peter Kussi, foreword by Arthur Miller

Apocryphal Tales
translated by Norma Comrada

Tales from Two Pockets
translated by Norma Comrada

Talks with T. G. Masaryk
translated by Michael Henry Heim

Three Novels
translated by M. & R. Weatherall

War with the Newts

by Karel Čapek

A New Translation from the Czech
by Ewald Osers

Catbird Press/UNESCO Publishing
A Garrigue Book

UNESCO Collection of Representative Works
UNESCO ISBN 92-3-103599-1

Original Title: Válka s mloky

Catbird Press, 16 Windsor Road, North Haven, CT 06473-3015
800-360-2391, catbird@pipeline.com, www.catbirdpress.com

Library of Congress Cataloging-in-Publication Data

Čapek, Karel, 1890-1938
[Válka s mloky. English]
War with the newts / Karel Čapek
translated from the Czech by Ewald Osers.
"A Garrigue book."
ISBN 0-945774-10-9 (pbk.)
PG5038.C3V33 1990
891.8'635--dc20   89-25373 CIP

Contents

BOOK ONE

Andrias Scheuchzeri

1

The Eccentricity of Captain van Toch

If you were to look for the little island of Tana Masa on a map you would find it right on the equator slightly to the west of Sumatra. But if you asked Captain J. van Toch of the *Kandong Bandoeng* what kind of place this Tana Masa was, the place off which he had just dropped anchor, he would curse for a while and then he would tell you that it was the filthiest hole in all the Sunda Islands, even more miserable than Tana Bala and at least as lousy a place as Pini or Banjak; that the only, if you'll excuse me, human being living there – disregarding, of course, those lousy Bataks – was a drunken agent, a cross between a Cuban and a Portuguese and an even greater thief, heathen and swine than a pure-bred Cuban and a pure-bred white man combined; and if there was something really lousy in this world then it was this lousy life on this lousy Tana Masa, yessir. Whereupon you might cautiously inquire why in that case he had dropped his lousy anchor, just as if he was going to stop here for three lousy days, he'd just snort irritably and mutter something to the effect that the *Kandong Bandoeng* would not have sailed here just for some lousy copra or palm oil, stands to reason, doesn't it?, and anyway what business is it of yours, sir?, but I've got my damned orders, sir, and will you kindly mind your own damned business. And he'd curse as richly and colourfully as you'd expect from a sea captain who was getting on a bit but was still in good shape for his years.

But if instead of asking such nosy questions you left Captain van Toch to grumble and curse to himself you'd probably learn a lot more. Can't you see that he needs to let off steam? Just let him be and his irritability will simmer down on its own. 'It's like this, sir,' the captain would burst out, 'those fellows back home in Amsterdam, those damned Jews at the top, suddenly say to you: pearls, that's what it is about, my man, you look out for pearls. People apparently go nuts over pearls and suchlike.' Here the captain expectorated angrily. 'Sure thing, put your money into pearls! That's because you people are always wanting to have wars or suchlike. Worried about your money, that's what it is. What's called a crisis, yessir.' Captain van Toch hesitated for a moment as to whether to embark on a discourse of the economy with you; after all, nobody talked about anything else these days. Except that out here, off Tana Masa, it's a little too hot and enervating for that. So Captain van Toch just waved his hand and grumbled: 'Easily said: pearls! In Ceylon, sir, they cleared them clean out five years ago and in Formosa they've put a ban on pearl-fishing. – Why then, Captain van Toch, you'd better find some new fishing grounds. You just sail to those damned little islands, for all you know you may find whole banks of shells there – .' The captain contemptuously blew his nose into a sky-blue handkerchief. 'Those rats back in Europe imagine you can still find something here that nobody else knows about! Christ Almighty, those nitwits! For two pins they'd have made me peer up the snouts of those Bataks in case they snot up pearls! New fishing grounds, my arse! There's a new brothel in Padang, for sure, but new pearl-fishing grounds? Why sir, I know these islands here like the back of my hand . . . all the way from Ceylon to that lousy Clipperton Island . . . If anyone thinks he can find something here to make money out of, well, good luck to him! I've been sailing these waters for thirty years and now those idiots want me to discover something new here!' Captain van Toch almost choked under this insulting demand. 'Why don't they send out some greenhorn, he'd discover things for them enough to make their eyes pop – but to expect Captain van Toch . . . well, sir, I ask you! In Europe you might still find something or other, but here? Surely people come down here only to sniff around for something they can guzzle up, or not even guzzle up, for something to buy and sell. Why sir, if there was anything left in these lousy tropics that was worth a brass farthing you'd find three agents standing over it and waving a dirty handkerchief to ships of seven nationalities to heave to. That's how it is, sir. I know these parts better than Her Majesty's Colonial Office, if you'll pardon me.' With an effort

Captain van Toch struggled with his righteous indignation and after some further storming managed to master it. 'See that pair of lazy bastards there? Those are pearl fishers from Ceylon, may God forgive me, Singhalese as the Lord made them – though why he should have done so beats me. That's what I carry now, sir, and wherever I come across a stretch of coastline that hasn't got a notice Agency or Bata Corporation or Customs Office I drop that lot into the water to rout out shells. That shorter rascal can dive to a depth of forty fathoms; over there on Princes Island he came up from forty-five fathoms with the handle of a film camera, yessir, but as for pearls – nope! Not a trace! Useless scoundrels, those Singhalese. That's the kind of lousy job I've got, sir: making out I'm buying palm oil and all the time searching for new pearl-fishing grounds. Next thing they'll expect me to do is discover some virgin continent, what? That's no job for the honest master of a merchantman, no sir. J. van Toch's not one of your damned adventurers, sir. No sir.' And so on; the sea is vast and the ocean of time is boundless: spit into it and it won't rise, or rant at your fate but you won't change it; and so, after many preliminaries and diversions, we've at last reached the point where Captain J. van Toch of the Dutch ship *Kandong Bandoeng* with a deep sigh and a curse climbs down into a boat to step ashore at the kampong on Tana Masa, in order to discuss a few business matters with the drunken cross between a Cuban and a Portuguese.

'Sorry, Captain,' finally said the cross between a Cuban and a Portuguese, 'but there are no pearl-oysters here on Tana Masa. Those filthy Bataks,' he said with infinite loathing, 'will even eat jellyfish, they're more at home in the water than on dry land, the women here stink of fish, you've no idea – what was I going to say? Ah yes, you were asking about the women.'

'And isn't there any stretch of shore,' the captain inquired, 'where those Bataks don't get into the water?'

The cross between a Cuban and a Portuguese shook his head. 'None, sir. Except of course Devil Bay, but that's no use to you.'

'Why not?'

'Because . . . no one's allowed there, sir. Top you up, Captain?'

'Thanks. Are there any sharks there?'

'Sharks and other things,' the half-breed muttered. 'It's a bad spot, sir. The Bataks wouldn't like to see anyone going there.'

'Why not?'

'There are devils there, sir. Sea devils.'

'What's a sea devil? A fish?'

'Not a fish,' the half-breed countered evasively. 'Simply a devil, sir. A deep-sea devil. The Bataks call them *tapa*. *Tapa*. They're said to have their town down there, those devils. Top you up?'

'And what does . . . this sea devil look like?'

The cross between a Cuban and a Portuguese shrugged. 'Like a devil, sir. I saw one once – that is, only his head. I was in my boat coming back from Cape Haarlem . . . and suddenly it pushed its ugly mug out of the water right in front of me.'

'Well? And what did it look like?'

'It's got a pate . . . like a Batak, sir, but bald as a coot.'

'You sure it wasn't a Batak?'

'Quite sure, sir. No Batak would ever go into the water at that spot. Besides . . . it blinked at me with its *lower lids*, sir.' The half-breed shivered with horror. 'With its lower lids which came up right over its eyes. That's a *tapa*.'

Captain J. van Toch twisted his glass of palm wine between his fleshy fingers. 'Sure you weren't drunk, eh? You weren't sloshed?'

'Of course I was, sir. Otherwise I wouldn't have rowed out there. The Bataks don't like people to . . . to disturb the devils.'

Captain van Toch shook his head. 'Come on, man, no such thing as devils. And if there were they'd look like Europeans. Probably was some fish or something.'

'A fish,' the cross between a Cuban and a Portuguese stammered, 'a fish hasn't got any hands, sir. I'm not a Batak, sir, I went to school in Badjoeng . . . perhaps I can still recite the Ten Commandments and other scientifically proved doctrines; an educated person can tell the difference between a devil and an animal. You ask the Bataks, sir.'

'Nigger superstitions, man,' the captain declared with the jovial superiority of the educated. 'Scientifically it's nonsense. Surely a devil can't live in water. What would he be doing there? Shouldn't listen to natives' gossip, man. Somebody called the bay Devil Bay and the Bataks have been afraid of it ever since. That's the long and the short of it,' said the captain, bringing his massive palm down on the table. 'There's nothing there, man; that's scientifically evident, isn't it?'

'Yes, sir,' agreed the half-breed who had been to school in Badjoeng. 'But no man in his right senses has any business in Devil Bay.'

Captain J. van Toch turned florid. 'What?' he shouted. 'You filthy Cuban, you think I'm scared of your devils? We'll see about that,' he said, rising to the full majesty of his ample fourteen stone. 'I'm not wasting my time here with you when I have business to attend to. But remember one thing: there are no devils in the Dutch colonies; if there are any at all, then they are in the French colonies. Yes, there might well be some there. And now get me the mayor of this lousy kampong.'

The dignitary referred to was not too difficult to find: he was squatting next to the half-breed's shop, chewing sugar cane. He was a naked elderly gentleman, and a lot thinner than mayors as a rule come in Europe. A short way behind him, keeping an appropriate distance, squatted the entire village, complete with women and children, evidently in expectation of being filmed.

'Now listen to me, man,' Captain van Toch addressed him in Malay (he might equally well have addressed him in Dutch or in English since the venerable old Batak did not understand a word of Malay and the whole of the captain's speech had to be interpreted into the Batak dialect by the cross between a Cuban and a Portuguese; but for some reason or other the captain regarded the Malay language as more suitable). 'Now listen to me, man, I need a few big strong brave fellows to go hunting with me. Understand? Hunting.'

The half-breed translated and the mayor nodded his head to indicate he understood. He thereupon turned to his wider audience and delivered a speech to them with obvious success.

'The chief says,' the half-breed interpreted, 'that the whole village will go hunting with the tuan captain, where the tuan wishes.'

'There you are. You tell them we'll go shell-fishing in Devil Bay.'

There followed about a quarter of an hour of excited discussion, with the whole village taking part, especially the old women. Eventually the half-breed turned to the captain. 'They're saying, sir, one can't go to Devil Bay.'

The captain grew red in the face. 'And why not?'

The half-breed shrugged his shoulders. 'Because of the tapatapa there. The devils, sir.'

The captain's face was beginning to turn puce. 'Tell them if they won't come . . . I'll knock all their teeth in . . . I'll tear their ears off . . . I'll hang them . . . and that I'll burn their lousy kampong down, d'you understand?'

The half-breed translated faithfully, whereupon another lively consultation took place. In the end the half-breed turned to the captain. 'They're saying, sir, they'll go and complain to the police in Padang that the tuan has threatened them. There are laws about this. The mayor says he won't leave it at that.'

Captain J. van Toch began to turn blue. 'Tell him then,' he roared, 'that he is . . .' And he spoke for a good eleven minutes without drawing breath.

The half-breed translated as much as his vocabulary permitted, and after another prolonged but businesslike consultation among the Bataks he interpreted to the captain: 'They're saying, sir, that they might be willing to drop legal proceedings if the tuan captain paid a fine to the local authorities. They say,' here he hesitated, '200 rupees; but that's a bit steep, sir. Why not offer them five.'

Captain van Toch's colour began to break up into russet blotches. At first he offered to massacre all Bataks the world over, then he came down to 300 kicks, and finally he would have settled for stuffing the mayor for the Colonial Museum in Amsterdam. The Bataks on their part came down from 200 rupees to one iron pump with a wheel and in the end insisted that the captain should, by way of a fine, give the mayor a petrol cigarette lighter. ('Give it to them, sir,' the cross between a Cuban and a Portuguese pleaded, 'I've got three lighters in stock but they've got no wick.') Thus peace was restored on Tana Masa but Captain J. van Toch realised that the honour of the white race was now at stake.

In the afternoon a boat put off from the Dutch ship *Kandong Bandoeng*: it contained, more particularly, Captain van Toch, a Swede called Jensen, an Icelander called Gudmunson, a Finn called Gillemainen and two Singhalese pearl-fishers. The boat made straight for Devil Bay.

At three o'clock, just as the low tide was turning, the captain was standing on the beach, the boat was bobbing up and down about a hundred yards offshore to keep a look-out for sharks, and the two Singhalese divers, each with a knife in hand, were waiting for the signal to jump into the water.

'OK, you first,' the captain ordered the taller one of the naked figures. The Singhalese jumped in, waded a few steps and disappeared under the surface. The captain glanced at his watch.

Four minutes and twenty seconds later a brown head broke surface some sixty yards to the left; in a curiously desperate and at the same time paralysed rush the Singhalese scrambled up on the rocks, in one hand his knife for cutting the shells loose and in the other a pearl-oyster.

The captain scowled. 'What's the matter?' he said sharply.

The Singhalese was still climbing over the boulders, gasping noisily with fright.

'What's up?' yelled the captain.

'Sahib, sahib,' the Singhalese managed to utter, sinking down on the shore and letting his breath out in gasps. 'Sahib . . . sahib . . .'

'Sharks?'

'Djins,' the Singhalese moaned. 'Devils, sir. Thousands and thousands of devils!' He dug his fists into his eyes. 'Nothing but devils, sir!'

'Let's see that shell,' the captain ordered. He opened it with a knife. It contained a small clear pearl. 'This is all you found?'

The Singhalese took out three more shells from the bag slung around his neck. 'There are shells there all right, sir, but those devils are guarding them . . . They were looking at me as I cut them loose . . .' His straggly hair bristled in horror. 'Not at this spot, sahib!'

The captain opened the shells; two were empty but the third contained a pearl the size of a pea, as round as a drop of mercury. Captain van Toch studied in turn the pearl and the Singhalese who was crouching in a heap on the ground.

'You, boy,' he said hesitantly, 'you wouldn't like to go down there once more?'

The Singhalese shook his head speechlessly.

Captain van Toch felt a strong itch on his tongue to blaspheme. But to his surprise he found that he was talking quietly and almost gently: 'Don't be afraid, boy. And what do those . . . devils . . . look like?'

'Like little children,' the Singhalese breathed. 'They've got a tail and they are this tall,' and he indicated about four feet from the ground. 'They stood all around me and watched what I was doing there . . . there was a whole ring of them around me . . .' The Singhalese began to tremble. 'Sahib! Not here, sahib!'

Captain van Toch reflected. 'And tell me, do they blink their lower lids, or what?'

'I don't know, sir,' the Singhalese croaked. 'There's . . . ten thousands of them there!'

The captain looked round for the other Singhalese. He was standing some 150 yards off, casually waiting with his arms folded over his shoulders. It is true, of course, that when a chap is naked he's got nowhere to put his hands except on his own shoulders. The captain made a silent signal to him and the short Singhalese jumped into the water. Three minutes and fifty seconds later he emerged again and with slippery hands slithered up the rocks.

'Well, get out then,' the captain shouted. But then he looked more closely and already he was leaping over the boulders towards those desperately groping hands; you'd never credit such a bulk with such agility. He just managed to snatch hold in time of one hand, and panting he dragged the Singhalese out of the water. Then he laid him down on a rock and mopped his sweat. The Singhalese was lying motionless: one of his shins was skinned to the bone, evidently by a rock, but otherwise he was in one piece. The captain lifted his eyelid: only the white of his upturned eyes was visible. He had no shells and no knife.

At just that moment the boat with the crew closed in towards the shore. 'Sir,' the Swede Jensen shouted, 'there are sharks here. Will you carry on fishing?'

'No,' said the captain. 'Pull in here and pick up these two.'

'Look, sir,' Jensen pointed out as they were returning to the ship; 'look how suddenly it gets shallow here. All the way from here to the shore,' he pointed out, poking his oar in the water. 'Just as if there was some kind of dam here under the water.'

Not till he was on the boat did the short Singhalese come round. He sat with his knees drawn up to his chin and was shaking all over. The captain sent the men away and sat down with his legs straddled.

'Well, let's have it,' he said. 'What did you see there?'

'Djins, sahib,' the short Singhalese whispered. Now even his eyelids were beginning to tremble and little pimples of gooseflesh erupted all over his body.

Captain van Toch cleared his throat. 'And . . . what do they look like?'

'Like . . . like . . .' A strip of white again began to appear in the Singhalese's eyes. With unexpected agility Captain van Toch slapped both his cheeks with the palm and the back of his hand to bring him round.

'Thanks, sahib,' the short Singhalese breathed, and his pupils again swam out in the white of his eyes.

'All right now?'

'Yes, sahib.'

'Any shells there?'

'Yes, sahib.'

Captain van Toch continued his cross-examination with a great deal of patience and thoroughness. OK, so there are devils there. How many? Thousands and thousands. They're about as tall as a child of ten, sir, and nearly black. They swim in the water and on the sea-bed they walk upright. Upright, sir, just like you and me, but they sway their bodies the while: like this, and like this, all the time . . . Yes, sir, they've got hands too, just like human beings; no, they've got no claws, more like the hands of children. No, sir, they haven't got any horns or any hair. Yes, they've got a tail, a bit like a fish but without a tail-fin. And a big head, a round head like the Bataks. No, sir, they didn't say anything; they only seemed to smack their lips. As the Singhalese was cutting off some shells at a depth of about fifty feet he had felt something touching his back – like small cold fingers. He'd turned round, and there were hundreds and hundreds of them all round him. Hundreds and hundreds, sir, swimming or standing on rocks, and all of them watching what the Singhalese was doing there. That was when he'd dropped his knife and the shells and had tried to swim to the surface. In doing so he'd collided with some of the devils who were swimming above him, and what happened next he didn't know, sir.

Captain van Toch gazed thoughtfully at the trembling little diver. That boy wouldn't be any use for anything, he thought to himself; he'd send him home to Ceylon from Padang. Growling and snorting he went back to his cabin. There he tipped out two pearls from the bag on to his table. One of them was as small as a grain of sand and the other was like a pea, with a silvery gleam and a touch of pink. And the captain of the Dutch ship snorted and took his Irish whisky from the cupboard.

Towards six o'clock he again had himself taken in the boat to the kampong, and made straight for that cross between a Cuban and a Portuguese. 'Toddy,' he said, and that was the only word he uttered; he sat on the corrugated iron verandah with a thick glass between his thick fingers, and drank and spat and peered from beneath his bushy eyebrows at the scrawny yellow hens which were pecking heaven knows what on the trampled dirt yard between the palms. The half-breed was careful not to say anything and merely filled the glasses. Gradually the captain's eyes became bloodshot and his fingers began to lack response. It was nearly dusk when he got to his feet and yanked up his trousers.

'Turning in already, captain?' the half-breed between the devil and Satan inquired courteously.

The captain stabbed his finger into the air. 'I'd be damned surprised,' he said, 'if there were any devils in the world whom I've yet to come across. You man, which way is bloody north-west?'

'That way,' the half-breed pointed. 'Where are you off to, sir?'

'To hell,' Captain J. van Toch growled. 'Going to have a look at Devil Bay.'

That evening marked the start of Captain J. van Toch's eccentricity. He did not return to the kampong until daybreak; he spoke not a single word and had himself rowed out to the ship, where he locked himself in his cabin until evening. So far nobody noticed anything out of the ordinary since the *Kandong Bandoeng* was busy enough loading some of the blessings of the island (copra, pepper, camphor, gutta-percha, palm oil, tobacco and labour); but when in the evening he was informed that all the cargo had been stowed he merely snorted and said: 'The boat. To the kampong.' And again he did not return until dawn. The Swede Jensen, who helped him on board, inquired, just from politeness: 'So we're sailing today, captain?' The captain spun round as if he had had a needle stuck in his behind. 'What the hell's that to you?' he snapped. 'Mind your own bloody business!' All day long the *Kandong Bandoeng* rode at anchor a cable's length off the shore of Tana Masa, doing nothing. As evening fell the captain rolled out of his cabin and commanded: 'The boat. To the kampong.' Zapatis, the little Greek, followed him with his one blind and one squinting eye. 'Boys,' he said; 'either the old man's got a girl there or he's gone clean off his rocker.' The Swede Jensen scowled. 'What the hell's that to you?' he snapped at Zapatis. 'Mind your own bloody business!' Then, together with the Icelander Gudmunson he took the little dinghy and rowed in the direction of Devil Bay. They pulled in behind some boulders and awaited developments. In the bay the captain was pacing up and down: he seemed to be waiting for somebody. Now and again he would stop and call out something like ts, ts, ts. 'Look,' Gudmunson said, pointing to the sea which was now blindingly red and golden from the sunset. Jensen counted two, three, four, six fins, sharp as a blade, making for Devil Bay. 'Shit,' muttered Jensen; 'all those sharks!' Every so often one of the blades would submerge, a tail would flap above the surface and the water would be churned up. At that point Captain J. van Toch began to hop about furiously on the beach, hurl curses and shake his fist at the sharks. Then a brief tropical dusk fell and the moon sailed out over the island. Jensen gripped his oars and brought the dinghy to within a furlong of the shore. The captain was now sitting on a boulder, going ts, ts, ts. Something was moving near him, but it was difficult to make out what it was. Looks like seals, Jensen thought, but seals crawl differently. Whatever it was emerged from the water among the boulders and waddled along the beach with a swaying motion like penguins. Jensen quietly pulled on his oars and stopped half a furlong from the captain. Yes, the captain was saying something, but the devil only knew what it was – probably Malay or Tamil. He was waving his arms as if he were throwing something to the seals (except that they weren't seals, Jensen reassured himself), and all the while he was jabbering away in Chinese or Malay. At that moment a raised oar slipped from Jensen's hand and slapped into the water. The captain raised his head, stood up and took about thirty paces towards the water. And suddenly there were flashes and cracks: the captain was firing his Browning in the direction of the dinghy. Almost simultaneously there was a rustling, swirling and splashing as if of a thousand seals diving into the water. But by then Jensen and Gudmundson were pulling on their oars and fairly whipping their dinghy round the nearest headland. When they got back to the ship they did not say a word to anyone. These Nordics know how to keep silent. The captain returned towards dawn: he was morose and angry, but he did not speak a word. Only as Jensen was helping him on board two pairs of blue eyes met in a cold searching stare.

'Jensen,' the captain said.

'Yes, sir.'

'We sail today.'

'Yes, sir.'

'You'll get your papers in Surabaya.'

'Yes, sir.'

That was all. That day the *Kandong Bandoeng* sailed for Padang. From Padang Captain J. van Toch sent a package to his company in Amsterdam, a package insured for £1,200 sterling. And simultaneously he telegraphed a request for a year's leave. Urgent reasons of health and that sort of thing. Then he knocked about Padang until he found whoever he had been looking for. He was a savage from Borneo, a Dayak whom English tourists would occasionally hire as a shark hunter, just in order to watch him at work, for the Dayak still operated in the old way, armed only with a long knife. He was evidently a cannibal but he had his fixed scale of charges: five pounds per shark, plus board. Otherwise he was hideous to behold, for his skin had been scraped off both his arms, his chest and his thighs by sharkskin, and his nose and ears were adorned with sharks' teeth. Everyone called him Shark.

With this Dayak Captain J. van Toch now set out for the island of Tana Masa.

2

Mr Golombek and Mr Valenta

It was hot and the height of the silly season, when nothing, but positively nothing, happens, when there are no politics, when there is not even a European crisis. Yet even then the newspaper readership, sprawled out in agonies of boredom on sandy beaches or in the dappled shade of trees, demoralised by the heat, by nature, by the rural tranquillity and just by the simple healthy life of being on holiday, expects, with hopes dashed anew every day, that at least in their paper they'll find something new and refreshing, some murder perhaps or a war or an earthquake, in short Something. And if they don't find it they throw down their papers and angrily declare that there isn't a thing, not a damned thing, in the paper, that it's not worth reading at all and that they'll stop taking it.

And meanwhile there are five or six lonely people sitting in the editorial office because all their colleagues are also on holiday, angrily throwing down their papers and complaining that there isn't a thing, not a damned thing, in the paper. And the printing shop foreman would emerge from his cubbyhole and say reproachfully: 'Gentlemen, gentlemen, we haven't got tomorrow's leader yet.'

'Well, why not use . . . let's say . . . that article on the economic situation in Bulgaria,' one of the lonely gentlemen suggested.

The foreman heaved a deep sigh: 'And who's going to read that stuff, Mr Editor? It'll be another day of Nothing-to-Read in the whole paper.'

The six lonely gentlemen raised their eyes to the ceiling as if they might discover Something-to-Read up there.

'If only Something would happen,' one of them suggested vaguely.

'Or maybe . . . some . . . interesting report from somewhere,' suggested another.

'What about?'

'I wouldn't know.'

'Or invent . . . some new vitamin,' growled a third.

'Now, in summer?' objected a fourth. 'Why, my dear fellow, vitamins are intellectual stuff, that's more like something for the autumn . . .'

'Christ, it's hot,' yawned a fifth. 'We should have something from the polar regions.'

'Yes, but what?'

'Anything. Something like that Eskimo Welzl. Frostbitten fingers, eternal ice – that sort of thing.'

'Easily said,' said a sixth. 'But where do we get it?'

A hopeless silence fell upon the editorial office.

'I was in Jevíčko on Sunday . . .', the printing shop foreman spoke up hesitantly.

'So?'

'It seems some Captain Vantoch is on leave there. Seems he was born in Jevíčko.'

'Who's that Vantoch?'

'Fat chap. Supposed to be a sea captain. They were saying he's been fishing for pearls.'

Mr Golombek looked at Mr Valenta.

'And where did he fish for them?'

'Off Sumatra . . . and Celebes . . . somewhere down there. Seems he's lived there for thirty years.'

'Hell, it's an idea,' Mr Valenta said. 'Could make a first-rate story. Golombek, shall we go?'

'Why not give it a try?' agreed Mr Golombek and slipped off the desk he was sitting on.

'That's the gentleman over there,' said the landlord in Jevíčko.

Sitting legs apart at a table in the garden was a fat gentleman in a white cap, drinking beer and thoughtfully drawing his fat forefinger over the table. The two gentlemen made straight for him.

'I'm Valenta.'

'I'm Golombek.'

The fat gentleman raised his eyes. 'Whassat? What?'

'My name's Valenta and I'm a journalist.'

'And I'm Golombek. Also a journalist.'

The fat gentleman lifted himself with dignity. 'Captain van Toch. Very glad to meet you. Sit down, boys.'

The two gentlemen obligingly sat down and placed their notepads before them.

'What are you drinking, boys?'

'Raspberry juice,' Mr Valenta said.

'Raspberry juice?' the captain repeated incredulously. 'Whatever for? Landlord, fetch some beer. Well, what is it you're after?' he said, planting his elbows on the table.

'Is it true, Mr Vantoch, that you were born here?'

'Sure. Born right here.'

'How on earth did you manage to go to sea?'

'Well, via Hamburg.'

'And how long have you been a captain?'

'Twenty years, my boy. Got my papers here,' he said, importantly tapping his breast pocket. 'Like to see them?'

Mr Golombek would have liked to see what a captain's papers looked like but he suppressed his curiosity. 'That means, captain, that in those twenty years you'll have seen a good deal of the world, what?'

'Sure. A good deal. Yes.'

'Whereabouts mostly?'

'Java. Borneo. Philippines. Fiji Islands. Solomon Islands. Carolines. Samoa. Damned Clipperton Island. A lot of damned islands, my boy. Why?'

'Well, because it's interesting. We'd like you to tell us more, you know.'

'That's all, is it?' The captain fixed his pale blue eyes on them. 'So you're from the police – that it?'

'No, we're not, captain. We're the press.'

'The press, is it? Reporters, eh? OK, take it down: Captain J. van Toch, master of the *Kandong Bandoeng* – '

'How's that again?'

'*Kandong Bandoeng*, home port Surabaya. Purpose of visit: *vacances* – how d'you say it?'

'Vacation.'

'Hell, yes, vacation. Well then, print it in your paper under "ships berthed". And now away with those notebooks, boys. Your health.'

'Mr Vantoch, we've come specially to seek you out, so you could tell us something about your life.'

'But why?'

'To write about it. People are interested in that sort of thing;

they like reading about faraway islands, [and about what a fellow-countryman of theirs, a Czech born in Jevíčko, has seen and experienced in foreign parts.]

The captain nodded his head. 'That's true enough. D'you know, I am the only sea captain in the whole of Jevíčko. That's a fact. I'm told there's also a Jevíčko-born captain in charge of . . . of . . . of boat swings, but,' he added confidentially, 'I don't believe he's a real captain. That goes by the tonnage, did you know?'

'And what tonnage was your ship?'

'Twelve thousand tons, young man.'

'So you were quite a big captain, what?'

'Sure. A big captain,' the captain said with dignity. 'Got any money, boys?'

The two gentlemen looked at each other a little uncertainly. 'Yes, but not a lot. You in need of money, captain?'

'Yes. I could do with some.'

'Well then. You tell us a nice lot and we'll write it up for the paper and then you'll get some money for it.'

'How much?'

'Could be as much as . . . a thousand or so,' Mr Golombek said generously.

'Pounds sterling?'

'No, only Czech Crowns.'

Captain van Toch shook his head. 'That's no use. That much I've got myself, young man.' He fished out a fat bundle of bank-notes from his trouser pocket. 'See?' Then he planted his elbows on the table and leaned across to the two gentlemen. 'Gentlemen, I could let you in on a big *Geschäft*. How d'you say that?'

'A big deal.'

'Sure. A big deal. But for that you'd have to give me fifteen . . . wait a minute, fifteen, sixteen million Crowns. How about it?'

Again the two gentlemen looked at each other uncertainly. Every journalist has had his experience of the oddest kind of lunatic, con man and inventor.

'Hold it,' said the captain. 'Got something to show you.' He fished with his fat fingers in his waistcoat pocket, pulled something out and placed it on the table. There were five pale pink pearls the size of cherry stones. 'Know anything about pearls?'

'How much are they worth?' Mr Valenta gasped.
'Plenty, my boy. But I'm carrying these around with me
merely . . . as samples, you know. Now then, feel like coming
in with me?' he asked, extending his massive hand across the
table.
Mr Golombek sighed. 'Mr Vantoch, that kind of money – '
'Stop,' the captain interrupted him. 'I know you don't know
me – but ask about Captain van Toch in Surabaya, in Batavia,
in Padang or anywhere you like. Go and ask, and everybody will
tell you: sure, Captain van Toch is as good as his word.'
'Mr Vantoch, we believe you,' protested Mr Golombek.
'It's just—'
'Wait,' the captain commanded. 'I realise you don't want
to throw your good money away just like that – I respect
you for that, my boy. But you'd put it in a boat, d'you see?
You'd buy that boat, you'd be the owner of that ship and
would come along. Sure, so you could watch me running
things. And the money we'd make there, that would be fifty-
fifty. That's an honest deal, isn't it?'
'But Mr Vantoch,' Mr Golombek at last groaned, a little
unhappily, 'we just don't have that sort of money!'
'Well, that's different,' said the captain. 'Sorry. But in that
case I don't see why you looked me up.'
'So you could give us a story, captain. You must have had
a lot of adventures – '
'That I have, my boy. Damned adventures I've had.'
'Ever been shipwrecked?'
'What's that? Shipwrecked? Oh no. What do you mean?
Give me a good ship and nothing can happen to her. Go and
ask around Amsterdam for my references. You go and ask.'
'What about natives? Meet any natives there?'
Captain van Toch shook his head. 'That's not a subject
for educated people. I'm not going to talk about that.'
'Tell us something else then.'
'Yeah, tell,' the captain growled mistrustfully. 'So you can
go and sell it to some company which will then send in its
own ships. Let me tell you, my lad, people are great crooks.
And the greatest crooks are those bankers in Colombo.'
'Have you often been to Colombo?'
'Sure. Often. And to Bangkok too, and to Manilla. Boys,'
he said suddenly; 'there's a ship I know about. A very handy

ship, and cheap at the price. Lying in Rotterdam. Come and look her over with me. Rotterdam, that's only just round the corner,' he pointed with his thumb over his shoulder. 'Ships are dirt cheap at present, boys. Like old iron. She's only six years old and runs on diesel. Would you like to look her over?'

'We can't, Mr Vantoch.'

'A queer lot you two are,' the captain sighed. Then he blew his nose noisily into a sky-blue handkerchief. 'And you wouldn't know of anybody who'd like to buy a ship?'

'Here, in Jevíčko?'

'Sure, here or hereabouts. I'd like this big deal to be clinched here, in my own country.'

'That's very nice of you, captain – '

'Sure. The others are all such big crooks. And they've got no money. You, being journalists and such, must surely know the big shots here – you know, bankers and shipowners and, how do you say, ship-makers, right?'

'Shipbuilders. No, Mr Vantoch, we don't know such people.'

'That's a pity,' the captain grew gloomy.

Mr Golombek remembered something. 'You don't by any chance know Mr Bondy?'

'Bondy? Bondy?' Captain van Toch reflected. 'Wait a minute, I should know that name. There's a Bond Street in London and only very rich people live there. Has he got some business in Bond Street, that Mr Bondy?'

'No, he lives in Prague, but I rather think he was born here, in Jevíčko.'

'Hell, yes,' the captain exclaimed happily; 'you're right, my boy! Had a draper's shop in the Market Place! Sure, Bondy – now what was his name? Max. Max Bondy. So he's got a business in Prague now?'

'No, that must have been his father. This man Bondy is called G. H. Bondy. President G. H. Bondy, captain.'

'G. H.,' the captain shook his head. 'No, there was no G. H. here. Unless, of course, he was Gussie Bondy. But he was no president. Gussie was a pimply little Jew. Can't be him.'

'That'll be him all right, Mr Vantoch. After all, it must be a good many years since you last saw him.'

'Well, that's true. A good many years,' the captain agreed. 'Forty years, my boy. Gussie could be a big man now. And what is he?'

'He's Chairman of the Board of MEAS – you know, a big company making boilers and suchlike – as well as president of some twenty companies and cartels. A very big man, Mr Vantoch. They call him a captain of industry.'
'A captain?' mused Captain van Toch. 'So I'm not the only captain from Jevíčko after all! Hell, that boy Gus is a captain too! I really ought to meet him. And has he got money?'
'What do you think? Piles of it, Mr Vantoch. Sure to have several hundred million. Richest man in the country.'
Captain van Toch turned profoundly serious. 'And a captain as well. I'm most grateful to you, my boy. I'll set course for that man Bondy straight away. Such a little Jew he used to be. And now he's Captain G. H. Bondy. Ah well, time does fly,' he sighed melancholically.
'Captain, we'll have to leave now or we'll miss the evening train – '
'I'll see you down to the harbour,' said the captain and began to weigh anchor. 'Jolly glad you hove to, gentlemen. I know an editor chap in Surabaya, a very sound lad and a good friend of mine. Frightful old soak. I could find you jobs on that Surabaya paper, if you'd like me to, boys. No? Just as you like.'
When the train pulled out Captain van Toch slowly and ceremoniously waved his huge blue handkerchief. As he did so a large irregular pearl dropped into the sand. A pearl nobody ever found.

3

G. H. Bondy and His Fellow Countryman

It is a well-known fact that the greater a man is the less he has on his door-plate. An old chap like Max Bondy in Jevíčko had to have large letters painted above his shop, on both sides of the door and on the windows, that this was the place of Max Bondy, merchant of all types of drapery, brides' trousseaux, canvas, towels, napery and household linen, printed cotton and flannel, top-quality cloth, silk, curtains, pelmets, braids and all kinds of sewing material. Founded 1885. His son, G. H. Bondy, a captain of industry, President of MEAS Incorporated, Commercial Counsellor, Stock Exchange Consultant, Vice-Chairman of the Federation of Industries, Consulato de la Republica Ecuador, member of numerous boards of directors, etc. etc., had on his house only a small black-glass plate with the gilt lettering

BONDY

Nothing more. Just Bondy. Let others write on their doors Julius Bondy, General Motors Representative; or Dr Med. Ervin Bondy; or S. Bondy & Co. – but there was just one Bondy who was simply Bondy without further particulars. (I believe that the Pope, on his front door, has simply the word Pius, without any title or numeral. And God has no shingle at all, on earth or in heaven. It's up to you to find out that He lives here. But this is all beside the point and mentioned only in passing.)

It was in front of that glass plate that on a scorching day a gentleman in a white sailor's cap stopped and with a blue handkerchief mopped the massive nape of his neck. A damned superior house, he was thinking to himself, and a little uncertainly tugged the brass bell-pull.

In the door appeared the doorman, Povondra: with his eyes he sized up the fat gentleman from his boots all the way to the gold braid on his cap and inquired with reserve: 'Yes?'

'I say, boy,' boomed the gentleman; 'does a Mr Bondy live here?'

'Your business?' Mr Povondra asked icily.

'Tell him that Captain van Toch from Surabaya wishes to speak to him. Oh yes,' he remembered. 'Here is my card.' And he handed Mr Povondra a visiting card which bore an embossed anchor and the printed name:

CAPTAIN J. VAN TOCH
E. I. & P. L. Co. S. Kandong Bandoeng

Surabaya   Naval Club

Mr Povondra inclined his head and hesitated. Should he tell him Mr Bondy was not at home? Or that, most regrettably, Mr Bondy was in an important conference? There are those visitors who had to be announced and others which a competent doorman dealt with himself. Mr Povondra experienced an embarrassing failure of the instinct which normally guided him on such occasions: somehow the fat gentleman did not fit into any of the customary categories of unannounced callers, he did not look either like a commercial traveller or like an official of some charitable organisation. Meanwhile, Captain van Toch was puffing and mopping his bald head with his handkerchief; at the same time he was guilelessly blinking his pale blue eyes. Mr Povondra abruptly decided to assume entire responsibility. 'Come in please,' he said. 'I'll announce you to the Counsellor.'

Captain van Toch was mopping his face with the blue handkerchief and looking around the hall. Hell, that Gussie had done all right for himself: why, it was just like the saloons on the ships which sailed between Rotterdam and Batavia.

Must have cost a packet. And such a pimply little Jew he used to be, the captain thought in wonderment.

Meanwhile, in his study G. H. Bondy was thoughtfully examining the captain's visiting card. 'What does he want?' he asked suspiciously.

'I don't know, sir,' Mr Povondra mumbled respectfully.

Mr Bondy was still fingering the visiting card. An embossed ship's anchor. Captain van Toch, Surabaya. Where the hell was Surabaya, anyway? Wasn't it somewhere on Java? Mr Bondy felt a breath of distant parts engulfing him. Kandong Bandoeng – sounds like a gong being struck. Surabaya. And today was just that kind of tropical day. Surabaya. 'Well, show him in,' decided Mr. Bondy.

In the doorway stood a massive man with a captain's cap, saluting. G. H. Bondy walked over to meet him. 'Very glad to meet you, Captain. Please come in,' he said in English.

'Hi! Hi, Mr Bondy,' the captain cheerfully exclaimed in Czech.

'You're Czech?' Mr Bondy was amazed.

'Sure. Czech. But we know each other, Mr Bondy. From Jevíčko. Vantoch the grocer, remember?

'Of course, of course,' G. H. Bondy loudly expressed delight but inwardly felt something approaching disappointment. (So he's not a Dutchman after all!) 'Vantoch the grocer in the Market Place, right? Haven't changed at all, Mr Vantoch. Always the same! And how's the grocery business going?'

'Thank you,' the captain said politely. 'Dad's been gone a long time – how do you say it – ?'

'Dead? Well, what do you know? Of course, you must be his son . . . Mr Bondy's eyes suddenly lit up in reminiscence. 'Good heavens, you must be the Vantoch who used to fight with me in Jevíčko when we were boys?'

'Sure, that'll have been me, Mr Bondy,' the captain agreed in all seriousness. 'That's why I was sent away from home to Moravská Ostrava.'

'We used to fight a lot. But you were always stronger than me,' Mr Bondy sportingly conceded.

'That I was. Of course, you were such a weak little Jew, Mr Bondy. And you got a lot of kicks up your arse. A lot.'

'Too right,' G. H. Bondy reminisced with emotion. 'Sit

down, sit down, fellow countryman! Good of you to remember me. Where have you sprung from?'

Captain van Toch sat down in a dignified manner in a leather armchair and put his cap on the floor. 'I'm here on leave, Mr Bondy. That's it. Yes.'

'Do you remember,' Mr Bondy delved deeper into his memories, 'how you used to shout after me: Jew, Jew, the devil take you?'

'Sure,' said the captain with feeling and blew into his blue handkerchief. 'Ah yes. Those were great days, oh boy! It's no use, time flies. Now we're both old men and both of us captains – '

'Of course, you're a captain,' Mr Bondy reminded himself. 'Who'd have thought it! Captain of Long Distances – is that how you say it?'

'Yes, sir. A High Sea captain. East India and Pacific Lines, sir.'

'A splendid profession,' Mr Bondy sighed. 'Change places with you any day, captain. You'll have to tell me about yourself.'

'That's just it,' the captain came to life. 'I'd like to tell you about something, Mr Bondy. A most interesting matter, old chap.' Captain van Toch looked around nervously.

'You looking for something, captain?'

'Yes. You wouldn't have any beer, Mr Bondy? I've worked up a huge thirst on the way up from Surabaya.' The captain began scrabbling in his copious trouser pocket and produced the blue handkerchief, a linen bag with something in it, a tobacco pouch, a knife, a compass and a bundle of banknotes. 'I'd like to send someone for some beer. Maybe that steward who brought me to your cabin.'

Mr Bondy rang a bell. 'Leave it, captain. Why don't you take a cigar in the meantime – ?'

The captain took a cigar with a red and gold band and smelled it. 'This tobacco comes from Lombok. They're frightful crooks there, believe me.' Whereupon, to Mr Bondy's horror, he squashed the precious cigar in his massive fist and crammed the tobacco into his pipe. 'Yes, Lombok. Or Sumba.'

Meanwhile, Mr Povondra had soundlessly appeared in the door.

'Bring some beer,' Mr Bondy ordered.

Mr Povondra raised his eyebrows: 'Beer? And how much?'

'A gallon,' growled the captain and ground a burnt match into the carpet. 'Boy, was it hot in Aden. But I've got some real news for you, Mr Bondy. From the Sunda Islands, see? There you could do a terrific *Geschäft*. A big deal. But I'd have to tell you the whole – how do you say – tale?'

'Story.'

'Sure. And what a story, sir. Wait.' The captain turned his forget-me-not-blue eyes to the ceiling. 'Hardly know where to start.'

(Another business deal, G. H. Bondy thought to himself. God, what a bore! He'll be telling me he could ship sewing machines to Tasmania or steam boilers and pins to Fiji. Terrific deal, I know. That's all I'm good to you for. To hell, I'm no shopkeeper. I'm a visionary. I'm a poet in my way. Tell me, Sindbad the sailor, about Surabaya or the Phoenix Islands. Have you not been drawn off course by the Magnetic Mountain? Have you never been carried off by the bird Roc? And are you not returning home with a cargo of pearls, cinnamon and bezoar? OK, man, let's have your lies!)

'Maybe I'll start with that scorpion,' the captain announced.

'What scorpion?' Commercial Counsellor Bondy wondered.

'That is, I probably mean lizard. You do say lizards, don't you?'

'Lizards?'

'Hell, yes, lizards. You should see those lizards out there, Mr Bondy.'

'Where?'

'On an island. Can't tell you its name, old boy. That's a great secret. Worth millions.' Captain van Toch mopped his forehead with his handkerchief. 'Damn it, where's that beer?'

'Be here in a minute, captain.'

'Yes. Very well then. Let me tell you, Mr Bondy, they are very nice and good animals, those lizards. I know them, old boy.' The captain brought his hand down sharply on the table. 'To say they're devils is a lie. A damned lie, sir. You'd sooner be a devil and I'd sooner be a devil – yes, I, Captain van Toch, sir. You may believe me.'

G. H. Bondy began to be alarmed. Delirious, he thought. Where the devil was Povondra?

'There are several thousands of them there, those lizards I mean, but a lot of them have been eaten by – hell, what do you call them?'

'Sharks?'

'That's it, sharks. That's why those lizards are so rare, sir, and why they are only found in that bay whose name I can't tell you.'

'So these lizards live in the sea?'

'Sure. In the sea. They only come ashore at night, but after a while they've got to go back into the water.'

'And what do they look like?' (Mr Bondy was playing for time pending that damned Povondra's return.)

'Well, about the size of seals, but when they's strutting on their hindlegs they're as tall as this,' the captain demonstrated. 'Can't say they're exactly pretty. But they've got no flakes on them.'

'Scales?'

'Sure, scales. They're entirely naked, Mr Bondy, like some kind of frog or those salamanders. And those front paws of theirs, they're just like children's hands, except that they have only four fingers. Poor little things,' the captain added compassionately. 'But extremely clever and nice animals, Mr Bondy.' The captain squatted on his heels and in this position began to shuffle along with a swaying motion. 'That's how they waddle, those lizards.'

The captain struggled to get his massive body into an undulating motion while in the crouch; simultaneously he held out his arms like a dog begging on its hindlegs and fixed his forget-me-not-blue eyes on Mr Bondy, who thought they were begging for sympathy. G. H. Bondy was deeply stirred and, in a way, shamed as a human being. To make matters worse, at just that moment the silent Mr Povondra appeared in the door with a jug of beer, raising scandalised eyebrows as he watched the captain's unseemly behaviour.

'Put the beer down here and leave us,' Mr Bondy hurriedly ejaculated.

The captain raised himself up and snorted. 'Well, that's what those creatures are like, Mr Bondy. Your health,' he said, taking a drink. 'Got good beer here, old chap. Truth to tell, the house you've got here – ' The captain wiped his moustache.

'And how did you come across those lizards, captain?'

'Well, that's just the story, Mr Bondy. It all started when I was pearl-fishing on Tana Masa – ' the captain checked himself. 'Or somewhere in those parts. Ah yes, it was some other island, but that's still my secret, old chap. People are great crooks, Mr Bondy, and a chap's got to watch his tongue. And as those two damned Singhalese were cutting off those pearl-oysters under water – '

'Pearl-oysters?'

'Sure. Those are shells which cling to the rocks as fast as the Jewish faith and you've got to prise them loose with a knife. Well, those lizards were watching the Singhalese, and the Singhalese thought they were sea devils. Very uneducated people they are, the Singhalese and the Bataks. They believe there are devils there. Yes.' The captain blew mightily into his handkerchief. 'Well, you know how it is – a chap wants to find out. I don't know if it's only us Czechs who are such an inquisitive nation, but wherever I've met one of our fellow countrymen he's just had to poke his nose into everything to find out what was behind it. I think it's because we Czechs don't want to believe in anything. So I got it into my silly old head that I'd have a look at those devils myself. Besides, I was sloshed, to be perfectly honest, but that was because I couldn't get those damned devils out of my mind. Anything, you know, is possible down there on the equator. So I went out in the evening to have a look at that Devil Bay – '

Mr Bondy tried to visualise a tropical bay lined with rocks and primeval forest. 'Well?'

'So I sat there, going ts-ts-ts, to make the devils come out. And, would you believe it, one such lizard came out of the sea after a little while, stood up on its hindlegs and twisted his whole body. And went ts-ts-ts at me. If I hadn't been sloshed I'd probably have fired at it; but, old chap, I was as drunk as a lord and so I said: Come here, you, come here, tapa-boy, I'm not going to hurt you.'

'You spoke Czech to it?'

'No, Malay. Malay is what's spoken most in those parts. He didn't say anything and merely shuffled from one foot to the other, squirming, just like a child being bashful. And all round in the water were several hundred of those lizards, poking their mugs out of the water and staring at me. And

I – as I said, I was sloshed – sat down on my heels and began to twist like that lizard, so he shouldn't be afraid of me, see? And then another lizard came out of the water, about as tall as a 10-year-old, and also started waddling. And in his front paw he was holding that pearl-oyster.' The captain took a drink. 'Cheers, Mr Bondy. Of course, I was absolutely pissed and so I said to him: OK, smart guy, you want me to open that shell for you? Well, come over here then, I can open it for you with my knife. But he didn't move, he was still afraid. So I started twisting again, as if I were a little girl who's bashful of somebody. Then he waddled up closer and I slowly put out my hand and took the shell from his paw. True, we were both scared, as you'll appreciate, Mr Bondy, but I of course was drunk. So I took out my knife and opened that shell. With my finger I felt if there was a pearl in it, but there wasn't, only that nasty snail, that slimy mollusc which lives in those shells. So I said: ts-ts-ts, eat it if you like. And I threw the shell to him. Boy, you should have seen him licking it clean. Must be a great tit-bit – what d'you call it – for those lizards.'

'A delicacy.'

'That's it, a delicacy. Except that those poor little buggers couldn't get inside those shells with their little fingers. It's a hard life, sure is.' The captain took another swig. 'So I turned things over in my mind a bit. When those lizards saw the Singhalese cutting off those shells they probably said to themselves: Aha, they eat those things – and they wanted to see how the Singhalese would open them. You know, a Singhalese like that, when he's in the water, looks a bit like a lizard, except that those lizards have more brains than a Singhalese or a Batak because they tried to learn something. Whereas a Batak will never learn anything except some crookery,' Captain van Toch added angrily. 'So when I went ts-ts-ts on the shore, and twisted like a lizard, they probably thought I was some kind of big salamander. That's why they weren't too frightened and came up to me to get me to open that shell. That's the kind of intelligent and trustful creatures they are.' Captain van Toch blushed. 'When I came to know them better, Mr Bondy, I stripped naked so as to be more like them, naked, you know. But they were still surprised that I had such a hairy chest and some other things. Yes.' The captain passed his handkerchief over his reddish neck. 'But maybe I'm getting a little too long-winded, Mr Bondy?' G. H. Bondy was enthralled. 'No, not at all. Go on, captain.' 'Well, OK. I will then. While that lizard was licking the shell clean the others were watching and crawling up the beach. Some of them also had shells in their paws – it's odd they managed to tear them off those rocks with such childish paws without thumbs. At first they were bashful but then they allowed me to take the shells from their paws. Of course, they weren't all pearl-oysters, there was all kind of rubbish, ordinary oysters and suchlike, but those I chucked into the water and said: No, children, these are no good, I'm not going to open those with my knife. But whenever there was a pearl-oyster I would open it with my knife and feel if there was a pearl inside. But I gave them the shell to lick out. By that time there were a few hundred of those lizards sitting around and watching me open the shells. And some of them even tried to do it themselves, to prise the shell open with a broken bit of shell that was lying around. That, old boy, I thought was very odd. No animal can handle tools; after all, an animal is just part of nature. True enough, at Buitenzorg I saw a monkey that could open a tin, a processed food tin, with a knife; but then a monkey isn't a real animal any more, sir. Sure, it seemed strange to me.' The captain took a drink. 'That night, Mr Bondy, I found something like eighteen pearls in those shells. Some were quite small, others were bigger, and three were the size of cherry stones, Mr Bondy. Cherry stones!' Captain van Toch nodded his head gravely. 'When I returned to my ship in the morning I kept saying to myself: Captain van Toch, you must have dreamt all that, sir, you were pissed, sir, and so on – but what the hell, there in my little pocket I had those eighteen pearls. Sure.'

'That's the best tale I ever heard,' Mr Bondy gasped.

'There you are, old boy,' the captain said happily. 'During the day I turned it over in my mind. I'm going to tame those lizards, see? Yes, tame them and train them, and they're going to fetch me those pearl shells. There must be heaps of them down there – shells, I mean, in Devil Bay. So I went out there again in the evening, but a little earlier. As soon as the sun starts setting those lizards push their mugs out of the water, first one here, then another one there, until the place fairly swarms with them. I'm sitting on the beach going ts-ts-ts. Suddenly I look up: a shark! You could only see his fin sticking out of the water. Then there was some splashing, and one of the lizards was gone. I counted twelve sharks, moving into Devil Bay in one evening. Mr Bondy, those brutes ate over twenty of *my* lizards,' the captain burst out and blew his nose furiously. 'Yes, over twenty of them! Stands to reason, doesn't it: how can a naked little lizard defend himself against them with only those little paws? I felt like crying as I sat watching it. You'd have to see that for yourself, old boy . . .'

The captain turned thoughtful. 'Thing is, I'm terribly fond of animals, old boy,' he said eventually, lifting his sky-blue eyes to G. H. Bondy. 'I don't know how you feel about these things, Captain Bondy – '

Mr Bondy nodded in token of agreement.

'That's all right, then,' Captain van Toch noted with pleasure. 'They're very good and clever, those tapa-boys; when you tell them something they pay attention, just like a dog listening to his master. And most of all those childish little hands – you know, old boy, I'm an old chap with no family of my own . . . An old man, you know, is rather lonely,' the captain muttered, trying to control his emotion. 'Very sweet those lizards are, dammit all. If only those sharks didn't hunt them so! When I began to throw stones at them, at the sharks I mean, *they began to throw stones too*, those tapa-boys. You won't believe this, Mr Bondy. True, they didn't throw very far, what with those short little hands. But it's odd all the same. If you're so clever, boys, I said to them, why don't you have a go at opening one of your shells with my knife here? And I put my knife down on the ground. For a bit they were shy, and then one of them tried and stuck the point of the knife between the two halves. You've got to lever, I said, lever, see? Twist the knife, like this, and you'll be all right. And he kept trying, poor little bugger, till it cracked and the shell opened. Well done, I said. Not so difficult after all, what? If a heathenish Batak or Singhalese can do it, why shouldn't a tapa-boy, what? Of course, I won't tell those lizards that it's a bloody marvel and quite wonderful that an animal can do such a thing. But now I can say it: I was – well – I was absolutely thunderstruck.'

'Like a vision,' Mr Bondy prompted.

'Too damn right. Like a vision. I couldn't get it out of my mind so I stayed there with my ship for another day. And at nightfall back to Devil Bay, and again I watched those sharks eating my lizards. That night, old boy, I swore that I'd do something about it. *Tapa-boys, Captain J. van Toch, beneath these terrible stars here, promises that he will help you.*

4

Captain van Toch's Business Enterprise

As Captain van Toch was relating this story the hair on the nape of his neck bristled with enthusiasm and excitement.

'Yes, sir, that's what I swore. Ever since, old boy, I've not had a quiet moment. I started my leave in Batavia and from there sent those Jews in Amsterdam 157 pearls – everything my creatures brought me. Then I found such a fellow, he was a Dayak and shark killer, one of those who kill sharks in the water with a knife. A fearful crook and assassin, that Dayak. And with him I took a small tramp steamer back to Tana Masa, and now, fellow, in you go and kill those sharks with your knife. I wanted him to kill off all the sharks there, so they left my lizards in peace. He was such an assassin and heathen, that Dayak, that he was not put out by those tapa-boys at all. Devil or not, he didn't care. And in the meantime I was making my observations and experiments with those lizards. Wait a minute, I've got my ship's log-book, where I wrote everything down each day.' From his breast pocket the captain produced a voluminous notebook and began to turn its pages.

'What's today's date, then? That's it, 25 June. So let's take 25 June, for example – that would be last year, of course. Here we are. The Dayak killed a shark. The lizards greatly interested in its corpse. Toby – that was one of the smaller lizards, but very clever,' the captain explained. 'I had to give them all names, see? So I could write this book about them. Well, Toby pushed his fingers into the hole made by the knife. In the evening they brought me dry twigs for my fire. That's nothing,' the captain grumbled. 'I'll find another day. Say, 20 June, OK? The lizards are still building that . . . that . . . what do you call it? Jetty?'

'A dam, perhaps?'

'That's it. A dam. A kind of dam. That is they were building a new dam at the north-western end of Devil Bay. Man alive,' he explained, 'that was a fantastic job. A perfect breakwater.'

'A breakwater?'

'Sure. They lay their eggs on that side of the bay and they wanted smooth water there. Get it? They worked out *for themselves* that they wanted to build such a dam there. And let me tell you that no official or engineer from the Waterstaat in Amsterdam could have drawn a better plan for such an underwater dam. An enormously clever job, except that the water washed it away. They even dig out deep holes into the shore, and that's where they live during the day. Terribly clever animals, sir, just like the *Biebers*'

'Beavers.'

'Sure. Those big mice that build those dams in rivers. They had *masses* of dams, big and small, in that Devil Bay, beautifully straight dams, it looked just like some city. And in the end they wanted to build a dam right across Devil Bay. Really did. They have already learned to roll blocks of stone with lever-jacks,' he read on. 'Albert – that was one of the tapa-boys – got two of his fingers crushed. The 21st: The Dayak *ate Albert*! But he was sick afterwards. Fifteen drops of opium. Promised never to do it again. Rain all day. 30 June: The lizards are building the dam. Toby doesn't feel like work. Yes, sir, he was a clever one,' the captain explained admiringly. 'The clever ones never like working. He was always plotting something, Toby was. What's the use, even among lizards there are great inequalities. 3 July: Sergeant got a knife. That was a big powerful lizard, that Sergeant. And very skilful to boot, sir. 7 July: With that knife Sergeant has killed a cuttlefish – that's a kind of fish which has that brown mess inside it, you know?'

'Sepia?'

'Yes, that's probably it. 20 July: Sergeant killed a big jelly-fish with his knife – that's a brute like aspic and it stings like a nettle. Revolting creature. And now watch out, Mr Bondy. 13 July: I've underlined the date. Sergeant killed a small shark with his knife. Weight seventy pounds. Well, there it is, Mr Bondy,' Captain van Toch announced solemnly. 'There it is in black and white. That was a great day, old boy. 13 July last year.' The captain shut his notebook. 'I'm not ashamed of it, Mr Bondy, but I went down on my knees right there on the beach and blubbed from sheer joy. Now I knew that my tapa-boys wouldn't knuckle under. That Sergeant got a fine new harpoon as a reward – a harpoon's the best thing, old boy, when you're trying to get sharks – and I said to him: Be a man, Sergeant, and show the tapa-boys that they can defend themselves. Now would you believe it,' the captain shouted, leaping to his feet and excitedly banging his fist on the table, 'three days later, old boy, there was a huge shark floating there dead, full of gashes – can you say that?'

'Full of wounds?'

'Full of holes from that harpoon.' The captain took such a large swig that it gurgled. 'So that was that, Mr Bondy. And now I made something . . . something like a contract with those tapa-boys. That's to say I gave them my word that if they would bring me those pearl-oysters I would give them those harpoons and knives to defend themselves with. See? An honest deal, sir. And why not? A man should be honest even with those creatures. I also gave them some wood. And two iron wheelbarrows – '

'Wheelbarrows? Trolleys?'

'That's it, kind of trolleys. So they could wheel the stones along for their dam. Poor buggers had to drag everything along with their little paws, see? Well, they got a lot of things. I'd never cheat them, that I wouldn't. Hold on, old boy; got something to show you.'

With one hand Captain van Toch lifted his belly and with the other he fished out a linen bag from his trouser pocket. 'Well, here it is,' he said, tipping out its contents on the table. There were getting on for a thousand pearls of all sizes: tiny ones like hemp seed, bigger ones like peas, and a few the size of cherries; perfect ones, drop-shaped ones, lumpy baroque ones, silvery ones, bluish ones, skin-coloured ones, some with a yellowish touch and others running to black and pink. G. H. Bondy was as if in a dream; he could not help it, he had to let them run through his hands, roll them between his finger-tips, cover them with his palms – '

'Beautiful, just beautiful,' he gasped. 'Captain, this is like a dream!'

'Sure,' the captain said unemotionally. 'They're pretty all right. And they killed some thirty sharks that year I was with them. Got it all written down here,' he said, tapping his breast pocket. 'But what about all those knives I gave them, and those five harpoons . . . Those knives cost *me* nearly two American dollars apiece. Damn good knives, old boy, made of that steel which won't rust.'

'Stainless steel.'

'That's it. Because they have to be submarine knives, for use under water. And those Bataks also cost a heap of money.'

'What Bataks?'

'They're the natives on that island. They believe that the tapa-boys are something like devils, and they're frightfully scared of them. And when they saw me talking to those devils of theirs they wanted to kill me there and then. For several nights there they were striking bells of some sort so as to drive the devils away from their kampong. Shocking din they made, sir. And each morning they demanded that I should pay them for their bell-ringing. For the work they had with it, you know. Well, what's the use, those Bataks are frightful crooks. But with those tapa-boys, sir, with those lizards, one might do some honest business. That's so, Excellent business, Mr Bondy.'

G. H. Bondy felt as if he was in a fairy-tale. 'Buy pearls from them?'

'That's it. Except that there aren't any pearls left in Devil Bay, and there aren't any tapa-boys anywhere else. And this, old boy, is the key to the whole thing.' Captain van Toch puffed out his cheeks triumphantly. 'That's exactly how I figured out that big business in my head. Why, old boy,' he said, stabbing the air with his fat finger, 'those lizards have multiplied enormously since I took them under my wing! They're now able to defend themselves, see? And there'll be more and more of them all the time! So how about it, Mr Bondy? Wouldn't that be a terrific deal?'

'I'm still not quite clear,' G. H. Bondy said uncertainly, '. . . how you're envisaging the thing, captain.'

'By shipping those tapa-boys to other pearl islands,' the captain finally let it out. 'I've found out that those lizards cannot get across the open sea under their own steam. They can swim for a while, and waddle on the seabed for a while, but at great depth the pressure's too much for them. They're rather soft, you see? But if I had the kind of ship where one could install a tank, a sort of water container, then I could ferry them about wherever I wanted to. Get it? And they'd be finding pearls there and I'd be sailing out to them, supplying them with knives and harpoons and whatever other stuff they might need. Those poor little buggers so multi-pigged themselves in Devil Bay – '

'Multiplied.'

'Sure, multiplied, so they can't get enough food there any more. They live on small fish and molluscs and some kind of water slugs – but they'll also eat potatoes and biscuits and ordinary things. So it would be possible to feed them in the tanks on the ship. And at suitable spots, where there aren't many people about, I'd release them into the water again and set up some kind of . . . sort of farms for my lizards. I'd like to make sure they can feed themselves, those little creatures. They're very fetching and clever, Mr Bondy. Soon as you see them, old boy, you'll be saying: Hello, Captain, you've got some very useful creatures there. Sure. People just now are crazy about pearls, Mr Bondy. So that's the big business I've thought up.'

G. H. Bondy was embarrassed. 'I'm frightfully sorry, captain,' he began hesitantly, 'but – I really don't know – '

Captain van Toch's sky-blue eyes filled with tears. 'That's too bad, old boy. I'd leave you all these pearls here as . . . as a surety for that ship, but I can't buy her myself. And I know of a very handy ship over there in Rotterdam . . . runs on diesel – '

'Why haven't you proposed this business to somebody in Holland?'

The captain shook his head. 'I know those people, old boy. I can't talk to them about it. Well, I could perhaps carry some other cargo on that ship as well, general merchandise, sir, and sell it on those islands. Sure, I could do that. I know a lot of people out there, Mr Bondy. And then at the same time I could have tanks on that ship, for my lizards – '

'Now that's something one might consider,' G. H. Bondy reflected. 'It so happens . . . Well, we've *got* to find new markets for our industry. And it so happens I spoke to a few people a little while ago – I'd like to buy a ship or two, one for South America and the other for eastern parts – '

The captain revived. 'I like that idea, Mr Bondy, sir. Ships are terribly cheap just now, you can buy a whole harbour full of them – ' Captain van Toch launched out on a technical exposition on where and at what price certain vessels and boats and tank steamers were on sale. G. H. Bondy was not listening but was merely studying him: G. H. Bondy was a judge of men. He did not for one moment take Captain van Toch's lizards seriously, but he thought the captain was worth considering. Honest, yes. And he knew conditions out there. He was mad, of course. But damned likable. In G. H. Bondy's heart some fantastic chord was touched. Ships carrying pearls and coffee, ships with spices and all the perfumes of Arabia, G. H. Bondy felt distracted – a sensation which seized him before every major and successful decision, a sensation that might be put into words like this: I don't know why, but I'll probably go for it. Captain van Toch's massive hands were meanwhile mapping out in the air some ships with awning-decks or quarter-decks, superb ships, old boy –

'Tell you what, Captain Vantoch,' G. H. Bondy said suddenly. 'You come and see me in a fortnight. We'll have another talk about that ship.'

Captain van Toch understood the full import of those words. He flushed with pleasure and stammered: 'And those lizards – shall I be able to take them along on my ship as well?'

'But certainly. Except that you should not mention them to anyone, if you please. People might think that you've gone off your rocker – and me too.'

'And I may leave these pearls here?'

'You certainly may.'

'Only I've got to pick out two rather nice ones to send to somebody.'

'To whom?'

'To two journalists, old boy. Oh shit, wait a minute.'

'What is it?'

'Shit! I've forgotten their names.' Captain van Toch thoughtfully blinked his sky-blue eyes. 'I've got such a stupid head, old boy. Can't remember those two boys' names.'

5

Captain J. van Toch's Trained Lizards

'Blow me down,' said a man in Marseilles, 'if it isn't Jensen.'
The Swede, Jensen, raised his eyes. 'Wait,' he said, 'and don't say anything till I've placed you.' He put his hand on his forehead. *Seagull*, no. *Empress of India*, no. Pernambuco, no. Got it: Vancouver. Five years ago in Vancouver, Osaka Line, Frisco. And your name's Dingle, you old villain, and you're Irish.'
The man flashed his teeth and sat down. 'Right, Jensen. And I drink any hard stuff that comes out of a bottle. Where've you sprung from?'
Jensen motioned with his head. 'I'm now sailing Marseilles–Saigon. And you?'
'I'm on leave,' boasted Dingle. 'So I'm on my way home to see how many more kids I've got.'
Jensen nodded earnestly. 'So they've given you the boot again, right? Drunk on duty and that sort of thing. If you went to the YMCA like me, man, you'd – '
Dingle grinned with pleasure. 'There's a YMCA here?'
'Never mind, it's Saturday today,' Jensen growled. 'And what route did you work?'
'On some tramp,' Dingle said evasively. 'All sorts of islands down under.'
'Captain?'
'Man called van Toch. Dutchman or something.'
Jensen the Swede grew thoughtful. 'Captain van Toch. Sailed under him myself, years ago, brother. Ship: *Kandong Bandoeng*. Line: from devil to Satan. Fat chap, bald head, can even swear in Malay, so there's more of it. Know him well.'
'Was he potty in your time too?'
The Swede shook his head. 'Old Toch's all right, man.'
'Did he ship those lizards around with him then?'

'No.' Jensen hesitated for a moment. 'I did hear something
. . . in Singapore. Some blabbermouth was drivelling on about
it.'

The Irishman seemed rather offended. 'That's no drivel,
Jensen. That's gospel truth about the lizards.'

'Man in Singapore also said it was the truth,' the Swede
muttered. 'Still got his face pushed in,' he added triumphantly.

'Well, let me tell you then,' Dingle said defensively, 'what
it's all about. After all, I ought to know, chum. I saw the brutes
with my own eyes.'

'Me too,' muttered Jensen. 'Nearly black, about four foot
six with their tail, and walk on two legs. I know.'

'Hideous,' Dingle shuddered. 'All warts, man. Holy
Mother of God, I wouldn't touch them. Bound to be
poisonous!'

'Why?' grumbled the Swede. 'Man, I've served on ships
packed with people. Upper and lower deck, all crammed full,
nothing but people, nothing but women and suchlike, and
there they were dancing and playing cards – I was a stoker
then, you know. And now tell me, you dummy, which is more
poisonous.'

Dingle spat. 'If they were caymans, man, I wouldn't say
anything. Once I even carried snakes for a zoo, from
Bandjermassin down there, and boy, did they stink! But these
lizards – Jensen, they are mighty queer animals. OK, during
the day they're in their water tanks, but at night they creep
out, tap-tap, tap-tap . . . The whole ship was swarming with
them. Standing on their hindlegs and turning their heads after
you . . .' The Irishman crossed himself. 'They go ts-ts-ts at
you, just like those whores in Hong Kong. May God not
punish me, but I think they're not quite right. If jobs weren't
so hard to come by I wouldn't stay there another minute,
Jensy. Not a minute.'

'So that's it,' said Jensen. 'That's why you're running home
to mummy, right?'

'Partly. Chap had to drink heavily to put up with it all,
you know, and the captain's a real bastard about that. Terrible
fuss because they said I'd kicked one of those brutes. OK,
so I kicked it, and with gusto at that – so much so I broke
its back. You should have seen the old man going on about
it: turned blue he did, picked me up by the scruff of my neck

and would have thrown me overboard if Gregory the mate hadn't been around. Know him?'

The Swede merely nodded.

'He's had enough sir, the mate said, and poured a bucket of water over my head. And in Kokopo I went ashore.' Mr Dingle spat in a long flat trajectory. 'The old man cared more for those brutes than for his crew. Did you know he taught them to speak? Cross my heart, he'd lock himself up with them for hours on end and talk to them. I think he's training them like for a circus. But the oddest thing is that afterwards he lets them out into the water. He'll heave to off some silly little island, sail the boat along the shore, taking depth soundings, then he'll lock himself up near those tanks, open the broadside hatch and let the brutes into the water. Man, they dive in through that little window, one after another, just like trained seals – always some ten or twelve. And then old Toch rows to the shore at night, with some little crates. No one's allowed to know what he's got in them. And then the ship sails on. That's how things are with old Toch, Jensy. Odd. Very odd.' Mr Dingle's eyes became fixed. 'God Almighty, Jensy, I was getting the wind up! I drank, man; I drank like a fish; and when there was this tapping at night and this waddling on hindlegs all over the ship . . . and that ts-ts-ts . . . well, sometimes I thought: Aha, Dingle, my boyo, that comes from drink. It happened to me once before, in Frisco, as you well know, Jensy: only then I was seeing nothing but spiders. De-li-rium, that's what the doctors at the Sailors' Hospital called it. So I don't know. But then I asked Big Bing if he'd seen anything at night, and he said he had. Said he saw with his own eyes how one of those lizards turned the door handle and went into the captain's cabin. So I don't know. Joe's a terrible soak too. D'you think, Jensy, that Bing had delirium? What do you think?'

Jensen the Swede merely shrugged.

'And that German, Peters, said that on Manihiki Islands, when he had rowed the captain ashore, he'd hidden behind some rocks to watch what old Toch was up to with those little packing cases. Man, he said those lizards opened them themselves if the old man gave them a chisel. And do you know what was inside? Knives, he said. Knives this long, and harpoons, and such stuff. Man alive, I don't really trust Peters because he wears glasses – but it's odd all the same. What do you think?'

The veins on Jens Jensen's temples began to stand out. 'Well, I'm telling you that this German of yours is poking his nose into something that's no business of his, understand? And I'm telling you that I wouldn't advise him to do that.'

'Why don't you write him a letter?', the Irishman mocked. 'Surest address will be Hell; he's bound to get it there. But do you know what seems strange to me? That old Toch goes and visits those lizards of his from time to time, at the spots where he dropped them. Cross my heart, Jensy. He has himself taken ashore at night and doesn't come back till morning. So you tell me, Jensen, who he's visiting there. And you tell me what's inside those packages he sends to Europe. Look, a package about this big, and he insures it for maybe £3,000.'

'How do you know that?' the Swede frowned, turning darker still.

'There are ways of finding out,' Mr Dingle said evasively. 'And do you know where old Toch is shipping those lizards from? Devil Bay, Jensy! I've got a friend there, he's an agent and an educated man, and he said to me: Man, those aren't trained lizards. Far from it! Don't be fooled, he said.' Mr Dingle winked meaningfully. 'That's how things are, Jensen – just so you know. And you're telling me Captain van Toch is all right!'

'Say that again,' the big Swede growled menacingly.

'If old Toch was all right he wouldn't be shipping devils all over the place . . . and he wouldn't be dropping them off all over those islands like fleas in a fur. Jensy, during the time that I was with him he shipped a good few thousand around. Old Toch's sold his soul, man. And I know what those devils give him in return. Rubies, pearls and suchlike. Stands to reason; he wouldn't have done it for nothing.'

Jens Jensen turned puce. 'And what business is it of yours?' he roared and banged the table. 'You mind your own bloody business!'

Little Dingle jumped with fright. 'Please . . .' he stammered in confusion; 'why are you all of a sudden . . . I'm only saying what I saw. And if you like I only dreamt it. That's because it's you. If you like I'll say I was delirious. Don't be angry with me, Jensen. You know quite well I had this before, in Frisco. A bad case, the doctors at the Sailors' Hospital said. But man, I could have sworn by my immortal soul that I did see those lizards or devils or whatever. But they weren't real.'

'They were, Pat,' the Swede said gloomily. 'I saw them myself.'

'No, Jensy,' argued Dingle. 'You were only delirious. Old Toch is all right, but he shouldn't ship those devils all over the place. Know what? When I'm home I'll have a Mass said for his soul. May I be struck dead if I don't.'

'We don't do that,' Jensen boomed melancholically, 'in my religion. And what do you think, Pat, does it do any good if a Mass is said for somebody?'

'A powerful deal of good, man,' the Irishman burst out. 'I've heard of cases back home where it did a deal of good . . . why, even in the most difficult cases. Especially against devils and suchlike, you know!'

'Then I shall have a Catholic Mass said too,' Jens Jensen decided. 'For Captain van Toch. But I'll have it said right here, in Marseilles. I suppose they do it cheaper in that big church – at wholesale price, like.'

'Could be. But an Irish Mass is better. Back home, man, we have devil priests who are downright wizards. Just like fakirs or witch doctors.'

'Look, Pat, I'd like to give you twelve francs for that Mass. But you're a rascal and'll spend it on booze.'

'Jensy, I wouldn't lay such a sin upon myself. But hold it, so you can trust me I'll give you an IOU for those twelve francs. OK?'

'That would do,' said the methodical Swede. Mr Dingle borrowed a piece of paper and a pencil and spread himself broadly over the table. 'What am I to write, then?'

Jens Jensen was looking over his shoulder. 'OK, at the top you put that it's a kind of receipt.'

And Mr Dingle, sticking out his tongue with the effort and licking his pencil, wrote down slowly:

Receet

I hereby sirtify that I have receevd

from Jens Jensen 12 franks for a
Mass for the sole of Capn Toch.

Pat Dingle

'OK like this?' Mr Dingle asked uncertainly. 'And which
of us should keep this document?'

'You, of course, you idiot,' the Swede said without
hesitation. 'That's so you don't forget that you've received
the money.'

Mr Dingle spent those twelve francs on drink at Le Havre,
and instead of sailing to Ireland he sailed to Djibouti. In short,
the Mass has not yet been said, and in consequence no higher
power has intervened in the natural course of events.

6

The Yacht in the Lagoon

Mr Abe Loeb screwed up his eyes into the setting sun; he would have liked to put into words how beautiful it all was but his Sweetiepie Li, alias Miss Lily Valley, more properly Miss Lilian Nowak, in short golden-haired Li, White Lily, long-limbed Lilian or whatever other names she had been given before she had reached seventeen, was sleeping on the warm sand, snuggled into a fleecy bath-robe and curled up like a sleeping dog. That's why Abe didn't say anything about the beauty of the world but merely heaved a sigh and wriggled the toes of his bare feet because there were grains of sand between them. Out there on the sea rode his yacht, the *Gloria Pickford*; this yacht had been given to Abe as a present by Papa Loeb for passing his finals. Papa Loeb was quite a guy. Jesse Loeb, film tycoon and suchlike. Abe, boy, why don't you invite a few pals and some girl friends and see something of the world, the old man had said. Papa Jesse was really quite a guy. There then, on the mother-of-pearl sea, rode the *Gloria Pickford* and here on the warm sand slept Sweetiepie Li. Sleeps like a little child, poor kid. Abe felt an immense yearning to protect her somehow. I suppose I *really* ought to marry her, young Mr Loeb was thinking; in his heart he experienced a beautiful and tormenting pressure, compounded of firm determination and fear. Ma Loeb probably wouldn't approve, and Papa Loeb would throw up his hands: You're crazy, Abe. Well, parents simply didn't understand, that was it. And Abe, sighing with tenderness, drew the corner of the bath-robe over the slender white ankle of Sweetiepie Li. A nuisance, he thought with embarrassment, that I've got such hairy legs!

God, how beautiful it is here, how beautiful it is! Pity Li doesn't see it. Abe gazed at the splendid curve of her hip and by some indistinct association began to think about art. After all, Sweetiepie Li is an artist. A film actress. She hasn't had a part yet but she has made up her mind that she'll be the greatest screen actress there ever was; and if Li makes up her mind about something she sure gets it. That's just what Ma Loeb won't understand; an artist is simply an artist, and can't be like other girls. Besides, other girls were no better, Abe decided. Take for instance that Judy on board the yacht: such a rich girl – and I know perfectly well that Fred visits her in her cabin. *Every* night, I ask you, whereas I and Li . . . Well, Li just isn't like *that*. I don't begrudge it to baseball Freddie, Abe thought magnanimously, he's a college friend; but every night – a girl as rich as *that* oughtn't to do that. I mean, a girl from a family such as Judy's. And Judy isn't even an artist. (The things those girls whisper about amongst each other, it occurred to Abe; how their eyes shine and how they giggle – *I* never talk about *such* things to Fred.) (Li shouldn't drink so many cocktails, she doesn't know what she's saying afterwards.) (Like this afternoon, that was unnecessary –) (I mean how she and Judy quarrelled about which of them had the prettier legs. Stands to reason that Li has. I should know.) (And Fred needn't have had that idiotic idea of holding a leg competition. You can do that some place on Palm Beach but not at a private party. And surely the girls needn't have lifted their skirts *that high*. And it wasn't *just* legs. At least Li shouldn't have done so. Especially in front of Fred! And a girl as rich as Judy shouldn't have done it either.) (And I guess I shouldn't have asked the captain to judge. That was dumb of me. The way the captain blushed and his moustache bristled and with You'll excuse me, sir, had slammed the door. Embarrassing. Terribly embarrassing. But the captain needn't have been *that* rude. After all, it's *my* yacht, ain't it?) (True enough, the captain's got no sweetiepie of his own with him, so why should the poor guy be made to look at *such* things? I mean if he's got to be on his own.) (And why did Li cry when Fred said that Judy's legs were prettier? And then she said Fred was so ill-mannered he was spoiling the whole cruise for her . . . Poor kid, poor Li!) (And now the two girls aren't on speaking terms. And when I tried to speak to Fred, Judy called him over to her like a little dog. After all, Fred's my best friend. Of course, if he's Judy's lover he's *got* to say she has the prettier legs! But he needn't have been so emphatic about it. That *wasn't* tactful towards poor Li; Li's right, Fred is a conceited lout. A frightful lout.) (Matter of fact, I'd visualised this voyage rather differently. I need that Fred like I need a hole in my head!)

Abe realised that he was no longer gazing in ecstasy at the mother-of-pearl-coloured sea but that he was very, very angry as he let the sand with its little shells run through his fingers. Papa Loeb had said, Go and see something of the world. Have we already seen something of the world? Abe tried to remember just what he had seen but he couldn't recall anything except Judy and Sweetiepie Li showing their legs and Fred, broad-shouldered Fred, kneeling in front of them, sitting back on his heels. Abe frowned even more. What was the name of this coral island? Taraiva, the captain had said. Taraiva or Tahuara or Taraihatuara-ta-huara. How about turning back home and me telling the old man, Dad, we went as far as Taraihatuara-ta-huara. (If only I hadn't summoned that captain, Abe thought irritably.) (Got to have a talk with Li, tell her not to do such things. God, how come I'm so *terribly* in love with her? When she wakes up I'll have a talk with her. Tell her we might get married –) Abe's eyes were full of tears; God, is that love or pain, or is this boundless pain part of my loving her?

Sweetiepie Li's shiny blue-shadowed eyelids, which looked like delicate shells, trembled. 'Abe,' a sleepy voice said, 'do you know what I'm thinking? That on this island here we could make a fan-tas-tic film.'

Abe piled some fine sand on his unfortunate hairy legs. 'Great idea, Sweetiepie. What sort of film?'

Sweetiepie Li opened her immensely blue eyes. 'Something like this: Imagine me being on this island like Robinson Crusoe. A girl Crusoe. Isn't that a terrific new idea?'

'Sure,' Abe said uncertainly. 'And how would you get to this island?'

'Easy,' said the sweet little voice. 'You know, our yacht quite simply got shipwrecked in a storm, and you'd all be drowned – you, Judy, the captain, the lot.'

'And Fred too? Remember Fred's a great swimmer.'

The smooth forehead was furrowed. 'So Fred would have to be eaten by a shark. That would be a marvellous episode,' Sweetiepie clapped her hands. 'Because Fred's got a divinely beautiful body, don't you think?'

Abe sighed. 'And what next?'

'I'd be cast up on the beach by a wave, unconscious. I'd be wearing those pyjamas with the blue stripes you liked so much the day before yesterday.' From between the delicate eyelids there escaped a half-closed glance suitably illustrating feminine seductiveness. 'Actually it would have to be in colour, Abe. Everybody says that blue goes awfully well with my hair.'

'And who would find you here?' Abe asked in a matter-of-fact way.

Sweetiepie reflected. 'Nobody. I wouldn't be a girl Crusoe if there were other people about,' she said with surprising logic. 'That's why it would be such a terrific part, Abe – I'd be on my own the whole time. Just imagine it – Lily Valley in the leading and altogether only part.'

'And what would you be doing all through the film?'

Li raised herself on an elbow. 'I got all that figured out. I'd bathe and I'd sing perched on a rock.'

'In your pyjamas?'

'Without,' said Sweetiepie. 'Don't you think that would be a terrific success?'

'Surely you can't play the whole film in the nude,' Abe grumbled with a strong sense of disapproval.

'Why not?' Sweetiepie was innocently astonished. 'What's wrong with that?'

Abe said something unintelligible.

'And then,' Li reflected, ' – wait a minute, I've got it. Then a gorilla would carry me off. You know, such a terribly hairy black gorilla.'

Abe blushed and tried to hide his unfortunate legs even deeper in the sand. 'But there are no gorillas here,' he objected without much conviction.

'Sure there are. There are altogether all kinds of animals around. You got to look at it artistically, Abe. A gorilla would go tremendously well with my complexion. Have you noticed what a lot of hair Judy's got on her legs?'

'No,' said Abe, unhappy about the subject.

'Horrid legs,' Sweetiepie opined, gazing at her own calves. 'And just as that gorilla was carrying me off in its arms a marvellously handsome young savage would come out of the jungle and shoot it down.'

'What would he be wearing?'

'He'd carry a bow,' Sweetiepie decided without a moment's

hesitation. 'And a garland on his head. That savage would seize me and take me to the camp of the cannibals.'

'There aren't any here,' objected Abe, trying to defend the little island of Tahuara.

'Sure there are. Those cannibals would want to sacrifice me to their idols and they'd be singing Hawaiian songs meanwhile. You know, like those negroes at the Paradise restaurant. But that young cannibal would fall in love with me,' Sweetiepie breathed, her eyes wide with amazement, '. . . and then some other savage would also fall in love with me, say the chief of those cannibals . . . and then a white man too – '

'Where would the white man spring from?' Abe asked, just to make sure.

'He'd be their prisoner. He could be a famous tenor who'd fallen into the cannibals' hands. That's so he could sing a lot in the film.'

'And what would he be wearing?'

Sweetiepie looked at her toes. 'He would be . . . without anything, like those cannibals.'

Abe shook his head. 'Sweetiepie, that's impossible. All famous tenors are frightfully fat.'

'That's a real shame,' Sweetiepie regretted. 'In that case Fred might act the part and the tenor would just do the singing. You know how they do those synchronisations in the film business.'

'But surely Fred was eaten by a shark!'

Sweetiepie was irritated. 'You mustn't be so terribly realistic, Abe. It's *quite* impossible to talk to you about art. And that chieftain would wind strings of pearls all round me – '

'Where'd he get them from?'

'There are *masses* of pearls around,' Li declared. 'And Fred, from jealousy, would have a boxing match with him on a cliff above the crashing waves of the sea – ' Sweetiepie suddenly brightened up. 'Now we could have that sequence with the shark. Think how furious Judy'd be if Fred was in a film with me! And I'd marry that handsome savage.' Golden-haired Li jumped up. 'We'd stand right here on the beach . . . against the sunset . . . quite naked . . . and the camera would slowly fade out – ' Li dropped her bath-robe. 'I'm going in.'

'. . . not got your swimsuit on,' Abe reminded her, aghast, turning towards the yacht to make sure no one was looking;

but Sweetiepie was already tripping over the sand towards the lagoon.

. . . actually looks better dressed, a brutally cold and critical voice suddenly spoke up inside the young man. Abe felt shattered by his lack of lover's adoration, he almost felt guilty; but . . . well, when Li's got her pretty clothes and shoes on it's . . . well, somehow nicer.

Perhaps you mean: more decent, Abe defended himself against that cold voice.

Well, that too. And also prettier. Why does she waddle so strangely? Why is that flesh on her legs wobbling so? Why this and why that . . .

Stop it, Abe defended himself in alarm. Li is the most beautiful girl ever! I'm terribly fond of her . . .

. . . even without her clothes on? the cold critical voice inquired.

Abe averted his eyes and gazed at the yacht on the lagoon. How beautiful she is, how trim and sleek all over! Pity Fred isn't here. You can talk to Fred about the beauty of the yacht.

Sweetiepie, meanwhile, was standing up to her knees in the water, raising her arms towards the setting sun and singing. Why the hell isn't she getting her swim over, Abe thought irritably. But it had been nice, having her lying there, all curled up and swaddled in her robe, with her eyes closed. Sweetiepie Li. And with a tender sigh Abe kissed the sleeve of her robe. Yes, he was terribly fond of her. So fond that it hurt.

Suddenly a piercing scream came from the lagoon. Abe raised himself on one knee to get a better view. Sweetiepie Li was squealing, waving her arms about and wading hurriedly towards the beach, stumbling and splashing all over the place . . . Abe leapt to his feet and ran over to her. 'What's up, Li?'

(Just look how strangely she is running, the cold critical voice nudged him. Flinging her legs about too much. Flapping her hands around too much. In short, it is *not* pretty. Moreover, she is cackling, yes, cackling.)

'What's happened, Li?' Abe called out, running to her aid.

'Abe, Abe,' Sweetiepie sobbed, and – flop – she was already hanging on him, all wet and cold. 'Abe, there was some kind of animal there!'

'That was nothing,' Abe soothed her. 'Probably some kind of fish.'

'But it had such a frightful head,' Sweetiepie squealed, burying her wet nose in Abe's chest.

Abe tried to pat her paternally on the shoulder, but on her wet body this turned into a rather noisy smack. 'Now, now,' he murmured; 'look, there's nothing there now.'

Li turned back towards the lagoon. 'It was horrid,' she breathed, and suddenly started squealing: 'There . . . there . . . see it?'

A dark head was slowly approaching the shore, its mouth opening and closing. Sweetiepie Li screeched hysterically and started desperately to run away from the water's edge.

Abe was in a quandary. Should he run after Li to stop her being frightened? Or should he stay put to show that he wasn't afraid of the beast? Naturally he decided on the second course; he moved closer, until he stood ankle-deep in the water, and with fists clenched looked the animal in the eyes. The black head halted, rocked strangely and said: 'Ts, ts, ts.'

Abe was feeling a little uneasy but he tried not to show it. 'What is it?' he said sharply in the direction of the head.

'Ts, ts, ts,' went the head.

'Abe, Abe, Aaa-be,' yelled Sweetiepie Li.

'Coming,' shouted Abe and slowly (to preserve his dignity) strode over to his girl. He stopped once and severely turned towards the sea.

On the beach, where the sea draws its perpetual and impermanent lace on the sand, some kind of dark animal with a round head was standing on its hindlegs, twisting its body. Abe stopped, his heart pounding.

'Ts, ts, ts,' went the animal.

'Aaa-be,' Sweetiepie squealed, almost in a swoon.

Abe backed away step by step, not letting the animal out of his sight; the creature did not move but merely turned its head towards him.

At last Abe had reached his Sweetiepie, who was lying face down and sobbing with terror. 'It's . . . some kind of seal,' Abe said uncertainly. 'Maybe we'd better get back to the boat, Li.' But Li was only shaking.

'It isn't anything dangerous at all,' Abe insisted. He would have liked to kneel down by Li but he had to stand chivalrously between her and the animal. If only I wasn't in my trunks, he was thinking, if only I had even a pocket-knife, or if I could find a stick . . .

Dusk was beginning to fall. The animal once more approached to within some thirty paces, and then stopped. Behind it five, six, eight identical animals rose from the sea and hesitantly, with a swaying motion, waddled to the spot where Abe was guarding Sweetiepie Li.

'Don't look, Li,' Abe breathed, but that was superfluous since nothing in the world would have made Li turn her head.

More shadows were emerging from the sea and advancing in a wide semicircle. There must be some sixty by now, Abe counted. That light thing over there was Sweetiepie Li's bath-robe. The robe she had been sleeping in a little while ago. The animals had by now advanced to that light thing spread on the sand.

At this point Abe did something obvious and nonsensical, just like that knight in Schiller's poem who walked into the lion's cage to retrieve his lady's glove. What of it; there are obvious and nonsensical things men will do as long as the world revolves. Without stopping to think, his head held high and his fists clenched, Abe walked amidst those animals to get Sweetiepie Li's bath-robe.

The animals retreated a little but did not run away. Abe picked up the robe, flung it over his arm like a bullfighter, and stopped.

'Aaa-be,' came a desperate whine from behind him.

Abe was conscious of boundless strength and courage within him. 'Well, then?' he addressed the animals, taking another step forward. 'What is it you want?'

'Ts, ts,' one animal smacked, but then, in a somewhat croaking and elderly voice, it barked: 'Nyfe!'

'Nyfe!' came a bark from nearby. 'Nyfe!' 'Nyfe!' 'Aaa-be!'

'Don't be afraid, Li!,' Abe called out.

'Li,' came a bark in front of him. 'Li.' 'Li.' 'Aaa-be!'

Abe thought he was dreaming. 'What is it?'

'Nyfe!'

'Aaa-be,' Sweetiepie Li moaned. 'Come back!'

'In a minute. You mean a knife? I haven't got a knife. I'm not going to hurt you. What else do you want?'

'Ts-ts,' an animal hissed and swayed closer to him.

Abe stood with his legs apart, the robe over his arm, but he did not retreat. 'Ts-ts,' he said. 'What do you want?' It looked to him as if the animal was offering him its front paw, but this did not appeal to Abe. 'What?' he said rather sharply.

'Nyfe,' the animal barked and from its paw dropped some whitish things, like drops of water. But they were not drops of water because they rolled in the sand.

'Abe,' stammered Li. 'Don't leave me here alone!'

By now Mr Abe felt no fear at all. 'Clear off,' he said and waved the robe at the animal. The animal retreated hastily and awkwardly. Abe could now have moved away without loss of face, but he wanted Li to see how brave he was. He bent down to the whitish things the animal had dropped from its paw, to get a closer look. They were three hard, smooth little globules with a matt sheen. Mr Abe lifted them to his eyes because it was getting dark.

'Aaa-be,' howled his deserted Sweetiepie. 'Abe!'

'Coming,' called Mr Abe. 'Li, I've got something for you! Li, Li, I'm bringing it over!' Swirling the bath-robe over his head Mr Abe Loeb raced across the beach like a young god.

Li was cowering in a heap, shaking all over. 'Abe,' she sobbed, her teeth chattering. 'How could you . . . how could you . . .'

Abe knelt down ceremoniously in front of her. 'Lily Valley, the gods of the sea, the Tritons, have come to pay tribute to you. I am to tell you that, since Venus emerged from the foam, no artist has made a deeper impression on them than you. As a token of their admiration they are offering you – ' here Abe extended his hand – 'these three pearls. Look.'

'Stop fooling, Abe,' Sweetiepie Li whimpered.

'Seriously, Li. Why don't you look: these are real pearls!'

'Let's see,' Li grunted and with trembling fingers reached out for the whitish beads. 'Abe,' she gasped, 'but these are *pearls*! Did you find them in the sand?'

'But Li, Sweetiepie, pearls aren't found in the sand!'

'Sure they are,' Sweetiepie insisted. 'And they're panned. See, I told you there were masses of pearls around!'

'Pearls grow in a kind of shell under the water,' Abe declared with something approaching assurance. 'Cross my heart, Li, these were brought for you by those Tritons.

You see, they saw you bathing. They'd have given them to you in person if you hadn't been so scared – '

'But they're so ugly,' Li blurted out. 'Abe, these are *marvellous* pearls! I'm awfully fond of pearls!'

(Now she is pretty, said the critical voice. The way she is kneeling there with those pearls in her palm – real pretty, got to admit it.)

'Abe, these were *really* brought to me by those . . . those animals?'

'Those aren't animals, Sweetiepie. Those are gods of the sea. They're called Tritons.'

Sweetiepie was not in the least surprised. 'That's real nice of them, isn't it? They're awfully sweet. What d'you think, Abe, should I thank them in some way?'

'You're no longer afraid of them?'

Sweetiepie shivered. 'Yes, I am. Please, Abe, take me away!'

'Look,' Abe said. 'We've got to get to our boat. Come along then, and don't be scared.'

'But . . . but they're standing in our way,' Li stammered. 'Wouldn't you rather go to them alone? But you mustn't leave me here on my own!'

'I'll carry you across in my arms,' Abe proposed heroically.

'That might do,' Sweetiepie breathed.

'But put that robe on,' Abe growled.

'Just a minute.' Miss Li straightened her famous golden hair with both hands. 'Isn't my hair *terribly* untidy? Abe, you wouldn't have any lipstick for me?'

Abe put the robe round her shoulders. 'Better come now, Li!'

'I'm scared,' Sweetiepie breathed. Mr Abe picked her up in his arms. Li felt as light as a little cloud. Hell, she's heavier than you thought, isn't she, the cold critical voice said to Abe. And now you've got both hands full, man – suppose those animals went for you now? What then?

'How about going at a trot?' Sweetiepie suggested.

'Sure,' puffed Mr Abe, scarcely moving his legs. By then it was getting dark rapidly. He approached the wide semicircle of the animals. 'Faster, run faster,' moaned Sweetiepie, kicking her legs hysterically and digging her silver-painted nails into Abe's neck.

'Hell, Li, stop it,' Abe howled.

'Nyfe' came a bark from his side. 'Ts-ts-ts.' 'Nyfe.' 'Li.' 'Nyfe.' 'Nyfe.' 'Nyfe.' 'Li.'

They were now clear of the semicircle and Abe felt his feet sinking into the damp sand. 'You can put me down now,' Sweetiepie breathed at the very moment when Abe's arms and legs gave way.

Abe was breathing heavily, wiping his sweaty brow with his forearm. 'Get back to the boat, quick,' he ordered Sweetiepie Li. The semicircle of dark shadows now turned to face Li and drew closer. 'Ts-ts-ts.' 'Nyfe.' 'Nyfe.' 'Li.' And Li did not scream. Li did not start running. Li raised her arms towards the sky, and the robe slid from her shoulders. Naked, Li waved both her arms to the swaying shades and blew them kisses. On her trembling lips there appeared something that anybody would feel bound to call an enchanting smile. 'You're so sweet,' said a stammering little voice. And her white arms again extended towards the swaying shadows.

'Give me a hand, Li,' Abe grumbled a little rudely, pushing the boat deeper into the water.

Sweetiepie Li picked up her bath-robe. 'Good-bye, darlings!' The shadows could be heard splashing in the water. 'Hurry up, Abe,' Sweetiepie hissed, wading towards the boat. 'They're here again!' Mr Abe Loeb was desperately trying to get the boat afloat. That's it – and now Miss Sweetiepie clambered aboard and waved her hand in salutation. 'Get on the other side, Abe; they can't see me.'

'Nyfe.' 'Ts-ts-ts.' 'Aaa-be!'

'Nyfe, ts, nyfe.'

'Ts-ts.'

'Nyfe!'

At last the boat was bobbing on the waves. Mr Abe struggled in and with all his strength pulled on the oars. One oar struck some slippery body.

Sweetiepie Li drew a deep breath. 'Don't you agree they're awfully sweet? And wasn't I just *perfect*?'

Mr Abe rowed for all he was worth, making for the yacht. 'Put that robe on, Li,' he said rather drily.

'I think it was a *tremendous* success,' Miss Li declared. 'And those pearls, Abe! How much do you think they're worth?'

Mr Abe stopped rowing for a moment. 'I think you needn't have shown yourself to them *quite like that*, Sweetiepie.'

Miss Li was rather offended. 'What's wrong with that? It's obvious, Abe, you're not an *artist*. Do go on rowing, please; I'm freezing in this robe!'

7

The Yacht in the Lagoon (continued)

That evening there were no personal quarrels on board the *Gloria Pickford* – only a noisy clash of scientific opinion. Fred (loyally supported by Abe) decided that they must *definitely* have been some kind of reptile whereas the captain came down in favour of mammals. There were no reptiles in the sea, the captain insisted fiercely; but the young gentlemen with a university education took no notice of his objections; reptiles, after all, were more sensational. Sweetiepie Li was quite happy to believe that they were Tritons, that they were positively delightful, and that the whole thing had been a *terrific* success. And Li (wearing the blue-striped pyjamas which Abe liked *such a lot*) dreamed with shining eyes of pearls and marine deities. Judy, of course, was convinced that the whole thing was a joke and a hoax, and that Li and Abe had thought it up together; she was furiously winking at Fred to let the matter rest. Abe was thinking that Li *might* have mentioned how he, Abe, had fearlessly walked right amidst those reptiles to pick up her robe; that's why he related three times how *superbly* Li had stood up to them while he, Abe, had been pushing the boat into the water, and he was just about to relate it for a fourth time. But Fred and the captain were not listening at all but were passionately arguing the case of reptiles versus mammals. (As if it mattered *what* they were, thought Abe.) In the end Judy yawned and said she was going to bed; she looked meaningfully at Fred, but Fred had just remembered that such funny old reptiles had existed before the Flood, what the hell were they called, diplosaurs, bigosaurs or something like that, and they had walked about on their hindlegs, yessir; Fred had seen them himself in a funny scientific illustration and a book as fat as this. A tremendous book, sir, you ought to see it.

'Abe,' Sweetiepie Li piped up. 'I've got a *marvellous* idea for a film.'

'What's that?'

'Something tremendously new. You know, our yacht might go down and I alone would save myself and get to that island. And I'd live there like a Girl Crusoe.'

'What would you be doing there?' the captain objected sceptically.

'Swim in the sea and that sort of thing,' Sweetiepie said simply. 'And those sea Tritons would fall in love with me . . . and bring me pearls and pearls. You know, just as it really was. It might even be an educational nature film, don't you think? Something like Trader Horn.'

'Li is right,' Fred suddenly declared. 'We ought to film those reptiles tomorrow evening.'

'You mean those mammals,' the captain corrected him.

'You mean me,' said Sweetiepie. 'Standing among those sea Tritons.'

'But in a robe,' Abe blurted out.

'I could put on that *white* swimsuit,' Li said. 'But Greta would have to do my hair properly. Today I looked a frightful mess.'

'And who'd do the filming?'

'Abe. That way, at least, he'll be some use. And Judy would have to provide some lighting in case it's dark by then.'

'And what about Fred?'

'Fred would be carrying a bow and wearing a wreath on his head, and if those Tritons tried to carry me off he'd mow them down.'

'Much obliged,' Fred grinned. 'But I'd rather have a revolver. And I think the captain should be present too.'

The captain's moustache bristled with fighting spirit. 'Don't concern yourself, please. I'll do whatever is necessary.'

'And what will that be?'

'Three men of the crew, sir. And well armed, sir.'

Sweetiepie was delightfully astonished. 'You think it'll be *that* dangerous, captain?'

'I don't think anything, kid,' the captain growled. 'But I've got my orders from Mr Jesse Loeb – at least as far as Mr Abe's concerned.'

The gentlemen threw themselves enthusiastically into the

technical details of the enterprise; Abe winked at Sweetiepie, time you went to bed and that sort of thing. Li obediently went off. 'You know, Abe,' she said in her cabin; 'I think this is going to be a *fantastic* film!'

'Sure will, Sweetiepie,' agreed Mr Abe; trying to kiss her.

'Not tonight, Abe,' Sweetiepie resisted. 'Surely you understand that I've got to concentrate *frightfully*.'

All next day Miss Li was intensely concentrating; her poor maid Greta was kept more than busy over it. There were baths with important salts and essences, hair-washing with Everblonde shampoo, massages, pedicure, manicure, hair-curling and brushing out, pressing and trying on of clothes, alterations, make-up and a variety of other preparations; even Judy was swept along with the rush and made herself useful to Sweetiepie Li. (There are moments of crisis when women can be surprisingly loyal to each other, for instance over dressing.) While all this feverish activity was going on in Miss Li's cabin the gentlemen made their own arrangements and, placing ashtrays and glasses of whisky about the table, laid down their strategic plan, where each of them would stand and what he would be responsible for in case anything happened; in the course of this the captain was several times deeply offended over the question of prestige in the matter of command. During the afternoon they transported everything to the shore: a film camera, a small machine-gun, a hamper with food, plates and cutlery, rifles, a gramophone and other military equipment; everything was superbly camouflaged with palm leaves. Just before sunset three armed crew members and the captain (in his role of commander-in-chief) took up position. Next a huge basket containing a few little requisites of Miss Lily Valley was brought ashore. After that Fred arrived by boat with Miss Judy. And then the sun began to set in all its tropical splendour.

By then Mr Abe was knocking at Miss Li's cabin door for the tenth time. 'Sweetiepie, it's *really* high time to be off!'

'In a second, in a second,' replied Sweetiepie's voice. 'Please don't hassle me! I've got to *dress*, haven't I?'

Meanwhile, the captain was taking stock of the situation. Out there on the surface a long straight band was shimmering, dividing the rippling sea from the still water of the lagoon.

Almost as if there was some dam or breakwater under the surface, the captain thought; maybe a sandbar or a coral reef, but it almost looked like an artificial structure. Queer spot, this. Above the still surface of the lagoon black heads were popping up here and there, moving towards the beach. The captain pressed his lips together and nervously fingered his revolver. Would have been better, he thought, if those women had stayed behind on the ship. Judy was beginning to tremble and frantically clutched Fred. How strong he is, she thought. God, how I love him!

Finally the last boat pushed off from the yacht. In it was Miss Lily Valley in a white swimsuit and a transparent dressing gown in which, apparently, she intended to be shipwrecked; also in the boat were Miss Greta and Mr Abe. 'Why are you rowing so slowly, Abe,' Sweetiepie criticised. Mr Abe had seen those black heads moving towards the shore and said nothing.

'Ts-ts.'

'Ts.'

Mr Abe dragged the boat up on the sand and gave a hand to Sweetiepie Li and Miss Greta. 'Run over to the camera, quick,' the artist whispered. 'And when I say "Now" you start shooting.'

'But it'll be too dark,' Abe objected.

'Then Judy must switch on the light. Greta!'

While Mr Abe took up position behind the camera the artist was lying down on the sand like a dying swan, and Miss Greta straightened the folds of her dressing gown. 'I want to show a bit of leg,' the castaway whispered. 'Ready? Be off, then! Abe, now!'

Abe started to turn the handle. 'Judy, lights!' But no light came on. From the sea emerged some swaying shadows and moved towards Li. Greta clapped her hands over her mouth to stop herself screaming.

'Li,' Mr Abe called out. 'Li, run away!'

'Nyfe!' 'Ts-ts-ts.' 'Li.' 'Li.' 'Abe!'

Someone was flicking back a safety catch. 'Dammit, don't fire', hissed the captain.

'Li,' Abe called out and stopped turning the handle. 'Judy, lights!'

Li rose slowly and softly to her feet and stretched her arms up towards the sky. The gossamer dressing gown slipped from her shoulders. Thus she stood there, lily-white Lily, her arms charmingly raised above her head, the way castaways do when they wake from a faint. Mr Abe furiously started to turn his handle. 'Damn it all, Judy, let's have the lights!'

'Ts-ts-ts.'

'Nyfe.'

'Nyfe.'

'Aaa-be!'

The black shadows were swaying and circling around white Li. Hold on, this wasn't play-acting any more. Li was no longer raising her arms skywards but pushing something away from her, squealing: 'Abe, Abe, it touched me!' At that moment a blinding light came on. Abe quickly turned the camera handle, Fred and the captain came running with their revolvers to help Li who was cowering and stuttering with terror. Just then the bright light revealed dozens and hundreds of those tall dark shadows hurriedly slipping into the sea. Also just then two swimmers flung a net over one of the fleeing shadows. Just then Greta fainted, falling like a sack. Just then two or three shots rang out, there was some commotion in the water, the two swimmers with the net were lying on something that twisted and wriggled under them, and the light in Miss Judy's hand went out.

The captain switched on his pocket torch. 'You all right, kid?'

'It touched my leg,' Sweetiepie moaned. 'Fred, it was horrible!'

By then Mr Abe had also arrived with his pocket torch. 'That went beautifully, Li,' he boomed; 'only Judy should have switched on sooner!'

'It wouldn't go on,' Judy stammered. 'Would it, Fred?'

'Judy was scared,' Fred made excuses for her. 'Honest, she didn't do it deliberately. Isn't that so, Judy?'

Judy was offended; but the two swimmers were now approaching, dragging in their net something that was struggling like a big fish. 'Well, here it is, captain. And alive.'

'The brute, it squirted some kind of poison at me. My hands are covered in blisters, sir. And they sting like hell.'

'It touched me too,' Miss Li whimpered. 'Shine your torch here, Abe! See if I've got a blister here.'

'No, you haven't Sweetiepie. Nothing there,' Abe assured her. He nearly kissed the spot above her knee which Li was anxiously rubbing. 'Such a cold touch, horrid,' Sweetiepie Li complained.

'You dropped a pearl, ma'am,' said one of the swimmers and handed Li the little bead he'd picked up from the sand.

'Heavens, Abe,' Miss Li exclaimed; 'they've brought me pearls again! Come on, kids, we'll look for pearls! There'll be *masses* of pearls here which those poor little things brought me! Aren't they delightful creatures, Fred? Here's another pearl!'

'And here!'

Three torches turned their beams towards the ground.

'I've found a whopper!'

'That belongs to me,' blurted Sweetiepie Li.

'Fred,' came Miss Judy's frosty voice.

'In a minute,' said Mr Fred, crawling in the sand on his hands and knees.

'Fred, I want to go back to the ship!'

'Somebody'll take you,' Fred suggested, preoccupied. 'Hell, this is fun!'

The three gentlemen and Miss Li continued to move across the sand like large fireflies.

'Three pearls here,' announced the captain.

'Show me, show me,' squealed Li ecstatically, hurrying after the captain on her knees. At that moment the magnesium light flared up and the camera handle rattled. 'Right. Now you're on it,' Judy announced vindictively. 'That'll be a great picture for the papers. American Society Hunting for Pearls. Marine Lizards Fling Pearls at Humans.'

Fred sat down. 'Hell, Judy's right. We just *must* get this into the papers, kids!'

Li sat down. 'Judy is a darling. Judy, do take us again, but from the front!'

'You wouldn't look nearly so good, darling,' opined Judy.

'We'd better go on searching, kids,' said Mr Abe. 'The tide's coming in.'

In the darkness at the water's edge a black swaying shadow was moving. Li screeched: 'Over there – over there – '

Three torches threw their circles of light in that direction. But it was only Greta on her knees, looking for pearls in the dark.

On Li's lap was the captain's cap with twenty-one pearls in it. Abe was fixing the drinks and Judy attended to the gramophone. It was an immense starry night accompanied by the eternal murmuring of the sea.

'So what's our headline going to be?', boomed Fred. MILWAUKEE INDUSTRIALIST'S DAUGHTER FILMS FOSSIL REPTILES.'

'ANTEDILUVIAN LIZARDS PAY HOMAGE TO YOUTH AND BEAUTY', Abe proposed poetically.

'THE YACHT GLORIA PICKFORD DISCOVERS UNKNOWN FAUNA,' advised the captain. 'Or THE MYSTERY OF TAHUARA ISLAND.'

'That's more like a subtitle,' said Fred. 'The headline should say something more.'

'For instance: BASEBALL FRED FIGHTS MONSTERS,' Judy spoke up. 'Fred was terrific as he charged towards them. Hope it comes out all right on the film!'

The captain cleared his throat. 'Actually, Miss Judy, *I* ran out first – but let it pass. I think the headline should have a scientific ring, sir. Sober and . . . in short, scientific. ANTILUVIAN FAUNA ON PACIFIC ISLAND.'

'Anteliduvian,' corrected Fred. 'No, antevidulian. Hell, which is right? Antiluvalian. Anteduvialian. No, that's no go. Got to give it some simpler headline, something everybody can pronounce. Judy's a brick.'

'Antediluvial,' said Judy.

Fred shook his head. 'Too long, Judy. Longer than those brutes including their tails. A headline's got to be snappy. But Judy's terrific, what? Don't you think she's terrific, captain?'

'Sure,' the captain agreed. 'A remarkable young lady.'

'As good as a fellow, captain,' the young giant said approvingly. 'Say kids, the captain's a great guy. But antediluvian fauna is garbage. That's no headline for a paper. Why not LOVERS ON PEARL ISLAND, or something like that.'

'TRITONS SHOWER WHITE LILY WITH PEARLS,' shouted Abe. HOMAGE FROM POSEIDON'S REALM! A NEW APHRODITE!'

'Garbage,' Fred protested angrily. 'There weren't any Tritons. That's all scientifically proved, old boy. And there wasn't any Aphrodite, was there, Judy? HUMANS CLASH WITH PRIMEVAL REPTILES! GALLANT CAPTAIN CHARGES ANTEDILUVIAN MONSTERS! Boy, that would be a scoop, this headline.'

'Special edition,' sang out Abe. 'FILM ACTRESS ASSAULTED BY SEA MONSTERS! A MODERN WOMAN'S SEX APPEAL TRIUMPHS OVER PREHISTORIC LIZARDS! FOSSIL REPTILES PREFER BLONDES!'

'Abe,' Sweetiepie Li spoke up. 'I've got an idea – '

'What idea?'

'For a film. That would be a marvellous thing, Abe. Imagine me bathing at the edge of the sea – '

'You look great in that swimsuit,' Abe blurted out in a hurry.

'Don't I? And those Tritons would fall in love with me and carry me off to the bottom of the sea. And I'd be their queen.'

'On the seabed?'

'Sure, under the water. In their mysterious realm, you know? Surely they've got cities there and everything.'

'But Sweetiepie, you'd be drowned there!'

'Don't worry, I can swim,' Sweetiepie Li said unconcernedly. 'But once a day I'd swim up to the beach to fill my lungs with air.' Li demonstrated a breathing exercise associated with a heaving of her bosom and soft arm movements. 'Something like this, see? And on the beach there could be ... a young fisherman who'd fall in love with me. And I with him. Terribly,' Sweetiepie sighed. 'You know, he'd be a handsome, strong man. And those Tritons would try to drown him, but I would save him and follow him to his hut. And the Tritons would besiege us – well, and then you could come and rescue us.'

'Li,' Fred said earnestly, 'this is so idiotic that it might really make a film, cross my heart. I'd be surprised if old Jesse didn't turn it into a film spectacular.'

Fred was right; in due course this was turned into a spectacular by Jesse Loeb Pictures, with Miss Lily Valley in the leading role; in addition the cast called for 600 young Nereids, one Neptune and 12,000 extras dressed up as various antediluvian reptiles. But before this came to pass a lot of water had to flow under the bridges and a great many events had to take place – in particular:

(1) The captured animal, kept in the tub in Sweetiepie Li's bathroom, enjoyed the lively interest of the entire company for two whole days; on the third day it stopped moving and Miss Li insisted that the poor little thing was pining away; on the fourth day it began to smell and had to be dumped in an advanced stage of decomposition.

(2) Of the shots taken by the lagoon only two were usable. On one of them Sweetiepie Li was cowering in terror, desperately waving her arms at the erect animals. Everybody insisted that this was a marvellous sequence. The other clip showed three men and a girl, on their knees, with their noses on the ground; they were all taken from behind and they looked as if they were kowtowing to something. This sequence was suppressed.

(3) As for the suggested newspaper headlines, nearly all of them were used (even that with the antediluvian fauna in it) in hundreds and hundreds of American and foreign dailies, weeklies and magazines; added to them was an account of the whole event with numerous details and photographs, such as Sweetiepie Li among the lizards, a separate picture of the lizard in the bath-tub, a separate picture of Li in her swimsuit, separate pictures of Miss Judy, Mr Abe Loeb, Baseball Fred, the captain of the yacht *Gloria Pickford*, a separate picture of Taraiva Island, and a separate picture of the pearls, laid out on black velvet. Thus Sweetiepie Li's career was assured; she even declined to appear in a variety show and declared to newspaper reporters that she intended to devote herself exclusively to Art.

(4) Admittedly there were some people who, on the pretext of a professional education, maintained that – as far as it was possible to judge from the pictures – the creatures were not prehistoric reptiles but some type of newt. People with even higher professional qualifications then maintained that this type of newt was not so far known to science and therefore did not exist. There was a prolonged discussion in the press, finally brought to an end by Professor J. W. Hopkins (Yale) with the announcement that he had examined the photographs submitted to him and that he considered them a fraud ('a hoax') or some trick photography; that the animals depicted

were somewhat reminiscent of the Giant Covered-Gilled Salamander (Cryptobranchus japonicus, Sieboldia maxima, Tritomegas Sieboldii or Megalobatrachus Sieboldii), but inaccurately, clumsily and downright amateurishly copied. In this way the matter was scientifically settled for some time to come.

(5) Eventually, at the appropriate time, Mr Abe Loeb married Miss Judy. His closest friend, Baseball Fred, was his best-man at a wedding staged with great pomp and in the presence of numerous outstanding figures from political, artistic and other circles.

8
Andrias Scheuchzeri

There is no limit to human curiosity. It was not enough for Professor J. W. Hopkins (Yale), the greatest living authority on reptiles, to declare those mysterious creatures to be an unscientific hoax and pure fantasy; an increasing number of reports began to appear both in specialised publications and in the daily press of the discovery of hitherto unknown animals, resembling giant salamanders, in the most various parts of the Pacific. Relatively reliable data referred to such discoveries in the Solomon Islands, on Schouten Island, on Kapingamarangi, Butarita and Tapeteuea, as well as on a whole group of lesser islands: Nukufetau, Funafuti, Nukonono and Fukaofu, and finally on Hiau, Uahuka, Uapu and Pukapuka. There were the legends of Captain van Toch's devils (mainly in the Melanesian region) and of Miss Lily's Tritons (more usually in Polynesia); so the papers concluded that these were probably different kinds of submarine and antediluvian monsters, especially as the silly season had begun and there was nothing else to write about. Submarine monsters are a sure-fire success with the reading public. In the United States, in particular, Tritons became fashionable; in New York the lavish review featuring Poseidon, with 300 of the prettiest girl Tritons, Nereids and Sirens ran to 300 performances; in Miami and on the Californian beaches young people wore Triton and Nereid swimsuits (i.e. three strings of pearls and nothing else), while in the Midwestern states and the Bible Belt the Movement for the Suppression of Immorality (MSI) recorded an extraordinary increase in support; in this connection mass demonstrations took place and a number of negroes were either hanged or burnt to death.

Finally there appeared in The National Geographic Magazine a report by the Columbia University Scientific Expedition (mounted at the expense of J. S. Tincker, known as the Tinned Food King); that report was signed by P. L.

Smith, W. Kleinschmidt, Charles Kovar, Louis Forgeron and D. Herrero, internationally renowned experts especially in the fields of fish parasites, ringworms, plant biology, infusorians and mites. We quote from their voluminous report:

On Rakahanga Island the expedition for the first time encountered the imprints of the hind-feet of an unknown giant salamander. The imprints show five digits with a toe length of 3 to 4 cm. Judging by the number of tracks the coast of Rakahanga Island would seem to be literally swarming with those salamanders. Because of the absence of fore-feet imprints (except for one four-digit print, apparently of a young specimen) the expedition concluded that these salamanders evidently move on their hindlegs.

It should be pointed out that there are no rivers or swamps on Rakahanga Island, so that these salamanders must live in the sea and are probably the only representatives of their order with a pelagic habitat. It is, of course, known that the Mexican axolotl (Amblystoma mexicanum) inhabits brackish lakes; however, there is no reference to any pelagic (sea-inhabiting) salamanders even in the classic work of W. Korngold *Caudate Amphibians (Urodela)*, Berlin 1913.

. . . We waited until the afternoon in order to capture or a least to catch sight of a living specimen, but in vain. Regretfully we left the charming little island of Rakahanga, where D. Herrero succeeded in discovering a beautiful new species of *Tingidae* . . .

We were much more fortunate on the island of Tongarewa. We were waiting on the beach with our rifles in our hands. After sunset the heads of salamanders emerged from the water: relatively large and slightly flattened. After a while the salamanders crawled up on the sand, walking on their hindlegs with a swaying gait but quite nimbly. When seated they were a little over a metre high. They sat down in a wide circle and with a strange motion began to twist their upper bodies; it looked as if they were dancing. W. Kleinschmidt stood up in order to get a better view. The salamanders turned their heads towards him and for a brief moment remained rigid; then they approached him at remarkable speed, uttering hissing and barking sounds. When they were about seven feet away from him we fired our rifles at them. They fled very quickly and flung themselves into the sea; they did not reappear that evening. Left on the beach were two dead salamanders and one with a broken spine, which uttered a strange sound like 'ogod, ogod, ogod'. He subsequently died when W. Kleinschmidt opened his pleural cavity with a knife . . . *(This is followed by anatomical details which would be incomprehensible to the lay reader; we refer the expert reader to the above-mentioned report.)*

It is clear, therefore, from the characteristics listed above, that we are concerned with a typical member of the order of caudate reptiles (Urodela), to which, as is well known, belongs the family of real salamanders (Salamandrida), which in turn comprises the genera of newts (Tritones) and salamanders (Salamandrae), as well as the family of perinnibranchs (Ichthyoidea), which in turn comprises the cryptobranchiate (Cryptobranchiata) and branchiate (Phanerobranchiata) forms. The salamander recorded on the island of Tangarewa would seem to be most closely related to the perinnibranch cryptobranchiates; in many respects, such as size, it resembles the Japanese Giant Salamander (Megalobranchus Sieboldii) and the American hellbender, known as the 'swamp devil', though it differs from these by its well-developed sensory organs and its longer and more powerful extremities, which enable it to move with marked agility both in the water and on dry land. *(This is followed by further comparative anatomical details.)*

Following the preparation of the slain animals' skeletons we made a most interesting discovery: the skeletons of these salamanders are an almost perfect match of a fossil imprint of a salamander skeleton found on a stone slab from the Oeningen quarry by Dr Johannes Jakob Scheuchzer and illustrated in his *Homo diluvii testis* published in 1726. For the benefit of less informed readers it should be explained that the above-mentioned Dr Scheuchzer regarded that fossil as the remains of *antediluvian man*. 'The figure here presented,' he writes, 'which I hereby submit to the world of learning, is beyond any doubt the image of Man who witnessed the Great Flood. These are not lines from which but a lively imagination must needs construe something

that would resemble Man, but everywhere there is complete
conformity and perfect concordance with the several parts
of the human skeleton. Petrified Man is here counterfeited
from the front: behold a memorial to an extinct human race
older than all Roman, Greek, and even Egyptian and other
oriental tombs.' Subsequently Cuvier identified the
Oeningen imprint as the skeleton of a fossilised salamander,
which was named Cryptobranchus primaevus or Andrias
Scheuchzeri Tschudi and considered to be a long-extinct
species. Osteological comparison now enabled us to identify
our salamanders as the prehistoric Andrias salamander
which had been presumed extinct. The mystery proto-
lizard, as the newspapers have dubbed it, *is nothing other
than the fossil cryptobranchiate salamander Andrias Scheuchzeri*; or,
should a new name be needed, Cryptobranchus Tinckeri
erectus or the Polynesian Giant Salamander.

. . . It remains a mystery why this interesting giant
salamander should, until now, have eluded scientific
attention, even though it occurs in large numbers at least
on the islands of Rakahanga and Tongarewa in the
Manihiki archipelago. It is not mentioned by Randolph
and Montgomery in their work *Two Years on the Islands of
Manihiki* (1885). The local population maintains that this
animal – which incidentally they believe to be venomous
– only began to show itself during the past six or eight
years. They claim that the 'sea devils' can talk (sic) and
that they build entire systems of barriers and dams in the
bays they inhabit, in the nature of submarine cities; they
say the water in these bays is as smooth as a millpond all
the year round; they also state that they dig out, under the
water, burrows and passages many metres long and that
they stay in these during the day; at night they are said
to steal sweet potatoes and yams from the fields, and even
carry off hoes and other tools. Altogether the people do not
like them and are even afraid of them; in a number of
instances they have actually preferred to move away to other
places. Obviously this is just a case of primitive legends
and superstitions based presumably on the repulsive
appearance and the erect quasi-human walk of these
harmless giant salamanders.

. . . Travellers' accounts according to which these

salamanders are found also on islands other than the Manihiki archipelago should be received with a good deal of reserve. On the other hand, there cannot be the least doubt about identifying a recent imprint of a hind-foot, found on the beach of Tongatabu Island and published by Capt. Croisset in *La Nature*, as belonging to Andrias Scheuchzeri. This find is of especial significance in that it links the animals' occurrence in the Manihiki Islands with the Australian–New Zealand zone, where so many survivors of an ancient fauna have been preserved: we need only think of the 'antediluvian' lizard Hatterii or Tuaturu, still living on Stephen Island. On these remote and for the most part sparsely populated little islands, almost untouched by civilisation, individual relics of animal types extinct elsewhere have succeeded in surviving. Thanks to Mr J. S. Tincker the fossil lizard Hatterii is now joined by an antediluvian salamander. The good Dr Johannes Jakob Scheuchzer would now have witnessed the resurrection of his Oeningen Adam . . .

This learned account should surely have been sufficient to illuminate scientifically the question of those mysterious marine monsters of which we have already spoken at length. Unfortunately, simultaneously with it, there appeared a report by the Dutch researcher van Hogenhouck, who classified these cryptobranchiate giant salamanders as belonging to the family of true salamanders or Tritons, naming them Megatriton moluccanus and establishing their occurrence on the Dutch Sunda Islands Dgilolo, Morotai and Ceram; there was also a report by the French scientist Dr Mignard, who classified them as typical salamanders, placed their original occurrence on the French islands of Takaroa, Rangiroa and Raroira, and named them quite simply Cryptobranchus salamandroides; then there was a report by H. W. Spence, who saw them as a new family, Pelagidae, native to the Gilbert Islands and capable of acquiring zoological existence under the generic name of Pelagotriton Spencei. Mr Spence succeeded in transporting a live specimen all the way to the London Zoo; there it became the object of further research, from which it emerged under the names of Pelagobatrachus Hookeri, Salamandrops maritimus, Abranchus giganteus, Amphiuma gigas, and a great number of others. Some scientists argued that Pelagotriton Spencei was identical with Cryptobranchus Tinckeri and that Mignard's salamander was nothing other than Andrias Scheuchzeri; there was a lot of argument about priority and about other purely scientific questions. Thus it came about that eventually the natural history of every nation had its own giant salamanders and was waging a furious scientific war against the giant salamanders of other nations. As a result, that whole important business of the salamanders was never sufficiently resolved on the scientific side.

9

Andrew Scheuchzer

One Thursday morning, when the London Zoo was closed to the public, it so happened that Mr Thomas Greggs, a keeper in the Lizard House, was cleaning out the tanks and enclosures of his charges. He was alone in the salamander section, whose exhibits consisted of the Japanese Giant Salamander, the American Hellbender, Andrias Scheuchzeri, and a great number of lesser newts, salamanders, axolotls, eels, sirenia and amphibians, pleurodeles and branchiates. Mr Greggs was busying himself with a broom and a cloth, and whistling Annie Laurie, when suddenly somebody behind him spoke with a croak:

'Look, mummy.'

Mr Thomas Greggs looked round, but there was nobody there; only the hellbender was smacking about in its swampy pool, and that big newt, that Andrias, was leaning with his forepaws on the edge of the tank and twisting its body. Must have dreamt it, thought Mr Greggs, and went on sweeping the floor for all he was worth.

'Look, a newt,' came a voice from behind him.

Mr Greggs spun round; that black newt, that Andrias, was looking at him, blinking its lower lids.

'Yuk, isn't it ugly?' the newt suddenly said. 'Let's go on, darling.'

Mr Greggs's mouth gaped in amazement. 'What's that?'

'Does it bite?' the newt croaked.

'You . . . you can talk?' stammered Mr Greggs, not believing his senses.

'I'm scared of it,' the newt jerked out. 'Mummy, what does it eat?'

'Say good morning,' said the startled Mr Greggs.

The newt twisted its body. 'Good morning,' it croaked. 'Good morning. Good morning. Can I feed him some cake?'

Confused, Mr Greggs fished into his pocket and produced a piece of roll. 'Here you are.'

The newt took the roll in its paw and started to nibble it. 'Look, a newt,' it grunted contentedly. 'Daddy, why is he so black?' Suddenly it slipped into the water, leaving only its head sticking out. 'Why is he in the water? Why? Yuk, isn't he horrid?'

Mr Thomas Greggs scratched his neck in surprise. I see, it repeats what it hears people say. 'Say Greggs,' he tried. 'Say Greggs,' the newt repeated.

'Mister Thomas Greggs.'

'Mister Thomas Greggs.'

'Good morning, sir.'

'Good morning, sir. Good morning. Good morning, sir.' It seemed the newt would never tire of talking; but Mr Thomas Greggs was not a very talkative person. 'OK, now you shut up,' he said. 'And when I'm through I'll teach you to talk.'

'OK, now you shut up,' the newt mumbled. 'Good morning, sir. Look, a newt. I'll teach you to talk.'

However, the Zoo management did not like the keepers to teach their animals any tricks; an elephant was different, but the rest of the animals were there for instructional purposes and not to perform any circus tricks. That was why Mr Greggs spent his time in the salamander section more or less surreptitiously, when everybody had left. As he was a widower nobody thought his recluse's life in the Reptile House at all odd. Everyone had his hobbies. Besides, the salamander section was not visited by a lot of people: the crocodile might enjoy universal popularity, but Andrias Scheuchzeri spent his days in relative seclusion.

One day – it was beginning to get dark – Sir Charles Wiggam, the Director of the Zoo, was touring some of the houses to make sure everything was all right. As he passed through the salamander section there was a splash in one of the tanks and somebody said in a croaking voice: 'Good evening, sir.'

'Good evening,' the Director replied in surprise. 'Who's that?'

'Excuse me, sir,' said the croaking voice. 'This isn't Mr Greggs.'

'Who's that?' the Director repeated.

'Andy. Andrew Scheuchzer.'

Sir Charles walked up closer to the tank. There was

only one erect and motionless newt sitting there. 'Who spoke?'

'Andy, sir,' the newt said. 'Who are you?'

'Wiggam,' Sir Charles blurted out in amazement.

'Delighted,' Andrias said politely. 'How are you?'

'Dammit,' Sir Charles roared. 'Greggs! I say, Greggs!' The newt flipped over and like lightning hid in the water.

Mr Thomas Greggs burst in, breathless and worried. 'Yes, sir?'

'Greggs, what's the meaning of this?' Sir Charles began.

'Is anything wrong, sir?' Mr Greggs stammered nervously.

'This animal here talks!'

'I'm sorry, sir,' Mr Greggs said, crestfallen. 'We shouldn't do that, Andy. I've told you a thousand times we don't annoy people with our chattering. I beg your pardon, sir, it won't happen again.'

'Was it you who taught this newt to talk?'

'But *he* started it, sir,' Greggs defended himself.

'I hope this won't happen again, Greggs,' Sir Charles said severely. 'I'll have my eye on you.'

Some time later Sir Charles was sitting beside Professor Petrov: they were discussing so-called animal intelligence, conditioned reflexes, and how popular belief overrated the intellectual activity of animals. Professor Petrov expressed his doubts about the Elberfeld horses which were credited with being able not only to do sums but to raise numbers to a higher power and find square roots; after all, how many normal educated people could do square roots, said the great scientist. Sir Charles remembered Greggs's talking newt. 'I've got a newt here,' he began hesitantly, 'it's that famous Andrias Scheuchzeri, and it's learned to talk like a parrot.'

'Impossible,' said the scientist. 'Surely newts have a reflexed tongue.'

'Why don't you come along and look,' said Sir Charles. 'It's cleaning day today, so the place won't be full of people.' And off they went.

At the entrance to the salamanders Sir Charles stopped. From inside they could hear the scratching of a broom and a monotonous voice awkwardly articulating something.

'Wait,' whispered Sir Charles Wiggam.

'IS MARS INHABITED?' the monotonous voice articulated. 'Want me to read that?'

'Something else, Andy,' replied another voice.

'WILL PELHAM BEAUTY OR GOBERNADOR WIN THIS YEAR'S DERBY?'

'Pelham Beauty will,' said the other voice. 'But read on.'

Sir Charles quietly opened the door. Mr Thomas Greggs was sweeping the floor with his broom; in the little pool sat Andrias Scheuchzeri, slowly and croakingly reading from an evening paper he was holding in his front paws.

'Greggs,' Sir Charles called out. The newt flicked its body and disappeared under the water.

Mr Greggs dropped his broom with fright. 'Yes, sir?'

'What is the meaning of this?'

'I beg your pardon, sir,' the unhappy Greggs stammered. 'Andy is reading to me while I do the sweeping. And when he sweeps I read to him.'

'Who taught him that?'

'He learns by himself by just watching, sir. I . . . I give him my paper so he doesn't talk so much. He was always wanting to talk, sir. So I thought he might as well learn to speak proper like – '

'Andy,' Sir Charles called out.

The black head appeared out of the water. 'Yes, sir,' it croaked.

'Professor Petrov here has come to take a look at you.'

'Pleased to meet you, sir. I'm Andy Scheuchzer.'

'How d'you know your name is Andrias Scheuchzer?'

'Why, it's written up here, sir. Andreas Scheuchzer, Gilbert Islands.'

'D'you read the paper often?'

'Yes, sir. Every day, sir.'

'And what interests you most in it?'

'Police Court news, horse racing, football – '

'Have you ever seen a football match?'

'No, sir.'

'Or a horse?'

'No, sir.'

'So why do you read about it?'

'Because it's in the paper, sir.'

'You're not interested in politics?'

'No, sir. WILL THERE BE WAR?'

'No one can tell, Andy.'

'GERMANY BUILDS A NEW TYPE OF SUB-
MARINE,' Andy said worriedly. 'DEATH RAYS CAN
TURN WHOLE CONTINENTS INTO DESERT.'

'You read that in the paper, didn't you?' asked Sir Charles.

'Yes, sir. WILL PELHAM BEAUTY OR GOBER-
NADOR WIN THIS YEAR'S DERBY?'

'What do you think, Andy?'

'Gobernador, sir. But Mr Greggs thinks Pelham Beauty.'
Andy nodded his head. 'BUY BRITISH, sir. SNIDER'S
BRACES ARE BEST. HAVE YOU GOT YOUR NEW
SIX-CYLINDER TANCRED JUNIOR? FAST, CHEAP,
ELEGANT.'

'Thank you, Andy. That will do.'

'WHO IS YOUR FAVOURITE FILM STAR?'

Professor Petrov's hair and beard were bristling. 'Excuse
me, Sir Charles,' he muttered, 'but I must be off.'

'Very well, we'll go. Andy, would you mind if I sent a few
learned gentlemen to take a look at you? I think they would
like to talk to you?'

'I shall be delighted, sir,' the newt croaked. 'Good-bye,
Sir Charles. Good-bye, professor.'

Professor Petrov was hurrying away, snorting and muttering
with irritation. 'Forgive me, Sir Charles,' he said at last. 'But
couldn't you show me some animal that *doesn't* read the paper?'

The learned gentlemen were Sir John Bertram, D.M.,
Professor Ebbigham, Sir Oliver Dodge, Julian Foxley and
others. We quote part of the report on their experiment with
Andrias Scheuchzer.

What is your name?

A.: Andrew Scheuchzer.

How old are you?

A.: I don't know. Do you want to look young? Wear
a Libella bra.

What is today's date?

A.: Monday. Lovely weather, sir. Gibraltar will be
running at Epsom this Saturday.

How much is three times five?

A.: Why?

Can you do arithmetic?

A.: Yes, sir. How much is seventeen times twenty-nine?

We shall ask the questions, Andrew. Give us the names of some English rivers.

A.: The Thames . . .

Any more?

A.: The Thames.

You don't know any others, do you? Who reigns over England?

A.: King George. God bless him.

Well done, Andy. Who is the greatest English writer?

A.: Kipling.

Very good. Have you read anything by him?

A.: No. How do you like Mae West?

We will ask the questions, Andy. What do you know of English history?

A.: Henry the Eighth.

What do you know about him?

A.: Best film in recent years. Marvellous decor. Terrific spectacle.

Have you seen it?

A.: I haven't. Want to see England? Buy a Baby Ford.

What would you most like to see, Andy?

A.: The Oxford–Cambridge boat race, sir.

How many continents are there?

A.: Five.

Very good. Which are they?

A.: England and the rest.

Which are the rest?

A.: The Bolsheviks and the Germans. And Italy.

Where are the Gilbert Islands?

A.: In England. England will not tie herself to the Continent. England needs ten thousand aircraft. Visit the English south coast.

May we look at your tongue, Andy?

A.: Yes, sir. Brush your teeth with Fresh. It saves you money, it's the best, and it's British. Do you want perfumed breath? Use Fresh toothpaste.

Thank you, that will do. And now tell us, Andy . . .

And so on. The report of the conversation with Andrias Scheuchzer ran to sixteen full pages and was published in *Natural Science*. At the end of the report the expert commission summed up the results of its experiment in these words:

(1) Andrias Scheuchzeri, the salamander kept at the London Zoo, can talk, though with something of a croak; it has a vocabulary of about four hundred words; it says what it has heard or read. There can, of course, be no suggestion of independent thought. Its tongue is sufficiently flexible; in the circumstances it was not possible to examine its vocal cords more closely.

(2) The same salamander can read, though only the evening papers. It is interested in the same things as the average Englishman and reacts to them in a similar manner, i.e. in the direction of established general views. Its intellectual life – in so far as one may speak of any – consists precisely of ideas and opinions current at the present time.

(3) There is absolutely no need to overrate its intelligence, since in no respect does it exceed the intelligence of the average person of our time.

In spite of this sober assessment by the experts the talking newt became the sensation of the London Zoo. Darling Andy was besieged by people anxious to discuss with him anything, from the weather to the economic recession and the political situation. In consequence he received so much chocolate and sweets from his visitors that he became seriously ill with an inflammation of the stomach and the intestines. In the end, the salamander section had to closed, but by then it was too late: Andrias Scheuchzeri, known as Andy, died of the consequences of his popularity. As can be seen, fame demoralises even newts.

10

The Fair at Nové Strašecí

Mr Povondra, the doorman at the Bondy residence, was for once spending his leave in his native town. The next day there was to be the annual fair; and when Mr Povondra stepped out of his house, leading his 8-year-old Frankie by the hand, the whole of Nové Strašecí was fragrant with cakes, and women and girls were scurrying about the streets carrying the freshly kneaded dough to the baker's. In the town square two toffee stalls had already been set up, as well as one with cheap glass and china, and one run by a loud-voiced woman selling all kinds of haberdashery. And then there was a square canvas tent, enclosed by sheets on all sides. Some slight little man was standing on a ladder, fixing a notice to the top.

Mr Povondra stopped to see what it would say.

The wizened little man climbed down from his ladder and looked with satisfaction at the lettering he had put up and Mr Povondra read with surprise:

> CAPTAIN J. VAN TOCH
>
> and
>
> HIS TRAINED NEWTS

Mr Povondra remembered the big fat man with the captain's cap whom he had admitted to Mr Bondy some time before. What a come-down, poor chap, Mr Povondra commiserated mentally: a ship's captain, and now he's having to tour the world with this miserable circus! Such a fine healthy man he was, too! Ought to look him up really, Mr Povondra reflected compassionately.

Meanwhile, the little man had fixed another banner by the entrance to the tent:

TALKING LIZARDS

THE GREATEST SCIENTIFIC SENSATION !!

Admission 2 Crowns. Accompanied children half price.

Mr Povondra hesitated. Two crowns, plus one for the boy, that seemed a bit steep. But Frankie did well at school, and seeing outlandish animals was really part of one's education. Mr Povondra was willing to make sacrifices for education, and so he stepped up to the wizened little man. 'Mate,' he said; 'I'd like to have a word with Captain van Toch.'

The little man blew out his chest under its striped sweatshirt. 'That's me, sir.'

'You are Captain van Toch?' Mr Povondra expressed surprise.

'Yessir,' said the little man and pointed to an anchor tattoed on his wrist.

Mr Povondra blinked thoughtfully. That captain could not have shrunk quite so much. Impossible. 'As it happens, I know Captain van Toch personally,' he said. 'My name's Povondra.'

'Well, that's different,' said the little man. 'But these newts really are Captain van Toch's, sir. Guaranteed real Australian lizards, sir. Why not step in, sir? The great performance is just starting,' he crowed, lifting the tarpaulin by the entrance.

'Come along, Frankie,' said Papa Povondra and stepped inside. An unusually large lady was hurriedly sitting down at a little table. An odd pair, Mr Povondra thought in amazement, paying his three crowns. Inside the booth there was nothing except a rather unpleasant smell and a tin bathtub.

'Where've you got those newts?' asked Mr Povondra.

'In that bath,' the huge lady said indifferently.

'Don't be scared, Frankie,' said Papa Povondra and stepped up to the bath. In it was something black and lethargic, as large as an old catfish; except that at the back of its head the skin expanded and contracted a little.

'So this is the antediluvian salamander we've read about in the newspapers,' Papa Povondra said didactically, not letting his disappointment show. (Been had again, he thought to himself, but the boy needn't know. Three crowns down the drain!)

'Dad, why is it in the water?' asked Frankie.

'Because salamanders live in the water, see?'

'And what does it eat?'

'Fish and such stuff,' Papa Povondra suggested. (Must eat something.)

'And why is it so ugly?' Frankie persisted.

Mr Povondra did not know what to say; but at that moment the little man came into the tent. 'Your attention, please, ladies and gentlemen,' he began hoarsely.

'You've only got that one salamander?' Mr Povondra inquired reproachfully. (With two of them I'd have had somewhat better value for my money.)

'The other one died,' said the little man. 'Now this is the famous Andrias, ladies and gentlemen, a rare and poisonous lizard from the Australian islands. In its homeland it grows to the height of a man and walks upright. 'You,' he said, poking a stick into that black lethargic mass lying motionless in the tank. The black mass wriggled and with an effort rose from the water. Frankie retreated a little, but Mr Povondra squeezed his hand: don't be scared, I'm with you.

Now it was standing on its hindlegs, its front paws resting on the edge of the tank. The gills behind its head were spasmodically twitching and its black mouth was yapping for air. Its skin, rubbed raw, was too loose and covered with warts, and every so often its round frog-like eyes were closed in pain by their membraneous lower lids.

'As you can see, ladies and gentlemen,' the little man continued hoarsely, 'this animal lives in the water; that's why it is equipped with both gills and lungs, so that it can breathe when it comes out on land. It has five toes on its hind feet and four on its front ones, but it can pick up objects with them. Here.' The animal gripped the stick in its fingers and held it up in front like some melancholy sceptre.

'It can also tie a knot in a piece of string,' the little man announced, taking the stick from the animal and handing it a dirty length of string. The animal held it in its fingers for a moment and then actually tied a knot.

'It can also beat the drum and dance,' the little man crowed, handing the animal a child's drum and a drumstick. The animal hit the drum a few times and twisted the upper part of its body; in doing so it dropped the drumstick in the water. 'Bloody brute,' the little man snapped and fished the drumstick out.

'And this animal,' he added, solemnly raising his voice, 'is so intelligent and talented it can talk like a human being.' At this he clapped his hands.

'Guten Morgen,' croaked the animal, painfully blinking its lower lids. 'Good morning.'

Mr Povondra was almost terrified, but Frankie did not seem particularly impressed.

'What do you say to our gracious audience?' the little man asked sharply.

'Welcome,' the newt bowed; its gills closed convulsively. 'Willkommen. Ben venuti.'

'Can you do sums?'

'I can.'

'How much is six times seven?'

'Forty-two,' quacked the newt with an effort.

'See, Frankie,' Papa Povondra pointed out, 'he can do sums!'

'Ladies and gentlemen,' the little man bellowed; 'you may put questions to it yourselves.'

'Ask him something, Frankie,' Papa Povondra nudged.

Frankie squirmed with embarrassment. 'How much is eight times nine?' he blurted out at last; evidently this seemed to him the most difficult of all possible questions.

The newt blinked slowly. 'Seventy-two.'

'What day is it today?' asked Mr Povondra.

'Saturday,' said the newt.

Mr Povondra shook his head in wonderment. 'Really just like a human. What's the name of this town?'

The newt opened its mouth and shut its eyes. 'He's tired out,' the little man hurriedly explained. 'What do you say to the ladies and gentlemen?'

The newt bowed. 'My compliments. My humble thanks. Good-bye. Hope to see you again.' And quickly it hid under the water.

'That's – that's a strange beast.' Mr Povondra was still amazed. But because three crowns was after all three crowns he added: 'And that's all you have to show the boy?'

The little man sucked his lower lip in embarrassment. 'That's all,' he said. 'I used to have monkeys in the old days, but they were rather a business,' he explained vaguely. 'Except that I could show you my wife. She used to be the fattest woman in the world. Mary, dear, come over here!'

Mary rose with difficulty. 'What is it?'

'Show yourself to the gentlemen, Mary, dear.'

The world's fattest woman put her head coquettishly to one side, put one leg forward and raised her skirt above her knee. There was a view of a red woollen stocking and in it something swollen and massive like a ham. 'Leg circumference at the top eighty-four centimetres,' the wizened little man explained; 'but what with today's competition Mary's no longer the fattest woman in the world.'

Mr Povondra dragged the aghast Frankie outside. 'My respects,' came a croaking voice from the tank. 'Come again. Auf Wiedersehen.'

'Well then, Frankie,' asked Mr Povondra when they were outside. 'Learnt something?'

'Yes,' said Frankie. 'Dad, why does that lady wear red stockings?'

11

Of Men-Lizards

It would certainly be an exaggeration to claim that about that time there existed no other subject of conversation or newspaper attention than the talking newts. People and newspapers were also concerned with the next war, with the depression, with the cup final, with vitamins and with fashion; nevertheless, the talking newts did enjoy a great deal of publicity, and moreover of uninformed publicity. That was why Professor Vladimir Uher, an outstanding scientist from Brno University, wrote an article for *Lidové Noviny*, in which he pointed out that Andrias Scheuchzeri's alleged ability to utter articulated speech was essentially just a parroting of spoken words and, from a scientific point of view, was not nearly as interesting as a number of other questions surrounding that unusual amphibian. the scientific mystery of Andrias Scheuchzeri lay elsewhere: for instance, where did it come from; where were its origins, the place where it survived entire geological periods; why had it remained unknown for so long when it was now appearing in large numbers virtually throughout the equatorial zone of the Pacific? It would seem that it had recently been multiplying with unusual rapidity; where did that enormous vitality come from in an ancient tertiary creature which, until not long ago, had led a totally unobserved, and hence presumably very sporadic and indeed probably geographically isolated, existence? Was it possible that the environmental conditions of this fossil newt had somehow changed in a biologically favourable direction, so that this rare Miocene relic was now enjoying a new and astonishingly successful evolutionary phase? In that case it could not be ruled out that Andrias would not only multiply quantitatively but also develop qualitatively, so that science would have a unique opportunity for witnessing, at least in one animal species, a major mutation *in actu*. That Andrias Scheuchzeri could croak a few dozen words and learn a few tricks – a fact which to the layman seemed evidence of some kind of intelligence – was not, in any scientific sense, a miracle. The miracle was the powerful vital *élan* which had so suddenly and extensively revived the arrested existence of an evolutionarily backward and indeed near-extinct creature. There were a number of special circumstances in this case: Andrias Scheuchzeri was the *only* newt living in the sea and – even more significantly – the *only* newt occurring in the Ethiopian-Australian zone, in mythical Lemuria. Might we not almost say that Nature was trying, belatedly and almost precipitously, to catch up on one of the biological potentialities and forms which, *in that zone*, it had omitted to develop or else been unable to bring to fulfilment? Moreover, it would be surprising if in the oceanic region lying between the Japanese giant salamanders on the one hand and the Alleghanian ones on the other, there existed no connecting link whatever. If Andrias did not exist, we would actually have to *postulate* its existence in the very places where it has been found; it is almost as if it filled the slot which, in accordance with geographical and evolutionary circumstances, it *should* always have occupied. Be that as it may, the learned professor's article concluded, on this evolutionary resurrection of a Miocene newt we observe, with respect and amazement, that the Genius of Evolution on our planet has by no means yet concluded its creative operation.

That article appeared in spite of the editorial board's silent but unshakable conviction that such learned stuff really had no place in a daily paper. As a result of its publication Professor Uher received a letter from a reader:

Dear Sir,
A year ago I bought a house in the Market Square in Čáslav. In the course of looking it over I found a box in the attic with valuable old publications, mostly scientific, such as two annual runs of Hýbl's periodical 'Hyllos' for 1821–22, Jan Svatopluk Presl's 'Mammalia', Vojtěch Sedláček's 'The Foundations of the Natural Sciences or Physics', nineteen annual runs of the encyclopaedic publication 'Krok' and thirteen annual runs of the 'Journal of the Bohemian Museum'. In Presl's translation of Cuvier's 'Dissertation on the Transformations of the Earth's

Crust' (dating from 1834) I found, inserted as a bookmark, a cutting from an old newspaper with a report
of some strange lizards.

Upon reading your splendid article about those
mysterious newts I remembered that bookmark and looked
it up. I believe that it might be of interest to you and
therefore, as an enthusiastic friend of nature and eager
reader of your writings, enclose it herewith.

Respectfully yours,

J. V. Najman

The enclosed cutting contained neither the name of the
paper nor a date; judging by the type and the orthography,
however, it clearly came from the twenties or thirties of the
last century; it was so yellowed and worn that it could only
be read with difficulty. Professor Uher was on the point of
throwing it into his wastepaper basket but somehow he was
touched by the antiquity of the printed page; so he began to
read. A moment later he gasped 'Christ!' and excitedly
adjusted his spectacles. This was the text:

Of Men-Lizards

We have read in a foreign newspaper that a certain
captain (commander) of an English warship, returning from
distant parts, made a report about strange reptiles which he
had found on a certain small island in the Australian ocean.
Upon that island there is a lake with salt water, although in
no way connected to the sea, and also most difficult of accefs,
where the said captain and the ship's surgeon were enjoying
their rest. There emerg'd from the lake some animals in the
manner of lizards, except that they walk'd upon two legs like
Men, and having the size of a sea-dog or seal, and
charmingly and strangely disported themselves in such manner
as though they were dancing. The commander and surgeon,
firing their rifles, slew two of these animals. These are said
to have slimy bodies devoid of fur or any scales, so that they
resemble salamanders. Returning for them on the following
day they had to leave them behind because of the great stench
and commanded certain swimmers to drag the lake with nets

anð to bring a couple of those Monsters back alibe on boarð the ship. Habing ðrawn the small lake the sailors slew all lizarðs in great numbers anð ðragg'ð but two of them back on boarð, relating that they hað a poisonous boðy that stung like nettles. Thereupon they plac'ð them into casks containing sea water, in orðer to carry them back to Englanð. But stay! As they sail'ð past the islanð of Sumatra the captibe lizarðs, habing crept out of the casks anð habing of themselbes open'ð the porthole on the steerage ðeck ðuring the night, hað flung themselbes into the sea anð banish'ð. Accorðing to the ebiðence of the Commanðer anð ship's surgeon these animals were pafsing strange anð cunning, walking upon two legs anð making strange barking anð smacking sounðs, though in no way ðangerous to Men. Wherefore we may surely by rights call them Men-Lizarðs.

Thus far the cutting. Christ, Professor Uher repeated excitedly, why isn't there a date or the name of the paper from which whoever it was cut this account? And what was that foreign newspaper, and what was the name of that certain captain or of that English warship? And which was the little island in the Australian ocean? Why couldn't people have been more specific then – and, well, a little more scientific? Surely this was a historical record of immense value –

A small island in the Australian ocean, all right. A little lake with salt water. That suggested a coral island, an atoll with a salt lagoon difficult of accefs: the very place where such a fossil animal might survive, insulated from an evolutionarily more advanced environment and undisturbed in its natural reserve. True, it could not multiply greatly because it would not find very much food in that little lake thereof. So much was clear, thought the professor, catching himself thinking in the archaic language of the newspaper cutting. An animal resembling a lizard, but devoid of scales and walking upon two legs in the manner of Men: that meant either Andrias Scheuchzeri or some other salamander closely related to it. Let's assume it was our Andrias. Let's assume that those damned swimmers slew all specimens in the little lake and that but one pair got on board the ship alive, the pair which, but stay!, escaped into the sea near the island of Sumatra. In other words, directly on the equator, in conditions biologically most favourable and in an environment offering unlimited food supplies. Was it possible that such a change of environment imparted to the Miocene newt that powerful evolutionary impulse? It was certain that it was used to salt water; let us imagine its new habitat as a calm, land-locked bay with a great profusion of food. So what happens? Having been transplanted into optimal conditions *the newt begins to flourish* with colossal vital energy. That was it! The scientist was jubilant. The newt gets down to evolving with boundless appetite; it hurls itself into life like crazy; it multiplies fantastically because its eggs and tadpoles have no specific natural enemies in the new environment. It colonises island after island – though it is odd that it somehow should skip certain islands in its advance. Otherwise it's a typical migration in search of food. And now comes the question: why didn't it evolve earlier? Isn't this perhaps connected with the evidence that in the Ethiopian–Australian zone no salamanders have been, or until quite recently were, recorded? Isn't it possible that in the course of the Miocene period some changes occurred in that zone which were biologically unfavourable to the salamanders? It's possible. Or could a specific enemy have appeared, one which simply exter- minated the newts? Only on *one* single small island, in a small enclosed lake, did the Miocene newt survive – though, of course, at the price of evolutionary arrest. Its evolutionary progress was halted. Just like a wound coil-spring which couldn't unwind. It's not impossible that Nature had great plans for that newt, that it was *meant* to evolve further and further, higher and higher, who could tell how high . . . (Professor Uher felt a slight shiver run down his spine at this thought; who could tell if Andrias Scheuchzeri had not in fact been meant to become Miocene Man?)

But stay! That *under-evolved* animal suddenly finds itself in a new, infinitely more promising, environment; the coiled spring of evolution within it is released. And watch that vital *élan*, that Miocene exuberance with which Andrias hurls himself forward along the road of evolution! How feverishly he makes up for the hundreds of thousands and millions of years of evolution he has missed! Is it conceivable that he will content himself with the evolutionary stage he has reached today? Will the generic upsurge we have witnessed now exhaust itself – or is Andrias still only on the threshold of his evolution and just getting ready to rise to further, and who can say to what, heights?

Such were the reflections and prospects which Professor Vladimir Uher, Doctor of Science, jotted down as he gazed on that yellowed old newspaper cutting, quivering with the intellectual excitement of discovery. I'm going to put it in the newspaper, he said to himself; no one reads scientific journals. Everybody should understand the great natural event we are witnessing! As a headline I'll have: DO THE NEWTS HAVE A FUTURE?

Except that the editorial staff at *Lidové Noviny* looked at Professor Uher's article and shook their heads. Those newts again! *I* believe that our readers are sick and tired of those newts. Time to give them something different. And anyway a daily paper is no place for this scientific stuff.

In consequence the article on the evolution and future of the newts was never published.

12

The Salamander Syndicate

The Chairman, Mr G. H. Bondy, rang his bell and rose to his feet.

'Gentlemen,' he began. 'I have the honour to declare this extraordinary general meeting of the Pacific Export Company open. Allow me to welcome all those present and to thank them for attending in such large numbers.'

'Gentlemen,' he continued with a shaking voice; 'it is my melancholy duty to acquaint you with some sad news. Captain Jan van Toch is no more. The man who, if I may put it that way, was our founder, the originator of the happy idea of establishing commercial relations with thousands of islands in the distant Pacific, our first captain and most zealous collaborator, has died. He passed away at the beginning of this year on board our ship *Šárka* not far from Fanning Island, as a result of a stroke he suffered in the performance of his duty.' (Probably had a row, poor bugger, was the thought that flashed through Mr Bondy's mind.) 'May I ask you to stand in tribute to his shining memory.'

The gentlemen rose, scraping their chairs, and stood in solemn silence, united by the hope that the general meeting would not go on for too long. (Poor old Vantoch, G. H. Bondy thought with genuine emotion. I wonder what he looks like now! Probably dropped him into the sea off a plank – what a splash that must have been! Well, he was a decent chap and he had such blue eyes –)

'Thank you, gentlemen,' he added briefly, 'for commemorating Captain van Toch with such piety; he was a personal friend of mine. I now call upon Mr Volavka, our Manager, to acquaint you with the financial performance which PEC may look forward to this year. The figures aren't final yet, but please don't expect them to change substantially by the end of the year. If you please.'

'Gentlemen,' Mr Volavka, the Manager, began to burble,

and then he came out with it. 'The situation in the pearl market is most unsatisfactory. After last year, when pearl production had increased by a factor of nearly twenty compared with a favourable year like 1925, the price of pearls began to slip disastrously, by as much as 65 per cent. That is why your Board has decided not to place this year's output of pearls on the market at all but to hold it in store until such time as demand hardens again. Unfortunately, pearls began to go out of fashion last autumn, probably because the price had dropped so much. Our Amsterdam branch at the present time holds a stock of over 200,000 pearls which for the time being are virtually unmarketable.'

'On the other hand,' Mr Volavka continued to burble, 'pearl production this year has been declining alarmingly. A number of sources had to be abandoned because their yield no longer justified the long voyage. Sources opened up two or three years ago seem to be more or less exhausted. Your Board has therefore decided to turn its attention to other deep-sea products, such as coral, shells and sponges. While it has been possible to stimulate the market in coral jewellery and other ornaments, it is Italian rather than Pacific corals which have so far benefited from this boom. Your Board is moreover examining the feasibility of deep-sea fishing in the Pacific. The main problem is transporting the fish from there to the European and American markets; the results of preliminary investigations are not too promising.'

'On the other hand,' the Manager read in a slightly raised voice, 'a slightly higher turnover has been recorded in respect of various *secondary* articles, such as exports of textiles, enamelled hollow-ware, wireless sets and gloves to the Pacific islands. This business is capable of further expansion and intensification; even in the current year it will entail only a relatively insignificant deficit. It is, of course, out of the question for PEC to pay out any dividends on its shares at the end of the year; that is why your Board begs to announce in advance that, *for this once*, it will waive all fees and commissions . . .'

A prolonged uncomfortable silence followed. (Wonder what this Fanning Island is like, G. H. Bondy mused. Died like a true seadog, good old Vantoch. Great shame. A really good chap. Wasn't all that old either . . . no older than me . . .)

Dr Hubka then asked for the floor – so why not just quote from the minutes of the extraordinary general meeting of the Pacific Export Company:

Dr Hubka asked whether liquidation of PEC had at all been considered.

G. H. Bondy replied that the Board of Directors had decided to await any suggestions on this point.

M. Louis Bonenfant criticised the fact that the collection of pearls at source was not being carried out by regular representatives permanently resident there, who would ensure that pearl-fishing was done as intensively and efficiently as possible.

Manager Volavka stated that this had in fact been considered but that it had been felt that this would raise overheads too much.

At least 300 salaried agents would be needed; besides, would the meeting please consider how one could ensure that these agents passed on all the pearls found.

M. H. Brinkelaer asked if the Newts could actually be trusted to hand over all the pearls they found; might they not hand them over to persons other than those authorised by the Company?

G. H. Bondy noted that this was the first public mention of Newts. It had been customary in the past not to mention any details of the methods by which the pearls were fished. In point of fact, that was why the inconspicuous title Pacific Export Company had been chosen.

M. H. Brinkelaer inquired why it should be inadmissible in this forum to mention matters which concerned the Company's interests and which, moreover, had long been known to the general public.

G. H. Bondy remarked that it was not inadmissible but a new departure. He welcomed the fact that it was now possible to speak more openly. As for Mr Brinkelaer's first question, he was able to state that, to the best of his knowledge, there was no reason to question the absolute honesty and working efficiency of the Newts employed in fishing for pearls and coral. But one had to expect that present sources of pearls either were, or in the near future would be, largely exhausted. As for new sources, our unforgettable collaborator Captain van Toch had died just as he was en route to hitherto unexploited islands. So far it had been impossible to replace him by somebody of equal experience and equal honesty, let alone dedication to the cause.

Col D. W. Bright fully acknowledged the merits of the late Captain van Toch. He pointed out, however, that the captain, whose demise everybody mourned, had pampered those Newts too much. (Hear, hear.) Surely there was no need to supply the Newts with knives and other tools of such high-class quality as had been done by the late van Toch. There was no need to feed them so expensively. It should be possible to cut down substantially on expenses incurred in the maintenance of the Newts and thus to improve cost-effectiveness of their enterprises. (Loud applause)

Vice-Chairman J. Gilbert agreed with Col Bright but pointed out that in Captain van Toch's lifetime this had not been feasible. Captain van Toch had insisted that he had personal obligations *vis-à-vis* the Newts. For a variety of reasons it had not been possible to flout the old man's wishes in that respect.

Curt von Frisch asked if it was not possible to employ the Newts on other and conceivably more profitable projects than fishing for pearls. One might bear in mind their natural, almost beaver-like, talent for the construction of dams and other submarine structures. It might be possible to use them for deepening harbours, building breakwaters and other hydraulic engineering projects.

G. H. Bondy informed the meeting that the Board of Directors was actively considering just this point; there was no doubt that a great potential existed along these lines. He announced that the number of Newts owned by the Company now totalled approximately 6 million; if one considered that each Newt pair produced about one hundred young each year the Company might have some 300 million Newts at its disposal next year; by the end of a decade the figure would be downright astronomical. G. H. Bondy asked what the Company should do with that enormous number of Newts, bearing in mind that it already had to supply its overcrowded newt farms with copra, potatoes, maize, etc., because of an insufficiency of their natural foodstuffs.

C. von Frisch inquired if the Newts were edible.

J. Gilbert: No. Nor is their skin any use at all.

M. Bonenfant wished to know what the Board actually intended to do.

G. H. Bondy (rising): 'Gentlemen, we called this extraordinary general meeting so we could openly draw your attention to the exceedingly unfavourable outlook for our Company which, if you will allow me to remind you, proudly

declared dividends of 20 to 23 per cent in recent years, in addition to setting aside ample reserves and amortisations. We have now reached a watershed: the kind of business that proved so successful in the past is virtually at an end. We have no choice but to seek new avenues.' (Applause)
'I would almost say that the passing of our excellent captain and friend J. van Toch at this very moment is the hand of fate. To his person was linked that romantic, beautiful and – let me be frank – slightly foolish little business with the pearls. I regard this as a closed chapter in our concern. It had its, how shall I put it, exotic charm, but it did not fit into our modern age. Gentlemen, pearls can never be the subject of a vast horizontal and vertical enterprise. To me, personally, that pearl business, was just a little entertaining diversion' – (Uneasiness) 'Yes, gentlemen, a diversion which earned you and me a nice profit. Besides, in the early stages of our enterprise those Newts had some kind of, let's say, charm of novelty. Three hundred million Newts will no longer have that charm.' (Laughter)
'I said: new avenues. So long as my good friend Captain van Toch was alive there could be no question of giving our enterprise a character different from what I would call Captain van Toch's style.' (Why not?) 'Because, sir, I have too much taste to mix different styles. Captain van Toch's style was, let us say, the style of the adventure novel. It was the style of Jack London, of Joseph Conrad and others. The old, exotic, colonial, almost heroic style. I do not deny that in its way it fascinated me. But after Captain van Toch's death we have no right to continue such adventurous or juvenile epics. What lies ahead of us, gentlemen, is not a new chapter but a whole new concept, a task for a new and substantially different imagination.' (You talk as if this was a novel!) 'Just so, sir; you're right. Personally, I am interested in business as an artist. Without some artistic touch, sir, you'll never come up with a new idea. We've got to be poets if we want to keep the world turning.' (Applause)
G. H. Bondy bowed. 'Gentlemen, it is with regret that I am closing this chapter, what I would call the van Tochian chapter. It enabled us to live out whatever there was young and adventurous in us. The time has now come to put an end to the fairy-tale of pearls and corals. Sindbad the sailor is dead, gentlemen. The question is: Where do we go from here?' (That's what we want to hear from you!) 'Very well, gentlemen. Pick up your pencils and write. Six million. Got that? Now multiply by fifty. That makes 300 million, correct? Now multiply by fifty

again. That makes 15 billion, correct? And now, gentlemen, would you kindly tell me what we are to do with 15 billion Newts in three years from now. How do we employ them, how do we feed them, and so on?' (Why not just let them die?) 'Yes, gentlemen, but wouldn't that be rather wasteful? Just think that every Newt represents some economic value, a workforce value waiting for exploitation? Gentlemen, with 6 million Newts we can just about manage. With 300 million things will be more difficult. But 15 billion Newts, gentlemen, is simply beyond us. The Newts will eat up the Company. That's how matters stand.' (That'll be your responsibility! You started the whole business with the Newts!)

G. H. Bondy straightened up. 'I fully accept that responsibility, gentlemen. Anyone so inclined can immediately divest himself of the Pacific Export Company's shares. I am willing to buy up every single share . . .' (At how much?) 'At par value, sir.' (Commotion. The chairman grants a ten minute adjournment.)

After the adjournment H. Brinkelaer requests the floor. He voiced his satisfaction over the way the Newts were rapidly multiplying, which meant that the Company's assests were growing. But of course it would be sheer madness to cultivate them without purpose; if they themselves had no appropriate employment for them, then he proposed, on behalf of a group of shareholders, that the Newts should simply be sold as labour to whoever planned to conduct any operations in or under water. (Applause) Feeding the Newts cost a few cents a day; if a pair of Newts, therefore, were sold for, say, 100 francs and even if a working Newt survived for just one year, this would be an investment that must easily pay for itself with any contractor. (Expressions of agreement.)

J. Gilbert observed that Newts attained an age considerably in excess of one year, even though experience so far was insufficient to establish their actual lifespan.

H. Brinkelaer amended his proposal to the effect that the price of a pair of Newts should be set at 300 francs f.o.b.

S. Weissberger inquired what kind of work the Newts could in fact perform.

Manager Volavka: 'By natural instinct and with their exceptional technical adaptability the Newts are especially suited to the construction of dams, dykes and breakwaters, the deepening of harbours and waterways, the removal of sandbars and mud deposits, and for keeping shipping lanes clear. They can secure and regulate marine coastlines, extend continents, and so on.

All these were instances of vast-scale works, requiring hundreds and thousands of labour units; moreover, these were projects of such magnitude that even modern engineering technology would never venture to embark on them unless an exceedingly cheap workforce were available.' (Hear, hear! Bravo!)

Dr Hubka objected that by selling off the Newts, which might then multiply in new locations, the Company would be losing its monopoly in them. He proposed that working parties of properly trained and qualified Newts should instead merely be *hired out* to hydraulic engineering contractors, on condition that any future progeny should continue to be the property of the Company.

Manager Volavka pointed out that it was impossible to guard millions or possibly billions of Newts in the water, let alone their progeny; unfortunately a lot of Newts had already been stolen for zoos and menageries.

Col D. W. Bright: 'Only male Newts should be sold, or else hired out, to prevent propagation outside the incubators and farms owned by the Company.'

Manager Volavka: 'We cannot claim that the Newt farms are the property of the Company. You cannot own or rent any part of the sea-bed. In point of law the question of who actually owns the Newts living in the territorial waters of, for the sake of argument, Her Majesty the Queen of the Netherlands, is exceedingly uncertain and could lead to a lot of litigation.' (Uneasiness) 'In most instances we do not even hold a title to fishing rights. We have, in fact, set up our Newt farms in the Pacific islands without legal title.' (Growing uneasiness)

Replying to Col Bright, J. Gilbert pointed out that, on past experience, isolated male Newts after a while lost their agility and value as labour units; they became lazy, apathetic and often pined away.

Von Fritsch inquired if it would not be possible to castrate or sterilise the marketable Newts.

J. Gilbert: 'That would come too expensive; there is simply no way of preventing the sold Newts from procreation.'

S. Weissberger, speaking as a member of the Society for the Prevention of Cruelty to Animals urged that any future sale of Newts should be executed in a humane manner and in a way that would not offend human feelings.

J. Gilbert thanked him for the suggestion; it was understood that the catch and transportation of Newts would be entrusted to trained personnel only and operated under proper supervision. One could not, of course, guarantee the manner in which contractors buying the Newts would treat them. S. Weissberger declared that he was satisfied with Vice-Chairman J. Gilbert's assurances. (Applause)

G. H. Bondy: 'Gentlemen, let us forgo the idea straight away that we could possibly maintain our monopoly in Newts in the future. Unfortunately, under existing regulations, we can't take out a patent on them.' (Laughter) 'We can and must maintain our privileged position with regard to the Newts in another way; an indispensable condition, of course, will be that we tackle our business in a different style and on a far greater scale than hitherto.' (Hear, hear!) 'Here, gentlemen, we have a whole batch of provisional agreements. The Board of Directors proposes that a new vertical trust be set up under the name of The Salamander Syndicate. The members of this Syndicate would be, apart from our Company, a number of major enterprises and financially powerful groups: for example, a certain concern which would manufacture special patented metal instruments for the Newts – ' (Are you referring to MEAS?) 'Yes, sir, I am referring to MEAS. Further, a chemical and foodstuffs cartel which would produce cheap patented feedingstuff for the Newts; a group of transportation companies which – making use of experience gained so far – would take out patents on special hygienic tanks for the transport of Newts; a block of insurance firms which would undertake the insurance of the animals purchased against injury or death during transportation and at their places of work; further various other interested parties in the fields of industry, export and finance which, for weighty reasons, we will not name at this stage. Perhaps it would be sufficient for you to know that this Syndicate would initially have at its disposal four hundred million pounds sterling.' (Excitement) 'This bundle here, my friends, are all contracts which are merely awaiting signature for one of the largest economic organisations of our century to come into being. The Board of Directors requests you, gentlemen, to authorise it to establish this giant concern, whose task will be the cost-effective cultivation and exploitation of the Newts.' (Applause and shouts of dissent)

'Gentlemen, I would ask you to reflect on the advantages of

such co-operation. The Salamander Syndicate will supply not only Newts but also all the tools and food needed by the Newts, that is maize, starch products, suet and sugar for the feeding of billions of animals; further the transport, insurance, veterinary services, and so on – all this at the lowest cost which would ensure if not a monopoly then at least an overwhelming superiority over any future competitor who might try to market Newts. Just let them try, gentlemen; they won't compete with us for long.' (Bravo!) 'And that's not all. The Salamander Syndicate will supply all the building materials for the hydro-engineering work to be done by the Newts. That's why heavy industry is backing us, cement, building timber, stone – ' (You don't know yet how well the Newts are going to work!) 'Gentlemen, at this very moment twelve thousand Newts are working in Saigon harbour on new docks, basins and jetties.' (You never told us that!) 'No. It is the first large-scale experiment. This experiment, gentlemen, has been most gratifyingly successful. The future of the Newts is now beyond any doubt.' (Enthusiastic applause)

'And that's not all, gentlemen. This does not by any means exhaust the tasks of the Salamander Syndicate. The Syndicate will be looking for work for millions of Newts throughout the world. It will supply plans and ideas for control of the seas. It will promote Utopias and gigantic dreams. It will supply projects for new coasts and canals, for causeways linking the continents, for whole chains of artificial islands for transoceanic flights, for new continents to be built in the oceans. That is where mankind's future lies. Gentlemen, four-fifths of the earth's surface is covered by seas; that is unquestionably too much; the world's surface, the map of oceans and dry land, must be corrected. We shall give the world the workforce of the sea, gentlemen. This will no longer be the style of Captain van Toch; we shall replace the adventure story of pearls by the hymnic paean of labour. We can either be shopkeepers or we can be creators; but unless we think in terms of continents and oceans we shall fall short of our potential. Somebody here mentioned the price of a pair of Newts. I would like you to think in terms of entire billions of Newts, of millions and millions of labour units, of transformation of the earth's crust, of a new Genesis and new geological epochs. We can speak today of a new Atlantis, of ancient continents which will stretch out further and further into the world's oceans, of New Worlds which mankind will build for itself. Forgive me, gentlemen, if this strikes you as utopian. Yes indeed, we are entering upon Utopia. We are right in it, my friends. We only have to work out the future of the Newts in technical terms – ' (And in economic terms!)

'Quite so. Especially in economic terms. Gentlemen, our Company is not big enough to exploit billions of Newts on its own; we are not capable of it financially – nor politically. Once the map of oceans and continents begins to change, gentlemen, the great powers will be interested in the business. But we will not discuss that; we will not mention the high quarters which are already adopting a very positive attitude to the Syndicate. I beg you, gentlemen, not to lose sight of the immense scope of the business that you will be voting on.' (Enthusiastic prolonged applause. Excellent! Bravo!)

It nevertheless proved necessary, before the vote was taken on the Salamander Syndicate, to promise that a dividend of at least 10 per cent would be paid out that year on the shares of the Pacific Export Company, drawn on the reserves. After that, the holders of 87 per cent of the shares voted in favour and a mere 13 against. The proposal of the Board of Directors was in consequence adopted. The Salamander Syndicate came into being. G. H. Bondy was congratulated.

'You put that very nicely, Mr Bondy,' old Sigi Weissberger complimented him. 'Very nicely indeed. But tell me, Mr Bondy, how did you hit on the idea?'

'How?' G. H. Bondy asked absent-mindedly. 'To tell you the truth, Mr Weissberger, it was because of old van Toch. He had such faith in his Newts – Poor fellow, what would he have said if we'd simply let those tapa-boys of his die or be done in?'

'What tapa-boys?'

'Why, those bloody Newts. Now at least they'll be decently treated – now that they have some value. Besides, Mr Weissberger, those brutes aren't fit for anything other than some Utopia.'

'I don't understand,' said Mr Weissberger. 'But have you ever seen a Newt, Mr Bondy? I don't actually know what a Newt is. Tell me, what do they look like?'

'I haven't a clue, Mr Weissberger. Why should I know what

a Newt is? Have I got time to worry what it looks like? I should be glad we've got that Salamander Syndicate sewn up.'

Appendix

The Sex Life of the Newts

One of the favourite occupations of the human mind is to speculate how the world and mankind will look in the distant future, what technological miracles will have been accomplished, what social problems solved, and what progress made by science and social organisation, and so on. Most of these Utopias, however, do not omit to exhibit a very lively interest in the question of what will be the future, in that better, more advanced or at least technologically more perfect world, of an institution as ancient yet ever popular as sex, propagation, love, marriage, the family, women's rights, and suchlike. Reference may be made on this point to the relevant literature, such as Paul Adam, H. G. Wells, Aldous Huxley, and many others.

By referring to the above examples, the author considers it his duty – now that he has cast a glance into the future of our globe – to discuss also the lines on which sexual matters will be arranged in that future world of the Newts. He is doing so now in order not to have to revert to the subject later on. Admittedly, the sex life of Andrias Scheuchzeri accords, in basic outline, with the propagation of other caudate amphibians: there is no copulation in the strict sense, the female lays her eggs in several stages, the fertilised eggs develop in the water into tadpoles, and so on; details may be found in any book on natural history. We shall therefore mention only a few peculiarities observed in that respect in Andrias Scheuchzeri.

In early April, H. Bolte records, the males associate with the females; in each sexual period the male as a rule sticks to the same female and, for a number of days, does not leave it even for a moment. During that time he takes in no food, whereas the female exhibits considerable voracity. The male pursues her in the water, trying to get his head close to hers. When he has succeeded in this he shoves his mouth a little way in front of her snout, possibly to prevent her from escaping, and becomes motionless. Thus, touching only with their heads while their bodies form an angle of about thirty degrees, the two animals float alongside each other without any movement. From time to time the male begins to writhe so violently that his flank strikes that of the female; thereupon he again becomes motionless, his legs wide apart, with only his mouth touching the head of his chosen mate who, meanwhile, with complete indifference, feeds on whatever she encounters. This, if we may so call it, kiss continues for several days; sometimes the female will tear herself away in her search for food, and the male will then pursue her in evident agitation and even anger. At last the female ceases any further resistance, she no longer tries to escape, and the pair float motionless in the water, like two dark logs lashed together. At that point the male's body is shaken by convulsive tremors, in the course of which he emits a copious, somewhat sticky sperm into the water. Immediately afterwards he leaves the female and hides away among the rocks, utterly exhausted; in that state his leg or tail might be cut off without defensive reaction on his part.

The female, meanwhile, remains for some time in her rigid, motionless position; then she arches her body vigorously and begins to expel from her cloaca concatenated eggs in a gelatinous sheath; in this she often assists herself with her hindlegs, in the manner of toads. These eggs number from forty to fifty and hang from the female like a tuft. With these eggs the female swims to sheltered spots and there attaches them to algae, seaweed or just stones. Ten days later the same female lays another set of eggs, numbering from twenty to thirty, although she has not been in contact with the male during that period; evidently these eggs were fertilised directly in her cloaca. As a rule a third and a fourth batch of eggs are laid after a further seven or eight days and fifteen to twenty days respectively; these range from fifteen to twenty in number. Within a period from one to three weeks agile tadpoles hatch out, with finely branched gills. After a year these tadpoles grow into adult Newts and are capable of further propagation.

Miss Blanche Kistemaeckers, on the other hand, observed two females and one male Andrias Scheuchzeri in captivity.

At mating time the male associated with only one of the females, pursuing her fairly brutally; whenever she eluded him he struck her viciously with his tail. He did not like to see her feed and tried to push her away from her food; it was obvious that he wanted to have her only for himself, and downright terrorised her. When he had emitted his semen he threw himself on the other female and tried to devour her; he had to be removed from his tank and accommodated elsewhere. Nevertheless, that second female also laid fertilised eggs, amounting to a total of sixty-three. However, Miss Kistemaeckers observed that in all three animals the rims of their cloacae were considerably swollen at that time. It would seem therefore, Miss Kistemaeckers writes, that in the case of Andrias fertilisation is accomplished neither by copulation nor externally, but by means of something that might be termed the *sexual milieu*. As has been seen, fertilisation of the eggs does not require even temporary association. This led the investigator to further interesting experiments. She separated the two sexes; when the appropriate moment arrived she squeezed out the sperm from the male and placed it in the water with the females. Thereupon the females began to lay fertilised eggs. In a further experiment Miss Blanche Kistemaeckers filtered the male's semen and introduced the filtrate from which the spermatozoa had been removed (a clear slightly acid fluid) into the water with the females; even then the females began to lay eggs, about fifty in number, of which the majority were fertilised and yielded normal tadpoles. This led Miss Kistemaeckers to the important concept of the sexual milieu, which represents a separate intermediate stage between parthenogenesis and sexual reproduction. Fertilisation of the eggs takes place simply through a chemical change of the environment (a certain increase in acidity which it has not so far been possible to bring about artificially), a change which seems to be connected somehow with the sexual function of the male. But evidently that function is not itself necessary; the fact that the male associates with the female appears to be a survival of an earlier developmental stage, when fertilisation in the case of Andrias took place in the same way as in other Newts. That association, as Miss Kistemaeckers rightly points out, is some kind of inherited illusion of paternity; in fact the male is not the father of the tadpoles but merely a certain – essentially impersonal – chemical factor of the sexual milieu which is the real fertilising agent. If we kept a hundred associated pairs of Andrias Scheuchzeri in one tank we might assume that a hundred individual fertilisation acts are taking place; in actual fact this is one single act, namely the collective sexualisation of the given environment, or, to put it more precisely, a certain increase in the acidity of the water, to which the ripe eggs of Andrias automatically react by developing into tadpoles. Produce that unknown acidity factor artificially, and no males will be necessary. Thus the sex life of the remarkable Andrias is revealed as a Grand Illusion; his erotic passion, his marriage and sexual tyranny, his temporary fidelity, his ponderous and slow ecstasy – all these are really unnecessary, outdated, almost symbolical actions accompanying or, in a manner of speaking, adorning the male's true impersonal sexual act which is the creation of the sexual milieu permitting fertilisation. The females' strange apathy with which they react to that pointless frantic personal courtship of the males clearly suggests that in the males' wooing the females instinctively see a purely formal ceremony or a prelude to their own mating act, in which they coalesce sexually with the fertilising environment; we might say that the Andrias female has a clearer idea of the state of affairs and a more down-to-earth approach to it, free from erotic illusions.

(Miss Kistemaeckers' experiments were supplemented by interesting experiments by the learned Abbé Bontempelli. He dried and ground up the sperm of Andrias and introduced the material into water containing females; in this case, too, the females began to lay fertile eggs. The same result was obtained when he dried and ground up the sex organs of Andrias or when he extracted them with alcohol or boiled them and poured the extract into the females' tank. He obtained the same result when he repeated the experiment with extracts of the cerebral hypophysis and even with extracts of the epidermal glands of Andrias, expressed when the animal was in heat. In all these instances the females initially failed to react to these additions; only after a little while did they cease to catch food and became motionless, and indeed rigid, in the water, whereupon, a few hours later, they began to eject gelatinous eggs roughly the size of broad beans.)

Mention should be made in this context of the strange ritual called the salamander dance. (We do not mean the Salamander Dance which became the rage at that time especially in the best society and which Bishop Hiram declared to be 'the most obscene dance he had ever heard of'.) What happened was that at the full moon (outside the breeding season) the Andriases would come up the beach in the evenings, but only the male ones, sit down in a circle and start twisting their upper bodies with a strange undulating movement. This was a movement typical of these giant newts even under different circumstances, but during their 'dances' they abandoned themselves to it frenetically, passionately, to the point of exhaustion, like dancing dervishes. Some scientists regarded this mad writhing and shuffling as a cult of the moon and hence as a religious ceremony; others, by contrast, saw this dance as essentially erotic and explained it by just that strange sexual pattern we have described. We have said that in the case of Andrias Scheuchzeri the real fertilising agent is the so-called sexual milieu as a collective and impersonal mediator between individual males and females. We have also said that the females accept this impersonal relationship in a far more realistic and matter-of-fact manner than the males, who – apparently from an instinctive male vanity and aggressiveness – wish to maintain at least the appearance of sexual conquest and therefore play-act amorous wooing and conjugal ownership. This is one of the great erotic illusions and it is compensated for, in a most interesting manner, by just these great male festivities, which are thus said to be nothing other than an instinctive attempt to perceive oneself as a Collective Male. That mass dance, it is argued, overcomes that atavistic and senseless illusion of male sexual individualism; that twisting, intoxicated, frenzied mass is nothing other than the Collective Male, the Collective Sex Partner and the Great Copulator, performing his famous nuptial dance and surrendering himself to a huge wedding ritual – with the curious exclusion of the females who are meanwhile smacking their lips over some small fish or squid they have just consumed. The well-known Charles J. Powell, who has called this Newt ritual the Dance of the Male Principle, further observes: 'And are these collective Newt rituals not the very root and mainspring of that strange Newt collectivism? Let us remember that real animal communities are found only where the life and development of a species is not based on the sexual pair: with bees, ants and termites. The community of the bees might be expressed as: I, the Maternal Hive. The community of the Newts can be expressed quite differently: We, the Male Principle. Only all males jointly, when at the given moment they almost exude from themselves their fertile sexual milieu, become that Great Male that penetrates into the womb of the females and copiously multiplies life. Their paternity is collective; that is why their whole nature is collective and finds expression in collective activity, while the females, having performed their egg-laying, lead a more or less dispersed and solitary life until the next spring. The males alone are the community. The males alone perform collective tasks. In no other animal species does the female play such a subordinate part as in Andrias; the females are excluded from collective action and in point of fact do not display the least interest in it. Their moment comes when the Male Principle saturates their environment with an acidity that is chemically barely perceptible but biologically so pervasive that it is effective even in the infinite dilution produced by the ocean tides. It is as if the Ocean itself became a male, fertilising millions of ova on its shores.'

'In spite of all the cockerel's pride,' Charles J. Powell continues, 'nature has, in the majority of animal species, tended to endow the female with vital superiority. The male exists for his own pleasure and in order to kill; he is a conceited and puffed-up individual, whereas the female represents the species in all its vigour and established virtues. In the case of Andrias (and partly also in Man) the relationship is substantially different; through the establishment of male collectivity and solidarity the male clearly acquires a biological superiority and determines the development of the species to a far greater extent than the female. Perhaps it is just this significant male trend in his evolution that makes Andrias display such engineering talent, i.e. a typically male talent. Andrias is a born technician with an inclination towards large-scale undertakings; these secondary sexual characteristics of the male, i.e. technical talent and a gift for organisation, are developing in him before our very eyes, and with such rapidity and success that we would regard it as a miracle of nature if we did not know that the most powerful vital agents are just these sexual determinants. Andrias Scheuchzer is an *animal faber* and in technical achievement it may well surpass even Man in the foreseeable future – and that only as a result of the natural circumstances that he has created a purely male community.'

BOOK TWO

Up the Ladder of Civilisation

1

Mr Povondra Reads His Paper

There are people who collect stamps and others who collect incunables. Mr Povondra, doorman at the G. H. Bondy residence, had for a long time failed to find a meaning to his life; for years he had wavered between an interest in prehistoric burial chambers and a passion for international politics; but one evening he unexpectedly realised what it was that his life had so far been lacking to make it truly fulfilled. Great things usually come unexpectedly.

That evening Mr Povondra was reading his paper, Mrs Povondra was darning Frankie's socks, and Frankie pretended to be learning the left-bank tributaries of the Danube. A pleasant silence reigned.

'Well, I'll be damned,' grunted Mr Povondra.

'What is it?' asked Mrs Povondra, threading her needle.

'Why, those Newts,' said Papa Povondra. 'It says here that seventy million of them were sold during the past three months.'

'That's a lot, isn't it?' remarked Mrs Povondra.

'You can say that again! Why, Mother, it's a colossal number. Just think: 70 million!' Mr Povondra shook his head. 'There must be a terrific profit in it. And look at the work that's done now,' he added after brief reflection. 'It says here that new land and new islands are being built at breakneck speed everywhere. Do you know, people can now build as many continents for themselves as they like. That's a great thing, Mother. I tell you, this is a greater step forward than the discovery of America.' Mr Povondra became thoughtful. 'A new era in history, that's what it is. Think what you like, Mother, but we're living in stirring times.'

A long domestic silence once more descended. Suddenly Papa Povondra puffed at his pipe more sharply. 'And to think that this whole business would never have come about but for me!'

'What business?'

'That business with the Newts. That New Age. If you look at it properly, it was really me who put it all together.'

Mrs Povondra looked up from the sock with the hole in it. 'What on earth do you mean?'

'That I admitted that captain to see Mr Bondy. If I hadn't let him in that captain would never have met Mr Bondy. Without me, Mother, this whole business would have come to nothing. Absolutely nothing.'

'Maybe the captain would have found someone else,' Mrs Povondra objected.

A contemptuous hiss came from Papa Povondra's pipe-stem. 'You don't know what you're talking about! Only Mr Bondy can do that sort of thing. Christ, that man can see further ahead than God knows who. Anyone else would have thought this thing was sheer lunacy or a con; but not Mr Bondy! That one's got a nose, and no mistake.' Mr Povondra grew thoughtful. 'And that captain, now what was his name, Vantoch – he didn't even look like it. Fat old man he was. Any other doorman would have told him, what an idea, my man, the master isn't in, and that sort of thing; but me, I can tell you, I had a kind of hunch or something. I'll announce him, I said to myself; maybe Mr Bondy'll tear a strip off me, but I'll take the responsibility and announce him. I always say a doorman's got to have a nose for people. Sometimes you get a chap ringing the bell, looks like a lord, and all the time he's a salesman for refrigerators. And another time you get a fat old chap, and just look what he's got in him. Need to understand human nature,' Papa Povondra meditated. 'Let this be a lesson to you, Frankie, of what a man in a humble position can achieve. Let it be an example to you and always try to do your duty same as me.' Mr Povondra nodded his head solemnly and with emotion. 'I could have sent that captain packing right at the front door, and I'd saved myself those stairs. Another doorman would have puffed himself up and slammed the door in his face. And by doing so he would have thwarted all this wonderful progress in the world. Always remember, Frankie, if everybody did his duty the world would be a fine place. And listen to me properly when I'm telling you something!'

'Yes, Dad,' Frankie grunted miserably.

Papa Povondra cleared his throat. 'Lend me those scissors, Mother. I ought to cut this out of the paper, so one day there'll be something to remember me by.'

Thus it came about that Mr Povondra started collecting newspaper cuttings about the Newts. To his zeal as a collector we owe a great deal of material which would otherwise have passed into oblivion. He cut out and filed away anything he found in print about the Newts; indeed no secret should be made of the fact that, after some initial inhibitions, he acquired the knack, in his regular café, of ransacking the papers whenever there was a mention of the Newts in them, and that he attained a special, almost prestidigitational, skill in inconspicuously ripping the relevant page from the paper and whisking it into his pocket right under the headwaiter's eyes. It is a well-known fact that all collectors are prepared to steal or do murder for the sake of acquiring a new piece for their collection; but this does not in any way reflect on their moral character.

Life now had a meaning for him, for it was the life of a collector. Evening after evening he would sort out and read his cuttings under the indulgent eyes of Mrs Povondra, who knew that every man was partly a nutcase and partly a little boy; why shouldn't he play with those cuttings instead of going to the pub and playing cards? In the end she even made room in her linen cupboard for the boxes which he himself glued together for his collection. What more could anyone expect from a wife and mother of a family?

G. H. Bondy himself was on some occasion or other surprised at Mr Povondra's encyclopaedic knowledge of anything concerning the Newts. Mr Povondra confessed, a little shamefacedly, that he collected everything that appeared in print about salamanders and showed Mr Bondy his boxes. G. H. Bondy was courteously complimentary about his collection; you can't deny it: only great men can be so gracious and only powerful men are able to make others happy without it costing them a penny; great men altogether have it made for them. Thus, for instance, Mr Bondy issued instructions that the offices of the Salamander Syndicate should send Povondra all such cuttings about the Newts as were not required for the firm's archives; in consequence, a blissfully happy if slightly overwhelmed Mr Povondra received whole stacks of documents every day, in all the languages of the world, of which especially the papers printed in the Cyrillic or Greek alphabet, or in Hebrew, Arabic, Chinese, Bengali, Tamil, Javanese, Burmese and Taalik script filled him with religious reverence. 'To think,' he would mutter over them, 'that none of these would have been without me!'

As we have said, Mr Povondra's collection has preserved a great deal of historical material about the whole story of the Newts; which is not to say that it could possibly satisfy a scholarly historian. For one thing, Mr Povondra, who had not had the benefit of specialised education in the ancillary historical sciences or in archival methods, did not furnish his cuttings with either a source reference or the appropriate date, so that for the most part we do not know where and when a certain document was printed. For another thing, because of the surfeit of material accumulating under his hands, Mr Povondra kept mainly the longer articles, considering them to be more important, while brief reports and journalist's cables he simply threw in the coal scuttle. As a result, an exceedingly small amount of reports and facts has come down to us about that entire period. Thirdly, there was a good deal of intervention on the part of Mrs Povondra: whenever Mr Povondra's boxes began to fill alarmingly she would quietly and surreptitiously extract some of the cuttings and burn them; this would happen several times a year. She would keep only those which did not accumulate too quickly, such as the cuttings printed in Malabar, Tibetan or Coptic script; these have come down to us almost in their entirety, but in view of certain gaps in our education they are not a lot of use to us. Hence the material available to us on the history of the Newts is essentially incomplete, rather like land registers from the eighth century AD or the collected works of the poetess Sappho; only by accident have the documents relating to one aspect or another of this great historic event been preserved for us. Yet in spite of all lacunae we shall attempt to map it out under the heading 'Up the Ladder of Civilisation'.

2
Up the Ladder of Civilisation

(The History of the Newts[1])

In the new epoch which G. H. Bondy inaugurated at the memorable general meeting of the Pacific Export Company, when he uttered his prophetic words about the beginning of Utopia,[2] historical events could no longer be measured in centuries or even decades, as had been customary in world history until then, but by the three-month periods for which the quarterly economic statistics were published.[3] Because the making of history, if we may so call it, was now taking place wholesale; in consequence the pace of history was accelerating quite extraordinarily (according to some estimates by a factor of five). Nowadays we simply cannot wait a few

[1] Cf. G. Kreuzmann, *Geschichte der Molche*; Hans Tietze, *Der Molch des XX. Jahrhunderts*; Kurt Wolff, *Der Molch und das deutsche Volk*; Sir Herbert Owen, *The Salamanders and the British Empire*; Giovanni Focaja, *L'evoluzione degli anfibi durante il Fascismo*; Léon Bonnet, *Les Urodèles et la Société des Nations*; S. Madariaga, *Las Salamandras y la Civilización*, and many others.

[2] Cf. *War with the Newts*, Book 1, Chapter 12.

[3] This is proved by the very first cutting in Mr Povondra's collection:

NEWT MARKET REPORT

(CTK) According to the latest report issued by the Salamander Syndicate at the end of the last quarter, sales of Newts have increased by 30 per cent. Over the past three months deliveries of Newts totalled nearly 70 million, chiefly to South and Central America, Indochina and Italian Somaliland. Projects scheduled for the near future include the deepening and widening of the Panama Canal, the dredging of the harbour of Guayaquil and the removal of all shoals and sandbars in the Torres Straits. These works alone, according to approximate estimates, involve the removal of 9 billion cubic metres of solid soil. Construction of solid aircraft islands on the Madeira–Bermuda route is expected to commence next spring. In-fill work in the Mariana islands under Japanese Mandate continues; so far 840,000 acres of new, so-called light, dry land has been won between the islands of Tinian and Saipan. In view of growing demand Newt prices are very firm: Leading 61, Team 620. Supplies are adequate.

hundred years for something good or bad to happen in the world. Take the migration of peoples which used to drag on over several centuries: today, with our present organisation of transport, it could be accomplished in three years; otherwise there would be no profit in it. The same is true of the liquidation of the Roman Empire, the colonisation of the continents, the extermination of the Red Indians, and so on. All these things could have been accomplished incomparably more speedily if they had been put in the hands of entrepreneurs with a lot of capital behind them. In that respect the huge success of the Salamander Syndicate and its powerful influence on world history undoubtedly points the way to the future.

The history of the Newts is thus characterised from the very outset by its perfect and rational organisation; the principal but not exclusive credit for this must go to the Salamander Syndicate; it should, however, be acknowledged that science, philanthropic endeavour, enlightenment, the press and other factors also played a considerable part in the spectacular spread and progress of the Newts. That said, it was the Salamander Syndicate which, so to speak, daily conquered new continents and new shores for the Newts, even though it had to overcome many an obstacle to that expansion.[4] The Syndicate's quarterly reports show how Indian and Chinese harbours are, one after the other, being settled by the Newts; how Newt colonisation is swamping the coast of Africa and leaping across to the American continent, where new, super-modern Newt incubators are fast springing up in the Gulf of Mexico; and how, alongside these vast waves of colonisation, smaller groups of Newts are sent out as pioneering vanguards of future exports. Thus the Salamander Syndicate made a present of 1,000 top-quality Newts to the Dutch Waterstaat; it presented

---

[4] Such obstacles are illustrated, for instance, by this report, cut from a newspaper without indication of date:

BRITAIN CLOSING THE DOOR TO NEWTS?

(Reuter) In reply to a Commons question by Mr J. Leeds MP, Sir Samuel Mandeville today stated that HM Government had closed the Suez Canal to all Newt transports; the Government did not intend to permit a single Newt to be employed on the coast or in the territorial waters of the British Isles. The reasons for these measures, Sir Samuel explained, were, on the one hand, the security of the British shores and, on the other, the continued validity of ancient laws and treaties on the abolition of the slave trade.

In reply to a question by Mr B. Russell MP, Sir Samuel stated that this practice did not of course apply to British Dominions or Colonies.

the city of Marseilles with 600 Newts for clearing out the Old Port, and similarly elsewhere. In short, unlike human colonisation of the globe, the spread of the Newts proceeded in accordance with a plan and on a generous scale; had it been left to nature it would have dragged on over hundreds and thousands of years. Say what you will, but nature is not, and never has been, as enterprising and purposeful as human production and commerce. It seems that the lively demand for Newts has even had an effect on their fertility; the spawn yield per female has risen to as much as 150 tadpoles per annum. Certain regular losses which sharks used to cause to the Newts ceased almost totally once the Newts had been equipped with underwater pistols and dum-dum ammunition for defence against predatory fish.[5]

Needless to say, the spread of the Newts did not take place equally smoothly everywhere; in some places conservative circles strongly objected to this introduction of a new workforce on the grounds that it represented unfair competition with human labour;[6] others expressed the anxiety that the Newts, feeding as they did on small marine organisms, would prove a threat to fisheries; others yet argued that with their submarine burrows and passages they were undermining coastlines and islands. To be perfectly honest, there were quite a few people who uttered outspoken warnings against the introduction of the Newts; but then this has happened from time immemorial – every innovation and every step forward

[5] The weapon used for this purpose almost universally was a pistol invented by the engineer Mirko Šafránek and manufactured by the Brno Armaments Works.

[6] Cf. this newspaper story:

STRIKE MOVEMENT IN AUSTRALIA

(Havas) Australian trade union leader Harry MacNamara has called for a general strike of all dockside, transport, power station and other workers. The unions demand that imports of working Newts to Australia be subject to strict quotas in accordance with immigration legislation. Australian farmers, on the other hand, are seeking a liberalisation of Newt imports since this would greatly stimulate sales of domestic maize and animal fats, especially mutton fat. The Government is trying to achieve a compromise; the Salamander Syndicate is offering to pay the trade unions six shillings as a contribution for every Newt imported. The Government is prepared to guarantee that the Newts will only be employed under water and that (for reasons of public morality) they will not surface beyond 16 inches, i.e. up to the chest. However, the trade unions insist on a 5-inch limit and demand a payment of 10 shillings per Newt, plus union membership due. It is thought that agreement will be reached with the aid of the Federal Exchequer.

have met with opposition and mistrust; this was so with machinery in the factories and this was now being repeated in the case of the Newts. In other places there were misunderstandings of a different kind,[7] but thanks to full support from the international press, which correctly assessed the enormous business potential of the Newts, and especially the profitable and extensive advertising that went hand in hand with it, the arrival of the salamanders in all parts of the world was widely welcomed with lively interest and indeed enthusiasm.[8]

The Newt trade was for the most part in the hands of the Salamander Syndicate, which conducted it by means of its own specially constructed tank ships; the centre of that trade and, in a manner of speaking, the Newt Exchange was the Salamander Building in Singapore.

Cf. the extensive and objective account which appeared on 5 October over the initials E. W.:

[7] Cf. the following remarkable document in Mr Povondra's collection:

THIRTY-SIX DROWNING PASSENGERS SAVED BY NEWTS

(From our special correspondent) Madras, 3 April. In the harbour here the steamship *Indian Star* collided with a ferryboat which was carrying about forty natives. The ferryboat sank instantly. Even before a police launch was able to set out for the spot some Newts employed on silt removal in the harbour hurried to the aid of the drowning and carried thirty-six of them to the bank. One salamander alone dragged three women and two children out of the water. In recognition of this gallant action the Newts have received a written expression of thanks in a waterproof case from the local authorities.

The native population, on the other hand, is most indignant that the Newts should have been allowed to touch drowning persons of higher caste, as they regard the Newts as unclean and untouchable. A crowd of a few thousand natives collected at the harbour, demanding the expulsion of the Newts. The police has the situation under control: only three persons have been killed and one hundred and twenty arrested. By 10 pm peace was restored. The salamanders are continuing their work.

[8] Cf. the following highly interesting cutting, unfortunately in an unknown language and therefore untranslatable:

Saht na kchi te
Salaam Ander bwtat

Saht gwan t'lap ne Salaam Ander bwtati og t'cheni bechri ne Simbwana m'bengwe ogandi sumkh na moimoi opwana Salaam Ander sri m'oana gwen's. Og di bwtat na Salaam Ander kchri p'we ogandi p'we o'gwandi te ur maswali sukh? Na, ne ur lingo t'Islami kcher oganda Salaam Andrias sahti. Bend op'tonga kchri Simbwana medh, salaam!

S-TRADE

'Singapore, 4 October. Leading 63. Heavy 317. Team 648. Odd Jobs 26-35. Trash 0.08. Spawn 80–132.'

This is the kind of report the reader will find in his newspaper every day in the business columns among the dispatches on commodity prices, such as cotton, tin or wheat. But do you in fact know what these mysterious figures and words mean? All right, the Salamander Trade or S-Trade – but how many readers have any clear idea of what that trade really looks like? They probably imagine some big market place swarming with thousands and thousands of Newts, with buyers in topees and turbans strolling about, inspecting the merchandise on offer and finally pointing a finger at some well-developed healthy young salamander and saying: 'I'll take this one; how much is it?'

In reality the salamander market looks quite different. In that marble building of the S-Trade in Singapore you will find not a single Newt but only busy smartly dressed clerks in white suits, accepting orders by telephone. 'Yes sir. Leading stands at 63. How many? 200? Very good, sir. Twenty Heavy and 180 Team. OK, understood. The ship sails in five weeks. Right? Thank you, sir.' The entire palatial S-Trade building is aloud with telephone conversations; the impression is that of a government office or a bank rather than of a market. And yet that noble white building with its Ionian-colonnade façade is more of a world market than the bazaar in Baghdad at the time of Haroun al-Rashid.

But to return to the market quotation at the top of this article and to its business jargon. *Leading* are quite simply specially selected intelligent Newts, as a rule three years old and carefully trained to be leaders and supervisors of Newt work teams. These are sold individually, regardless of body weight; it is their intelligence that counts. Singapore Leading, with a good command of English, are considered top quality and most reliable; occasionally other grades of leading Newts are also marketed, such as the so-called Capitanos, Engineers, Malayan Chiefs, Foremanders, etc., but Leading are priced highest. Currently they will fetch around sixty dollars apiece.

Heavy means ordinary heavy, athletically built Newts, as a rule two years old, with a weight ranging from 100 to 120 pounds. These are sold only in gangs, or 'bodies', of six. They are trained to perform the heaviest kind of physical work, such as breaking rocks, rolling away boulders and suchlike. If the above quotation says 'Heavy 317' this means that a six-specimen gang or 'body' costs 317 dollars. Each body of Heavy Newts normally has one Leading Newt as its foreman and supervisor.

Team are ordinary working Newts weighing from eighty to 100 pounds. These are sold only in work teams of twenty; they are intended for collective work and find their best employment in dredging and in the construction of banks, dams, etc. Each team of twenty requires one Leading.

Odd Jobs represent a category of their own. These are Newts which for some reason or other have not undergone either collective or specialised training, for instance because they have grown up away from the big, properly managed Newt farms. They are in effect semi-wild Newts, but are often very gifted. They are marketed individually or by the dozen and employed on various auxiliary jobs or lesser projects which do not warrant the use of entire Newt gangs or teams. If Leading represent the élite among the Newts, Odd Jobs are something like the lower proletariat. Lately they have become popular as Newt raw material to be further developed by individual entrepreneurs and then classified into Leading, Heavy, Team or Trash.

Trash or rubbish (refuse, crap) are inferior, weak or physically deficient Newts. These are not marketed individually or in definite quantities but collectively by weight, usually by entire tens of tons; one kilogramme live weight currently costs from seven to ten cents. It is not really clear what purpose they serve or why they are purchased – possibly for some less demanding work in the water. To avoid any misconceptions, readers are reminded that Newts are not fit for human consumption. This Trash is almost entirely bought up by Chinese dealers; where they are shipped has never been established.

Spawn is quite simply Newt fry or, more accurately,

tadpoles up to one year old. These are bought and sold by the hundred; trade in them is very lively, mainly because they are cheap and their transportation is least costly. Only when they have reached their destination are they nurtured and trained until fit for work. Spawn is shipped in barrels because the tadpoles do not leave the water, unlike the grown Newts which have to emerge every day. It often happens that exceptionally gifted individuals develop from Spawn, even surpassing the standard Leading type; this lends transactions in Spawn a particular interest. Highly talented Newts are then sold for several hundred dollars apiece; the American millionaire Denicker has actually paid 2,000 dollars for a Newt that was fluent in nine languages, and had it transported to Miami by special boat; that transport alone cost nearly 20,000 dollars. Purchase of Spawn has lately become popular for so-called Newt stables, where fast sporting Newts are selected and trained; these are then harnessed in teams of three to flat-bottomed boats shaped like a shell. Newt-shell racing is now the vogue in America and the favourite pastime of American youngsters at Palm Beach, in Honolulu or in Cuba; they are called 'Triton races' or 'Venus regattas'. In a light, prettily decorated shell, skimming over the sea's surface, stand the girl racers in the scantiest possible and most charming swimming attire, holding the silken reins of their salamandric three-in-hand, competing for the title of Venus. Mr J. S. Tincker, known as the Tinned Food King, bought his daughter a team of three racing Newts, Poseidon, Hengist and King Edward, for no less than 36,000 dollars. But this is really outside the scope of the S-Trade proper, which is concerned only with the worldwide supply of reliable working Leadings, Heavies and Teams.

We have mentioned Newt Farms. The reader would be wrong to visualise vast livestock buildings or pens. They are in fact several kilometres of empty foreshore with just a few corrugated-iron huts scattered about. One of these is for the veterinary surgeon, another for the manager, and the rest are for the supervisory staff. It is only at low tide that the long dams running out from the shore to the sea are visible, subdividing the coastline into several basins.

One is for the small fry, another for the Leading category, and so on; each type is fed and trained separately. Both these activities take place at night. At dusk the Newts emerge from their burrows under the shore and assemble round their instructors; as a rule these are retired servicemen. First there is a speaking lesson; the instructor says a word to the Newts, for instance 'dig', and demonstrates its meaning to them. He then arranges them into columns of four and teaches them to march; next follows half an hour's physical training and a brief rest in the water. After the break comes instruction in the handling of various tools and weapons, followed by three hours' practical work on hydro-engineering jobs under the supervision of the instructors. Thereafter the Newts return to the water where they are fed Newt biscuits consisting mainly of maize flour and suet; Leading and Heavy Newts receive an additional ration of meat. Laziness or disobedience are punished by withdrawal of food; there are no other physical punishments; besides, the salamanders' susceptibility to pain is slight. At sunrise a dead silence falls over the Newt farms; the staff go to bed and the Newts vanish below the sea's surface.

This drill is changed only on two occasions each year. Once at breeding time, when the Newts are left to their own devices for a fortnight, and once when the Salamander Syndicate's tank ship calls at the farm with instructions to the farm manager on how many Newts of each category are to be recruited. This recruitment is done at night; a ship's officer, the farm manager and the veterinary surgeon sit at a small table with a lamp on it, while the supervisors and the ship's crew block the salamanders' retreat to the water. One Newt after another steps up to the table and is pronounced fit or unfit for service. The recruited Newts then board the boats which take them out to the tank ship. Most of them volunteer to go, that is they go in response to a single sharp command; only occasionally is mild force needed, such as shackling. Spawn or fry, of course, are fished out by nets.

Just as humane and hygienic is the actual transportation of the Newts in tank ships; the water in their tanks is changed by pumping every other day and they are most amply fed. The death-rate during transportation scarcely reaches 10 per cent. At the request of the Society for the Prevention of

Cruelty to Animals there is a chaplain on board every tank
ship to ensure the salamanders are treated humanely; every
night he delivers them a sermon which exhorts them in
particular to show respect to humans and to show obedience
and love to their future employers whose one desire is to
exercise paternal care for their well-being. It is undoubtedly
rather difficult to explain this paternal care to the Newts
since the concept of paternity is unknown to them. Among
the more highly educated salamanders the ship's chaplain
has earned for himself the title of 'Papa Newt'. Educational
films have also proved extremely successful: in these the
Newts are acquainted with, on the one had, the miracles
of human engineering and, on the other, their own future
work and duties.

There are people who translate the abbreviation S-Trade
(for Salamander Trade) as 'Slave Trade'. However, as
unbiased observers we can only say that if the slave trade
in the past had been as well organised and as hygienically
practised as the present Newt trade, the slaves could have
been congratulated. The more expensive salamanders are
really treated very decently and considerately, if only
because the ship's captain and crew have to vouch with their
own salaries and wages for the lives of the Newts in their
charge. The writer of the present article personally
witnessed how even the toughest sailors on board the tank
ship SS 14 were deeply affected when two hundred and forty
top-quality Newts in one of the tanks became ill with violent
diarrhoea. They would go down to look at them, and with
eyes almost filled with tears would give vent to their human
sentiments in the rough words: 'Why the hell do we have
to have this stinking lot wished on us?'

With the growing turnover in Newt exports there arose,
naturally enough, also an irregular trade. The Salamander
Syndicate could not possibly control and administer all the
Newt incubators which the late Captain van Toch had set up
all over the place, especially on the tiny remote islands of
Micronesia, Melanesia and Polynesia, so that numerous bays
were left to their own devices. The result was that, alongside
the organised breeding of salamanders there developed – and
on quite a considerable scale – the hunting of wild Newts,

reminiscent in many respects of seal hunting expeditions in
the past; this hunt was to some extent illegal, but in the absence
of legislation on Newt hunting prosecution, at best, was for
unauthorised encroachment of the sovereignty of this state or
that. And since the Newts proliferated quite enormously on
those islands and here and there caused damage to the natives'
fields and orchards, this irregular hunting of Newts was tacitly
regarded as a natural regulation of the Newt population.
We quote here an authentic contemporary account:

BUCCANEERS OF THE TWENTIETH CENTURY
E. E. K.

The time was eleven o'clock in the evening when our ship's
captain gave orders for the national flag to be hauled down and
the boats to be lowered. It was a moonlit night with a silvery
haze; the little island we were heading for was, I think, Gardner
Island in the Phoenix Archipelago. On such moonlit nights the
Newts come up the beach and dance; you can approach them
closely and they will not hear you, so intent are they on their
silent collective dance. There were twenty of us, stepping ashore
with our oars in our hands and, strung out in single file, we began
to encircle the dark crowd that was swarming on the beach in
the milky light of the moon.
  It is difficult to describe the impression produced by that dance
of the Newts. Perhaps 300 animals are sitting on their hindlegs
in an absolutely perfect circle, facing inwards; the inside of the
circle is empty. The Newts do not move, they seem quite rigid;
the impression is that of a circular palisade surrounding some
mysterious altar; but there is no altar and no deity. Suddenly
one of the animals utters a smacking sound: 'Ts-ts-ts-ts' and
starts swaying and twisting the upper half of its body; this
fluctuating movement spreads further and further, and within
seconds all the Newts are twisting their upper bodies without
moving from the spot: faster and faster, soundlessly, more and
more frenetically, in a mad and intoxicated swirling. After about
a quarter of an hour one of the Newts will tire, then another,
and a third; they are now swaying exhaustedly and stiffly; and
now they are again all of them sitting motionless like statues;
after a while a quiet 'ts-ts-ts' is heard from somewhere, another
Newt starts writhing, and his dancing spreads rapidly to the
entire circle. I realise that this account sounds rather mechanical:

but add to it the chalky light of the moon and the regular slow murmur of the tide. There was something immensely magical and almost enchanted about the whole thing. I stopped with my throat gripped by an involuntary sense of terror or amazement. 'Get a move on, man,' my neighbour snapped at me, 'or you'll make a gap!'

We tightened our circle round the dancing animals. The men were holding their oars across and talking in low voices, more because it was night than for fear the Newts might hear them. 'Move in now, at the double,' called the commanding officer. We ran towards the writhing circle; with a dull thud the oars struck the Newts' backs. It was only then that the Newts took fright, retreating towards the centre or trying to slip out between our oars to regain the sea; but blows from the oars threw them back, shrieking with pain and terror. We forced them back with our oars, towards the middle, crowded together, packed tightly, climbing over each other in several layers; ten men penned them in a palisade of oars and another ten prodded or beat those which tried to slip underneath the oars or break out. It was a mass of squirming, confusedly croaking black flesh, upon which dull thuds were falling. Then a gap opened between two oars; a Newt slipped through and was stunned by a blow on the back of its head; a second and a third followed, and a moment later some twenty were lying there. 'Close it up,' commanded the officer and the gap between the oars closed once more. Bully Beach and the halfbreed Dingo with each hand grabbed a leg of one of the stunned Newts and dragged them like lifeless sacks through the sand to the boats. Sometimes a dragged body would get caught between the stones; then the sailor would give a violent and vicious jerk and a leg would come off. 'Never mind,' muttered old Mike who was next to me. 'He'll soon grow another.' As they were flinging the stunned Newts into the boats the officer said curtly: 'Get the next lot ready.' And again the blows fell on the necks of the Newts. That officer, Bellamy was his name, was an educated, quiet man and an excellent chess player; but this was a hunt, or more accurately a matter of business, so let's have no fuss. In this way over two hundred stunned Newts were captured; about seventy were left behind, probably dead or not worth dragging away.

On board the captured Newts were flung into tanks. Our ship was an old tanker; the badly cleaned tanks reeked of crude oil and the water in them had a rainbow skin of grease; only the cover had been taken off to admit air; with the Newts thrown in it looked thick and repulsive like some kind of noodle soup. Here and there was a faint and pitiful movement, but for the first day the Newts were left undisturbed to enable them to recover. On the following morning four men arrived with long poles and poked around in that 'soup' (it really is called soup in the trade); they stirred those densely packed bodies and identified those which did not move or whose flesh was falling off; these were then fished out of the tank with boathooks. 'Is the soup clear now?' asked the captain. 'Yes, sir.' 'Run some more water into it!' 'Yes, sir.' This cleaning of the soup had to be repeated daily; each time six to eight items of 'damaged goods' – as they called it – were thrown overboard. Our ship was accompanied by a procession of big and well-fed sharks. There was a terrible stench around the tanks; in spite of the occasional changing of the water it was yellow and dotted with excrement and sodden biscuits; in it, languidly splashing or apathetically floating, were painfully gasping bodies. 'They're well off here,' old Mike assured me. 'I saw a ship once which carried them in tin benzene drums; the whole lot of them pegged out there.'

Six days later we took new merchandise on board off Nanomea island.

This, then, is what the Newt trade is like; an illegal trade, admittedly, or more precisely a modern form of piracy that has sprung up virtually overnight. It is said that nearly one-quarter of all Newts bought and sold are captured in this manner. There are Newt breeding places which for the Salamander Syndicate are not worth operating as regular farms; on the lesser Pacific islands the Newts have multiplied on a scale that has made them a downright nuisance; the natives object to them and claim that with their burrows and passages they riddle entire islands; that is why not only the colonial authorities but the Salamander Syndicate itself turn a blind eye to these marauding raids on Newt localities. It is estimated that not far short of four hundred pirate ships are engaged in marauding alone. Apart from small-scale entrepreneurs, there are whole shipping companies which practise this modern buccaneering: the biggest of these is the Pacific Trade Company with its head office in Dublin; its president is the respected Mr Charles B. Harriman. Conditions were rather worse a year ago when a certain Teng, a Chinese bandit, with three ships made an outright raid on some Syndicate farms and did not even flinch from massacring their staff when they offered resistance; last autumn Teng with his small fleet was shot to pieces off Midway island by the American gunboat *Minnetonka*. Since then Newt piracy has been less savage in character and has even enjoyed a steady boom. Certain practices have come to be accepted, and with them the illegal trade is now tacitly tolerated: thus, for example, the ship's national naval ensign shall be lowered before an attack is made on foreign territory; Newt piracy shall not be used as a cover for the import or export of other commodities; the captured Newts shall not be dumped at uneconomic prices, and they shall be described in the trade as 'seconds'. In the illegal trade these Newts are marketed at twenty to twenty-two dollars apiece; they are regarded as an inferior but tough type, considering that they have survived terrible treatment on the pirate ships. It is estimated that on an average between 25 and 30 per cent of the captured Newts survive transportation; those that do are a particularly hardy lot. In business jargon they are called Macaroni; lately they have actually been quoted in the regular commodity market reports.

Two months later I was playing chess with Mr Bellamy in the lounge of the Hotel France in Saigon. By then, of course, I was no longer a hired hand on his ship.

'Look here, Bellamy,' I said. 'You're a decent sort of chap – what's called a gentleman. Doesn't it ever go against the grain to make a living from what, essentially, is the shabbiest kind of slave trade?'

Bellamy shrugged. 'Newts are Newts,' he grunted evasively.

'Two hundred years ago people said Niggers were Niggers.'

'And how right they were,' said Bellamy. 'Check!'

I lost that game. It suddenly seemed to me that every move on the board was old and had been made by someone before. Maybe our history has likewise been played through already and we are merely moving our chessmen to the same squares for the same defeats as in the past. Maybe just such a decent quiet chap as Bellamy once hunted Negroes on the Ivory Coast, shipped them to Haiti or Louisiana, and let them die like flies below deck. He had nothing evil in mind, that Bellamy. Bellamy never has anything evil in mind. That's why he is incorrigible.

'Black has lost,' Bellamy announced complacently and got up to stretch himself.

Alongside a well-organised Newt market and extensive press publicity, the major factor in the spread of the Newts was a huge wave of technological idealism which then flooded the whole world. G. H. Bondy had correctly predicted that the human intellect would start to operate in terms of entire new continents and new Atlantises. Throughout the Newt Age a lively and fruitful argument reigned among the technologists: should heavy continents be built with reinforced concrete coasts or lightweight continents of piled up sea sand? Almost daily giant new projects hit the headlines: Italian engineers were proposing, on the one hand, the construction of a Greater Italy which would take up virtually the entire Mediterranean all the way to Tripolitania, the Balearic Islands and the Dodecanese and, on the other, the establishment of a new continent, to be known as Lemuria, to the east of Italian Somaliland which would, one day, take up the whole of the Indian Ocean. In point of fact, with the aid of a whole army of Newts, a new little island was piled up opposite the Somalian port of Mogadishu, measuring thirteen and half acres. Japan had projected, and indeed partly completed, a big new island in place of the former Mariana group and was planning to link the Carolinas and Marshall Islands into two large islands, named in advance New Nippon; in fact each of these was to have an artificial volcano installed, to remind future inhabitants of the sacred Mount Fuji. There were rumours that German engineers were secretly developing a heavy concrete continent in the Sargasso Sea, to be the Atlantis of the future and capable of threatening French West Africa; but it seemed that no more than is foundations were completed. In Holland, steps were taken to drain Zeeland dry; France, on Guadeloupe, was linking up Grande Terre, Basse Terre and La Désirade into one blessed isle; and the United States had begun to construct the first aircraft island on the 37th meridian (two storeys, with a gigantic hotel, a sports stadium, a Fun Park and a cinema seating five thousand). In short, it seemed that the last barriers had fallen which the world's oceans had erected to human progress; it was the dawn of a joyous new age of amazing technical projects; man was beginning to realise that only now was he truly becoming the Master of the World, thanks to the Newts who had appeared on the world stage at the right moment and, in a manner of speaking, out of historical necessity. There can be no doubt that the immense proliferation of the Newts would not have come about if our age of technology had not provided for them such a wealth of tasks and such a vast field of permanent employment. The future of the Workers of the Sea seemed to be secure for centuries.

A significant part in the favourable development of the Newt trade was also played by science which soon turned its attention to investigating the physical and psychological aspects of the Newts.

We are quoting here an account of a scientific congress in Paris, written by an eye-witness, R. D.:

Ier Congrès d'Urodèles

Its short title is Caudate Amphibian Congress but its official title is rather longer: First International Congress of Zoologists for Psychological Research into Caudate Amphibians. Except that a real Parisian does not care for titles as long as your arm; the learned professors in session in the amphitheatre of the Sorbonne are to him simply *Messieurs les Urodèles*, the Caudate Amphibian Gentlemen, and that is all. Or still more briefly and irreverently *Ces Zoos-là*.

So we set out to have a look at *ces Zoos-là*, more out of curiosity than from a journalistic sense of duty. Curiosity, so you don't get me wrong, not about those mostly elderly and bespectacled academic luminaries but about those . . . creatures (why do we baulk at the term 'animals'?) about which such a lot has been written, from fat scholarly tomes down to frivolous jingles, and which, according to some, are a newspaper hoax or, according to others, creatures in many ways much more gifted than the Master of the Animal Kingdom and the Crown of Creation, as Man is to this day – I mean: after the Great War and other historical events – labelled. I had hoped that the distinguished gentlemen attending the congress on the psychological investigation of caudate amphibians would be able to give us laymen a clear and definitive answer to the question of what that much-vaunted learning ability of Andrias Scheuchzeri was really like; that they would be able to tell us: yes, this is an intelligent creature or at least one as capable of civilisation as you or me, and therefore we must expect to have him around in the future, just as we must expect to have alongside ourselves human races formerly considered savage and primitive . . . But let me tell you: no such answer has come from the congress, and indeed no such question has been put; contemporary scholarship is much too . . . professional to concern itself with that kind of problem.

Very well, let us be informed on what scientists call the psychological life of animals. That tall gentleman with the flowing sorcerer's beard, who is at this moment thundering from the rostrum, is the famous Professor Dubosque; he seems to be demolishing some perverse theory of some esteemed colleague, but that side of the argument is difficult for us to follow. It took us a little while to realise that the impassioned sorcerer is talking about Andrias's perception of colours and about his ability to distinguish different shades of colours. I don't know if I understood it properly, but I came away with the impression that while Andrias Scheuchzeri may be a little colour-blind, Professor Dubosque must be terribly shortsighted, judging by the way he raised his papers right up to his thick wildly flashing spectacles. He was followed by a smiling Japanese scientist, Dr Okagawa: it was something about a reaction curve and the phenomena which arise when some sensory canal in Andrias's brain is severed; he then described how Andrias would behave if the mechanism corresponding to the labyrinth of the inner ear were crushed. Professor Rehmann next explained in detail Andrias's reaction to electrical stimulation. Thereupon some heated argument erupted between him and Professor Bruckner: a short, irascible and almost alarmingly overactive man; among other things he observed that Andrias was just as ill equiped in the sensory respect as man and exhibited the same lack of instincts; seen in purely biological terms, it was just as decadent an animal as man, and like him it tried to overcompensate its biological inferiority by what was called the intellect. It seemed, however, that the other experts did not take Professor Bruckner too seriously, probably because he had not cut any sensory canals or sent electric shocks into Andrias's brain. Next Professor van Dietan, speaking in an almost liturgical tone, described the disturbances which had appeared in an Andrias whose right frontal or left occipital lobe had been removed. Then the American Professor Devrient explained –

You must forgive me, I really have no idea what he explained. Because just then a thought flashed through my mind: what kind of disturbances would appear in Professor Devrient if I removed his right frontal lobe? And how would the smiling Dr Okagawa react if I stimulated him electrically? And how would Professor Rehmann behave if someone were to crush his inner-ear labyrinth? I was also feeling a little uncertain about my own ability to distinguish colours and about the *t* factor in my motor reactions. I was tormented by doubt on whether we were entitled (in the strict scientific sense) to speak about our (I mean: human) mental life unless we first removed each other's cerebral lobes and cut each other's sensory canals. Strictly speaking, we should pounce on each other, scalpel in hand, to study each other and our own mentality. As for me, I would be quite prepared, in the interests of science, to smash Professor Dubosque's spectacles or to send electric shocks into Professor Dieten's bald head, after which I would publish a paper on their reactions. Actually, I can visualise their reactions quite well. I am less clear about what went on in Andrias's psyche during those experiments – but it is my impression that he is an exceedingly patient and good-natured creature. None of the distinguished lecturers mentioned that poor Andrias had ever become violent.

I have no doubt that the First Congress of Caudate Amphibians represents a remarkable scientific success; but when I get a day off I'll go to the *Jardin des Plantes* and straight to Andrias Scheuchzer's tank, in order to say to him softly: 'You, Newt, when your day comes . . . heaven forbid you should take it into your head to investigate scientifically the psychological life of *homo sapiens*!'

Thanks to such scientific investigation the Newts ceased to be regarded as some kind of marvel; in the sober light of science the salamanders lost much of their original nimbus of being something exceptional and extraordinary; under psychological testing they exhibited very average and uninteresting characteristics; their outstanding gifts were relegated by science to the realm of fantasy. Science established the Normal Salamander, a rather boring and mediocre creature; only the press now and again still discovered a Miracle Newt, capable of multiplying five-digit numbers in its head, but even that ceased to amuse the public when it was shown that, given appropriate training, this skill might even be acquired by a mere human. In short, people began to regard the Newts as something just as natural as a calculating machine or some other mechanical gadget; they no longer considered them something mysterious that had risen from the depths of the sea, heaven only knew why and what for. Besides, people never regard anything that serves and benefits them as mysterious; only the things which damage or threaten them are mysterious. And since the Newts proved to be highly useful creatures in a great variety of ways, they were simply accepted as something that was part and parcel of the natural and rational order of things.

The usefulness of the Newts was investigated in particular by the Hamburg researcher Wuhrmann, from whose writings on the subject we quote here, at least in brief synopsis, his:

Bericht über die somatische Veranlagung der Molche

The experiments I conducted with the Pacific Giant Salamander (Andrias Scheuchzeri Tschudi) in my Hamburg laboratory pursued a very definite aim: to examine the Newts' resistance to ambient changes and other external factors, and thereby to demonstrate their practical utility in different geographical regions and under different environmental conditions.

The first series of experiments was designed to determine how long a Newt can live outside water. The experimental animals were kept in dry tanks at a temperature between 40° and 50°C. After a few hours they exhibited obvious signs of fatigue; if they were sprinkled they revived. After twenty-four hours they lay motionless, moving only their eyelids; their heartbeat was slowed down and all body activity reduced to a minimum. The animals were clearly suffering and the slightest movement entailed a great effort. After three days a state of cataleptic rigor (xerosis) set in: the animals did not react even to burning with the electric cautery. When the humidity of the air was increased they exhibited at least a few signs of life (they shut their eyes to bright light, etc.). If, after seven days, such a desiccated Newt was thrown into the water it recovered after some considerable time; with more prolonged desiccation, however, the major part of the experimental animals perished. In direct sunlight they die within a few hours.

Other experimental animals were made to turn a shaft in the dark in a very dry environment. After three hours their performance began to decline but it rose again the moment they were copiously sprinkled with water. With frequently repeated sprinkling the animals managed to turn the shaft for seventeen, twenty, and in one instance twenty-six hours without interruption, whereas a control human would show considerable exhaustion after a mere five hours of identical mechanical performance. These experiments justify the conclusion that Newts are eminently suitable even for work on dry land, subject only to two conditions: that they are not exposed to direct sunlight and that they are hosed down with water over the whole surface of their bodies at frequent intervals.

The second series of experiments was concerned with the resistance which the Newts, originally tropical animals, would show to cold. A sudden chilling of the water caused them to die of intestinal inflammation; if, however, they were gradually acclimatised to a cooler environment they adapted quite easily; after eight months they remained active even at a water temperature of 7°C, provided more fats were included in their diet (150 to 200 grammes per animal daily). If the water temperature was lowered below 5°C they dropped into a state of hypothermic rigor (gelosis); in that condition they were refrigerated and kept frozen into a block of ice for several months; when the ice was melted and the water temperature rose to 5°C they again started to show signs of life, and at 7° to 10°C they began to seek food eagerly. This allows the conclusion that Newts can quite easily become adapted also to our climate and indeed as far north as northern Norway and Iceland. Polar climatic conditions would require further experiments.

By contrast, the Newts exhibit considerable sensitivity to chemical factors: in experiments with greatly diluted alkali, industrial effluent, tanning agents, etc., their skin peeled off in strips and the experimental animals died of some kind of gangrene of the gills. This means that the Newts are not in fact suited to our rivers.

In a further series of experiments we succeeded in determining how long a Newt can survive without food. They can go hungry for three weeks and more without showing any signs other than a certain lethargy. I let one experimental Newt starve for six months; for the final three months it slept incessantly and motionlessly; when I finally threw chopped liver into his tank it was so weakened that it failed to react at all and had to be artificially fed. After a few days it ate normally and was suitable for further experiments.

The final set of experiments was concerned with the Newts' powers of regeneration. If a Newt has its tail cut off it will grow a new one within a fortnight; with one Newt we repeated this experiment seven times with the same result. Likewise it will grow any severed legs again. In the case of one experimental animal we amputated all its four extremities and its tail; within thirty days it was again complete. If a Newt's femur or shoulder-blade is broken its whole limb drops off and a new one grows in its place. The same is true if one of its eyes is removed or its tongue cut out; it is a matter of some interest that a Newt whose tongue we removed forgot how to talk and had to be taught afresh. If a Newt's head is cut off or its body severed between its neck and pelvic bone the animal dies. On the other hand it is possible to remove its stomach, part of its intestines, two-thirds of its liver and other organs without damage to its vital functions; it can therefore be stated that an all but eviscerated Newt is still capable of life. No other animal has such resistance to all sorts of injury as a Newt. In that respect it would make a first-rate, almost indestructible, warfare animal; unfortunately its peacefulness and defencelessness militate against such use.

Alongside these experiments my assistant Dr Walter Hinkel investigated the Newt's value in terms of useful raw materials. He established in particular that the Newts' bodies contain an exceptionally high proportion of iodine and phosphorus; it is not impossible that in case of need these important elements could be extracted industrially. The skin of Newts, inferior in itself, can be ground up and fed into powerful presses to produce an artificial leather that is light, reasonably strong and could serve as a substitute for ox-hide. Their fat is unfit for human consumption because of its revolting flavour but it is suitable as an industrial lubricant on account of its very low solidification point. Their flesh has also been considered to be unfit for consumption and indeed poisonous; when eaten raw it causes acute pain, vomiting and sensual hallucinations. Dr Hinkel established after numerous experiments conducted on himself that these harmful effects disappear if the cut meat is scalded with hot water (as in the case of some toadstools) and after thorough rinsing is pickled for twenty-four hours in a weak permanganate solution. After that it can be boiled or steamed, and will taste like inferior beef. In this way we consumed a Newt we used to call Hans; it was an educated and clever animal with a special talent for scientific work; it used to be employed in Dr Hinkel's department as his laboratory assistant and it could be trusted with the most exacting chemical analyses. We used to have long chats with it in the evenings, amused by its insatiable thirst for knowledge. We were sorry to lose our Hans but he had lost his sight in the course of my trepanation experiments. His meat was dark and spongy but there were no unpleasant after-effects. There is no doubt that in the event of war Newt meat might make a welcome and cheap substitute for beef.

Besides, it was only natural that the Newts should have ceased to be a sensation once there were some 6 million of them in the world; the public interest they had aroused while they were still a novelty was echoed for a while in cartoon films (Sally and Andy, the Good Salamanders) and in cabaret, where singers and crooners endowed with particularly poor voices appeared in the roles of croaking and semi-grammatical Newts. The moment the Newts had become a mass-scale and commonplace phenomenon the whole question of the Newts, if we may so call it, underwent a change.[9] The simple truth

[9] A typical illustration is provided by an opinion poll organised by the *Daily Star* on the subject: DO NEWTS HAVE SOULS? We quote here the answers (without warranty of their authenticity) received from some prominent personalities:

Dear Sir,
My friend, the Rev. H. B. Bertram, and I spent some time observing salamanders building a dam at Aden; two or three times we actually talked to them but did not discover any indication whatever of higher sentiments such as Honour, Faith, Patriotism, or a spirit of Fair Play. And what else, I ask you, sir, can with any justification be called soul?

Yours truly,

John W. Britton (Colonel)

I have never seen a Newt, but I am convinced that creatures which have no music do not have a soul either.

Toscanini

Let's leave the question of a soul aside; but from what I can discover about Andrias I'd say that they have no individuality; they seem to be all alike, equally hard-working, equally capable – and equally nondescript. In short: they fulfil a particular ideal of modern civilisation, i.e. the Average.

André d'Artois

They certainly have no soul. In this they resemble man.

Yours G. B. Shaw

Your question embarrasses me. I know, for instance, that my little Chinese dog Bibi has a delightful little soul, so has my little Persian cat Sidi Hanum, and what a fine and cruel soul it is! But Newts? Oh yes, they are *most* talented and intelligent, poor little things; they can talk, do sums and be *terribly* useful; but they are *so* ugly!

Yours Madeleine Roche

is that the great Newt sensation gave way to something different and, in a way, rather more solid: the *Newt problem*. The protagonist of the Newt problem – as so often before in the history of human progress – was, of course, Woman. It was Mme Louise Zimmermann, the directrice of a young ladies' finishing school in Lausanne, who, with quite unusual energy and unflagging enthusiasm, propagated all over the world her noble slogan: *A proper education for the Newts!* For a long time she met with a lack of understanding from the public when she unceasingly pointed, on the one hand, to the Newts' inborn capacity for learning and, on the other, to the danger that might arise to human civilisation if the salamanders were not given a careful moral and intellectual education. 'Just as the Roman civilisation collapsed with the invasion of the Barbarians, so our own learning would be extinguished if it remained just an island amidst a sea of spiritually oppressed creatures who are precluded from sharing in the highest ideals of present-day humanity,' she exclaimed prophetically at the 6,300 lectures she gave to women's clubs throughout Europe and America, as well as in Japan, China, Turkey and elsewhere. 'If our civilisation is to survive it must be the learning of all. We cannot peacefully enjoy the gifts of our civilisation or the fruits of our culture while all around us there are millions and millions of wretched lower creatures deliberately kept in an animal state. Just as the slogan of the

 Who cares if they are Newts. So long as they're not Marxists.

Kurt Huber

They have no sex appeal. So they can't have a soul.

Mae West

They have a soul, just as every creature and every plant has a soul, and everything that lives. Great is the mystery of all life.

Sandrabhârata Nath

They have an interesting technique and style of swimming; there is a lot we can learn from them, especially in long-distance swimming.

Tony Weissmüller

nineteenth century was the emancipation of women, so the slogan of our age must be: PROPER SCHOOLS FOR THE NEWTS!' And so on. Thanks to her eloquence and incredible zeal Mme Louise Zimmermann mobilised women throughout the world and drummed up sufficient financial funds to endow the First Grammar School for Newts at Beaulieu (near Nice), where the young fry of salamanders working at Marseilles and Toulon were taught French language and literature, rhetoric, social deportment, mathematics and the history of civilisation.[10] Rather less successful was a Girls' School for

[10] For details see the book: *Mme Louise Zimmermann, sa vie, ses idées, son oeuvre* (Alcan).

We quote from it the reminiscences of a devoted Newt who was one of her first pupils:

She would recite to us Lafontaine's fables, sitting by our simple but clean and comfortable tank; although she suffered from the damp she disregarded her own discomfort: so dedicated was she to her educational task. She used to call us 'mes petits Chinois' because, like the Chinese, we were unable to pronounce the consonant *r*. After a while, however, she got so used to it that she herself pronounced her name Mme Zimmelmann. We tadpoles adored her: the little ones who had not yet properly developed lungs and therefore could not leave the water would cry that they could not accompany her on her strolls through the school garden. She was so gentle and kind and, as far as I know, she got angry only once; that was when our young female teacher of history on a hot summer day put on her swimsuit and got into the water tank with us, to lecture us on the Low Countries' wars of independence, sitting up to her neck in the water. On that occasion our dear Mme Zimmermann got really angry: 'Go and have a bath at once, Mademoiselle, at once, at once,' she exclaimed with tears in her eyes. To us this was a delicate but readily understood lesson that, when all was said and done, we were not the same as humans; later we were grateful to our spiritual mother for having inculcated in us this realisation in such a firm yet tactful manner.

When we did well she would reward us by reading to us some modern poetry, like Francois Coppé. 'Yes, it is a little *too* modern,' she would say, 'but even that is now part of a good education.' At the end of the academic year we had a public Speech Day, to which Monsieur le Préfect was invited from Nice, as well as other prominent figures. Advanced and gifted students who already had lungs were dried by the school beadle and dressed in a kind of white gown; then, behind a thin curtain (so as not to frighten the ladies), they recited Lafontaine's fables, mathematical formulae and the succession of the Capet dynasty, complete with all dates. Thereupon Monsieur le Préfect, in a lengthy and beautiful speech, expressed his thanks and compliments to our dear directrice; that concluded the joyful day. Our physical well-being was cared for just as much as our spiritual progress: once a month the local vet inspected us and every six months we were all weighed to make sure we were the prescribed weight. Our esteemed directrice appealed to us in particular to put aside that shameful and dissolute custom of the Lunar Dances; I am ashamed to say that some of the older students nevertheless secretly indulged in that bestial and low practice. I hope that our motherly friend never heard of it: it would have broken her great, noble and loving heart.

Newts in Menton, where the syllabus consisted mainly of music, dietary cookery and fine needlework (subjects on which Mme Zimmermann insisted mainly on paedagogical grounds); these encountered a striking lack of enthusiasm if not indeed a stubborn lack of interest on the part of the young female Newt students. By way of contrast, the first public examinations for Young Newts proved such an astonishing success that a Naval Polytechnic for Newts was immediately set up in Cannes and a Newt University in Marseilles (both at the expense of the Society for Prevention of Cruelty to Animals); it was at the latter institution that the first Newt was subsequently to be awarded the degree of Doctor of Law.

The issue of Newt education now began to develop rapidly and along predictable lines. Those teachers who were more progressive raised a number of serious objections to the exemplary Écoles Zimmermann: it was argued in particular that the outdated classical grammar school education for human pupils was inappropriate for young Newts. Teaching of literature and history was emphatically rejected and it was recommended instead that the greatest possible scope and time should be devoted to practical and modern subjects, such as the natural sciences, workshop practice, the technological training of the Newts, physical education, and so on. This so-called Reformed School was in turn passionately attacked by the adherents of classical learning: they argued that the only way to bring the Newts closer to human cultural values was through a grounding in Latin, and that it was not enough merely to teach them to speak unless they were also taught to recite poetry and declaim with Ciceronian eloquence. It was a long and rather heated dispute, and it was eventually solved by the salamander schools being taken over by the state and the schools for young humans being reformed with a view to bringing them as near as possible in line with the Reformed School for Newts.

Naturally the call for regularised and compulsory education for the Newts under state supervision was now also raised in other countries. This was effected step by step in all maritime countries (with the exception, of course, of Great Britain), and because these Newt schools were not burdened with the old classical traditions of the human schools and were able, therefore, to utilise the most up to date methods of psychotechnical instruction, premilitary training and all the latest achievements of educational research generally, they soon became the most modern and scientifically advanced educational establishments in the world and objects of the justified envy of human pedagogues and pupils. Hand in hand with Newt education the language question emerged. Which of the world languages should the salamanders learn first? The original Newts from the Pacific islands, of course, expressed themselves in pidgin English, as they had picked it up from natives and sailors; many spoke Malay or some local dialect. Newts bred for the Singapore market were taught to speak Basic English, that scientifically simplified form of English which managed with a vocabulary of a few hundred words and dispensed with obsolete grammatical fuss; thus reformed standard English came to be known as Salamander English. At the exemplary Écoles Zimmermann the Newts expressed themselves in the language of Corneille – not out of nationalistic motives but because it was part of a higher education. At the Reformed Schools, on the other hand, Esperanto was taught as a means of communication. In fact, some five or six new Universal Languages came into being just then, designed to supplant the Babylonian confusion of human tongues and provide the whole world with one common mother tongue. There was a lot of argument about which of these International Languages was the most efficient, the most melodious and the most universal. In the event, what happened was that a different Universal Language was championed in each country.[11]

---

[11] Among other proposals there was one from the famous philologist Curtius in *Janua linguarum aperta* to the effect that Latin of the golden age of Virgil be adopted as a single universal language for the Newts. It is now in our power, he exclaimed, to ensure that Latin, that most perfect of languages, the one richest in grammatical rules and the one best researched by scholars, once more becomes a living world language. If educated humanity will not seize this opportunity, why not then do it yourselves, *Salamandrae, gens maritima*! Choose *eruditam linguam latinam* as your mother tongue, the only language worthy of being spoken by the whole *orbis terrarum*. It would redound to your everlasting merit, *Salamandrae*, if you resuscitated anew the eternal language of gods and heroes; for with that language, *gens Tritonum*, you will one day assume the inheritance of Roman world rule.

On the other hand, a certain Latvian telegraph clerk named Wolteras, in cooperation with the pastor Mendelius, invented and developed a special *language for Newts*, called *pontic lang*; in it he made use of elements of all the world's languages, especially of African dialects. This Newtese (as it was also called) achieved a certain measure of currency especially in the Nordic countries, though unfortunately only among humans; in Uppsala a Chair of Newt Language was actually set up. But as far as is known not a single Newt spoke that language. The fact was that Basic English was the most common language among the Newts and subsequently became the official Newt language.

With the nationalisation of Newt education the whole business was simplified: Newts in each country were simply taught in the national language. Although the salamanders picked up foreign languages rather quickly, and with enthusiasm, their linguistic skill exhibited some peculiar shortcomings, due, on the one hand, to the configuration of their vocal organs and, on the other, to what one might call psychological reasons. They had difficulties, for instance, with the pronunciation of long polysyllabic words and tried to shorten them to one syllable which they then uttered in a brief and rather croaky manner. They said 'l' instead of 'r' and tended to lisp their sibillants. They dispensed with grammatical endings, never learned to differentiate between 'I' and 'we', and they could not care less whether a word was of feminine or masculine gender (maybe this reflected their sexual frigidity outside mating time). In short, every language was characteristically transformed in their mouths and somehow economically reduced to its simplest and most rudimentary form. It is worth noting that their neologisms, their pronunciation and their primitive grammar were rapidly being adopted by the dregs of dockside humanity, on the one hand, and by what is known as society, on the other. From there this manner of expression spread to the newspapers and soon became general. Even among humans grammatical gender often disappeared, endings were dropped, inflexion became extinct. The *jeunesse dorée* suppressed the 'r' and attempted a lisp; hardly any educated person was still able to say what indeterminism or transcendentalism meant, simply because these words had become too long and unpronounceable for humans too.

In short, whether well or badly, the Newts were able to speak languages of virtually anywhere in the world, according to what coast they inhabited. About that time an article appeared in our press (I believe in the Right-wing *Národní Listy*), questioning with some asperity why the Newts should not also learn Czech, considering that there were already some salamanders who spoke Portuguese, Dutch or languages of other small nations. True, the article conceded, our nation lacked a marine coastline and we therefore had no marine Newts; but just because we had no sea of our own this did not imply that we did not possess a culture equal, and in many respects superior, to that of many nations whose language was being learned by thousands of Newts. It would be no more than fair to allow the Newts to acquaint themselves with our spiritual life also: but how could they do this if there was not one among them who had command of our language? Why should we wait for someone in the outside world to acknowledge that cultural debt and set up a chair of Czech language and Czechoslovak literature at some Newt educational establishment? As the poet says, 'Mistrust the world from end to end, for nowhere do we have a friend.' Let us ourselves provide the remedy, the article appealed. Whatever we have achieved in this world we have achieved through our own efforts! It is our right as well as our duty to win friends also among the Newts. Our Ministry of Foreign Affairs, however, does not appear to be greatly interested in ensuring appropriate publicity for our name and our manufactures among the Newts, yet many other and often smaller nations are spending millions on opening up their cultural treasures to the Newts and, at the same time, arousing their interest in their industrial manufactures. The article caused considerable attention mainly among the Federation of Industries and at least resulted in the publication of a small manual, *Czech for Newts*, complete with examples of Czechoslovak *belles-lettres*. It may sound incredible, but over seven thousand copies of that little book were actually sold; all in all, therefore, it was a remarkable success.[12]

The question of the Newts' education and language was only one aspect of the general Newt problem, a problem that, as it were, grew under people's hands. One question that emerged rather early on was how the Newts should be treated in, if one may so put it, social terms. In the early years, almost the prehistoric years, of the Newt Age it was chiefly Societies for the Prevention of Cruelty to Animals that saw to it that the Newts were not cruelly or inhumanly treated; it is due to their efforts that police and veterinary regulations applicable to other farm animals were upheld with regard to the Newts. Conscientious objectors to vivisection also signed a lot of protests and petitions urging the banning of scientific experiments on live Newts. In a number of states such a law

[12] Cf. the feuilleton from the pen of Jaromír Seidl-Novoměstský preserved in Mr Povondra's collection.

OUR FRIEND ON THE GALAPAGOS ISLANDS

While engaged on a round-the-world trip with my wife, the poetess Henrietta Seidlová-Chrudimská, in order to find at least partial solace for the painful loss of our dear aunt, the writer Bohumila Jandová-Střešovická, in the magic of so many new and profound impressions, we found ourselves one day on the lonely Galapagos islands, a group steeped in legend. We only had two hours to spare, and we used that time to take a walk along the beach of that barren archipelago.

'Behold the beautifully setting sun,' I said to my wife. 'Is it not as though the entire firmament were drowning in a flood of gold and blood?'

'Why, the gentleman would seem to be a Czech!' a voice unexpectedly came from behind us in correct and pure Czech.

In astonishment we glanced in that direction. There was no one there, except a big black Newt sitting on some rocks, with what looked like a book in its hands. On our trip round the world we had already caught sight of a number of Newts but so far we had had no opportunity of conversing with any. The gentle reader will therefore appreciate our amazement when on such a deserted coast we encountered a Newt and, what is more, heard a remark in our native language.

'Who is that talking?' I exclaimed in Czech.

'I took the liberty, sir,' the Newt replied, courteously rising to its feet. 'I was unable to resist the temptation, hearing for the first time in my life a conversation in Czech.'

'How is it possible,' I gasped; 'you can really speak Czech?'

'I have just been amusing myself with the conjugation of the irregular verb "to be",' the Newt replied. 'That verb, as a matter of fact, is irregular in all languages.'

'How, where and why,' I pursued my questions, 'did you learn Czech?'

'Chance carried this book into my hands,' the Newt answered, offering me the book it had been holding in its hand; it was *Czech for Newts*, and its pages bore witness to frequent and diligent use. 'It arrived here with a shipment of books of an instructional character. I had the choice of Geometry for the Senior Forms of Secondary Schools, History of Military Tactics, a Guide through the Dolomites, and The Principles of Bimetallism. However, I chose this little book and I have grown very fond of it. I already know it by heart, yet I keep finding in it ever new sources of enjoyment and instruction.'

My wife and I expressed our unfeigned delight and amazement at the creature's correct, and indeed almost intelligible, pronunciation. 'Alas, there is no one here to whom I could speak Czech,' our new friend remarked modestly, 'and I am not even quite sure whether the instrumentative case of the word *kůň* is *koni* or *koňmi*.'

'*Koňmi*,' I said.

'Oh no, *koni*,' my wife exclaimed with animation.

'Would you be good enough,' our delightful interlocutor inquired eagerly, 'to tell me what news there is in Mother Prague, the City of a Hundred Towers?'

'It's growing, my friend,' I replied, pleased at his interest, and in a few words outlined to him the prosperous growth of our golden metropolis.

'What joyful tidings these are,' the Newt said with undisguised satisfaction. 'And are the severed heads of the decapitated Czech nobles still stuck up on the Bridge Tower?'

'No, they haven't been for a long time,' I said, somewhat (I admit) taken aback by his question.

'That is a great pity,' the Newt observed sympathetically. 'That was indeed a precious historical relic. It is a pity crying to high Heaven that so many splendid memorials have perished in the Thirty Years' War! Unless I am mistaken, the Czech land was then turned into a desert drenched with blood and tears. How fortunate that the genitive of negation did not die out then as well! It says in this book that it is on the point of extinction. I am deeply distressed to learn it, sir.'

'So you are fascinated also by our history,' I exclaimed joyfully.

'Certainly, sir,' the Newt replied. 'Especially by the disaster of the White Mountain and the three hundred years of servitude. I have read a lot about it in this book. No doubt you are very proud of your three hundred years of servitude. That was a great period, sir!'

'Yes, a hard period,' I agreed. 'A period of oppression and grief.'

'And did you groan?' our friend inquired with keen interest.

'We groaned, suffering inexpressibly under the yoke of the savage oppressors.'

'I am delighted to hear it,' the Newt heaved a sigh of relief. 'That is exactly what it says in my book. I am happy to find it is true. It is an excellent book, sir, better than Geometry for the Senior Forms of Secondary Schools. I should like one day to stand on that memorable spot where the Czech nobles were executed, and on other glorious spots of cruel injustice.'

'You should come and see our country,' I cordially suggested to him.

'Thank you for your courteous invitation,' the Newt made a bow. 'Unfortunately I am not an entirely free agent . . .'

'We would buy you,' I exclaimed. 'What I am saying is, maybe we could have a nationwide collection to provide the financial means that would enable you . . .'

'You are most kind,' our friend muttered, evidently touched. 'However, I have heard that the water of the Vltava is not good. The fact is we develop an unpleasant kind of dysentery in river water.' He paused for a short while and then added: 'I would also find it difficult to leave my beloved little garden.'

'Ah!' exclaimed my wife. 'I too am a passionate gardener! How grateful I would be to you if you could show us the children of the local Flora!'

'With the greatest pleasure, dear lady,' the Newt replied with a polite bow. 'That is, if you do not mind that my pleasure garden is under the water.'

'Under the water?'

'Yes. Twelve metres deep.'

'And what flowers do you grow there?'

'Sea anemones,' replied our friend; 'several rare varieties of them. Likewise sea stars and sea cucumbers, not to mention the coral bushes. Happy the man who's grown a rose, just one fair scion for his land, as the poet has it.'

Sadly we had to make our adieux, for our ship was sounding its siren in token of its imminent departure. 'And what message, Mr . . . Mr . . .' I said, not knowing our friend's name.

'My name is Boleslav Jablonský,' the Newt shyly informed us. 'In my opinion it is a beautiful name, sir. I chose it from my book.'

'And what message, Mr Jablonský, would you like to send to our nation?'

The Newt thought for a while. 'Tell your fellow countrymen,' he finally said with deep emotion, 'tell them . . . not to fall back into the age-old Slav discord . . . but to keep the Battle of Lipany and especially the White Mountain was in fact enacted.[13] But with the rising educational level of the salamanders there was increasing embarrassment at simply bracketing the Newts with other animals; for some (not entirely clear) reasons this seemed rather inappropriate. It was then that an international League for the Protection of Salamanders was founded under the patronage of the Duchess of Huddersfield. This League, with over 200,000 members mainly in England, did important and praiseworthy work for the salamanders. Above all else it ensured that special Newt recreation areas were set up for them on sea coasts, where, undisturbed by curious spectators, they might hold their 'meetings and sporting events' (meaning presumably the secret Moon Dance); that students at all schools (and even at Oxford University) were enjoined not to throw stones at Newts; that measures were taken to ensure, up to a point, that young tadpoles were not overworked at school; and finally that Newt work camps and hutments were surrounded by tall wooden fences to protect the Newts against all kinds of molestation, but mainly to ensure that the world of the salamanders was sufficiently segregated from the human world.[14]

in grateful memory! Goodbye, my compliments,' he suddenly concluded, trying to control his feelings.
    We departed in the boat, deep in thought and full of emotions. Our friend was standing on a cliff, waving his hand to us and seeming to call out something.
    'What's that he's calling?' asked my wife.
    'I can't be sure,' I replied, but it sounded like Remember me to Dr Baxa, the Lord Mayor of Prague.'

[13] In Germany, in particular, all vivisection was strictly prohibited – though only to Jewish researchers.

[14] It appears that certain issues of morality were also involved. Among Mr Povondra's papers a *Proclamation* was found in a number of languages, evidently published in newspapers throughout the world and signed by the Duchess of Huddersfield herself. This stated:

The League for the Protection of Newts addresses itself mainly to you, women, to request you, in the interest of decency and good morals, to contribute with the work of your hands to a great programme aimed at providing suitable clothing for the Newts. Most suitable for this purpose is a small skirt 40 cm long, with a waist of 60 cm, preferably with sewn-in elastic. We recommend a pleated skirt, which is both attractive and allows freedom of movement. For tropical areas a short apron with strings would be sufficient, made of simple washable material, possibly from some of your own cast-off clothes. Thus, with your help, those poor Newts who work near humans will not have to

Soon, however, these praiseworthy private initiatives to regulate the relations between human society and the Newts in a respectable and humane manner proved insufficient. Although it was easy enough to fit the salamanders into, as it was called, the production process, it was far more complicated and difficult to fit them, somehow or other, into the existing social order. The more conservative of the population denied the existence of any legal or public problems: the Newts were simply the property of their employers who were responsible for them and who were liable for any damage that might be caused by the Newts. In spite of their undeniable intelligence (these people argued) the salamanders were no more than a legal object, a chattel or an item of property, and any special legislative arrangement

expose themselves unclothed, which is bound to offend their sense of propriety and would embarrass any decent person, more especially all women and mothers.

It seems that this initiative did not meet with the hoped-for response. There is no record of the Newts ever having chosen to wear little skirts or aprons; probably these would have been a hindrance for them under water or else they would not stay up. Once the Newts were segregated from humans by wooden fences any cause for embarrassment or awkwardness on either side naturally disappeared.

As for our reference to the need to protect the Newts against various kinds of molestation, what we had in mind were, above all, dogs. These were never reconciled to the Newts and pursued them furiously even in the water, regardless of the fact that their salivary glands became infected whenever they bit a fugitive Newt. Occasionally the Newts would resist, and more than one valuable dog was killed with a hoe or a pickaxe. All in all there developed a permanent and downright deadly enmity between dogs and Newts which did not diminish in the least and, if anything, was intensified and consolidated by the construction of partitions between them. Which is what usually happens, and not only with dogs.

Incidentally, those tarred fences, extending in some places over hundreds and hundreds of kilometres of shoreline, were utilised for educational purposes: along their entire length they were painted in huge letters with slogans suitable for Newts. For instance:

YOUR WORK IS YOUR ACHIEVEMENT. DON'T WASTE A SECOND! THE DAY HAS ONLY 86,400 SECONDS! AN INDIVIDUAL'S WORTH IS THE VALUE OF HIS WORK. YOU CAN BUILD ONE METRE OF DAM IN 57 MINUTES! HE WHO WORKS SERVES THE COMMUNITY. HE WHO DOES NOT WORK, NEITHER SHALL HE EAT!

And so on. If we bear in mind that these close-boarded fences all over the world totalled over three hundred thousand kilometres of seashore, we can get an idea of the amount of exhortatory and generally useful slogans that could be placed on them.

concerning the Newts would be interference with the sacred rights of private ownership. The opposite view was held by those who objected that the Newts, as intelligent and, to a considerable degree, responsible creatures, were capable of deliberately (and in a great variety of ways) infringing the existing law. Was it reasonable to hold the owner of Newts responsible for a possible offence committed by his salamanders? Such a liability would surely undermine private initiative in the field of Newt operations. There were no fences in the sea, it was argued; you can't shut the Newts in to keep them under surveillance. That was why it was necessary to take legislative measures to make it incumbent upon the Newts themselves to respect the human legal system and observe the regulations which would be issued for them.[15]

As far as is known, the first laws for salamanders were enacted in France. Article One laid down the duties of the Newts in the event of mobilisation and war; the second law (called Lex Deval) stipulated that Newts could settle only in

[15] Cf. the first *Newt suit*, heard in Durban and much commented on in the international press (see Mr Povondra's cuttings). The Harbour authority in A. had employed a Newt work gang. In due course, the Newts multiplied to such an extent that there was no room for them in the port; a few tadpole colonies therefore settled on the nearby coast. The landowner B., to whose property that stretch of coast belonged, demanded that the port authority remove its salamanders from his private beach, because that was his own bathing place. The port authority took the view that the matter did not concern it; as soon as the Newts settled on the plaintiff's land they had become his private property. While this lawsuit was dragging on in the usual manner the Newts (partly from inborn instinct and partly from work zeal inculcated into them by training) began to build dams and harbour basins off Mr B.'s beaches without appropriate orders or permission. Mr B. thereupon sued the authority for causing damage to his property. The lower Court dismissed the case on the grounds that Mr B.'s property had not been damaged by the dams but actually improved. The higher Court, however, found in favour of the plaintiff on the grounds that no one was obliged to tolerate a neighbour's farm animals on his land, and that the port authority in A. was responsible for all the damage caused by the Newts, in the same way as a farmer had to make good the damage caused to a neighbour by his cattle. The defendant objected that it could not be held responsible for the salamanders because they could not be locked up under the sea. Thereupon the judge declared that in his opinion the damage caused by the Newts should be viewed in a similar manner to damage caused by hens, which were likewise impossible to lock up because they could fly. Attorney for the port authority asked in what way his client could transfer the Newts, or induce them to leave Mr B.'s beach of their own volition. The judge replied that this was not the business of the Court. Attorney then asked how His Honour would react if the defendant port authority had the undesirable Newts shot. To this the judge replied that as a British gentleman he would regard this as a highly improper proceeding and moreover as a violation of

those seashore localities that were assigned to them by their owner or local administrative authority; the third stated that Newts were unconditionally obliged to obey all police instructions; in the event of their failure to do so the police were entitled to punish them by detention in a dry and well-lit place or even by depriving them of work for a lengthy period. Thereupon the Left-wing parties tabled a motion in the Assembly that a social welfare law be drafted for salamanders: this would define their working duties and place certain obligations on their employers in dealing with working Newts (such as granting a fortnight's leave during the spring mating period); the extreme Left, by contrast, demanded that the Newts be altogether expelled as enemies of the working people: in the service of capitalism they were working too hard and for virtually nothing, thereby threatening the living standards of the working class. To lend weight to that demand a strike was declared at Brest and major demonstrations took place in Paris; there were a large number of wounded and the Deval Ministry was forced to resign. In Italy, the Newts were placed under a special Newt Corporation, composed of employers and the authorities; in Holland, they were administered by the Ministry of Hydro-Engineering. In short, each country tackled its Newt problem in its own particular way; yet a lot of official decrees governing the public duties of the Newts, and suitably curtailing the animal freedom of the Newts, were virtually identical everywhere.

Needless to say, the moment the first laws on the Newts were passed there were people who, in the name of juridical

Mr B.'s shooting rights. The defendant was therefore obliged, on the one hand, to remove the Newts from the plaintiff's private property and, on the other, to make good the damage caused there by the dams and coastal structures; this was to be done by restoring that stretch of coastline to its original condition. Attorney for the defendant thereupon asked whether salamanders might be used for that demolition work. The judge gave it as his opinion that they could not be so used unless the plaintiff agreed; but the plaintiff's wife found the Newts revolting and was unable to swim from the salamander-infested beach. The plaintiff pointed out that without Newts it was impossible to remove the dams built below the surface. Whereupon the judge ruled that the Court neither wished nor was competent to discuss technical details; Courts existed to protect property rights and not to adjudicate what was and what was not feasible.

This was the end of the suit from a legal point of view; it is not reported how the port authority in A. extricated itself from its tricky position. However, the case had shown that it would after all be necessary to regulate the Newt question by means of new legal instruments.

logic, argued that if human society was placing certain obligations upon the salamanders then it must also grant them certain rights. Any state enacting laws for the Newts *ipso facto* recognised them as responsible and free individuals, as legal subjects, and indeed as its citizens, in which case there was a need to regularise their civic status *vis-à-vis* the state under whose legislation they were living. It would, of course, be possible to regard the Newts as foreign immigrants, but the state could not then impose on them certain services or duties during periods of mobilisation or war, as was being done throughout civilised countries everywhere (with the exception of Britain). We would surely expect the Newts to defend our coastline in the event of a warlike conflict, in which event we could not deny them certain civil rights, such as the vote, the right of assembly, representation on various public bodies, and so on.[16] It was even proposed that the salamanders should have some kind of submarine autonomy; but these and

[16] Some took Newt equality so literally that they demanded that salamanders should be able to hold any public office in water or on land (J. Courtaud); or that fully armed submarine Newt regiments should be set up, under their own deep-sea commanders (General, retd, Desfours); or indeed that mixed marriages should be allowed between humans and Newts (Maître Louis Pierrot, a lawyer). Zoologists, of course, pointed out that such marriages were not even possible, but Maître Pierrot declared that what was at stake was not a natural possibility or impossibility but a legal principle, and that he himself was willing to take for his wife a female Newt to demonstrate that the reform of matrimonial law he advocated should not just remain on paper. (Maître Pierrot subsequently became an attorney much in demand for divorce cases.)

(This may be the place to report that, especially in the American press, reports cropped up from time to time of girls who claimed to have been raped by Newts while bathing. In consequence, there occurred increasingly frequent instances in the United States of Newts being caught and lynched, mostly by burning at the stake. In vain did scientists protest against this popular custom by pointing out that on anatomical grounds such an offence on the part of salamanders was physically impossible; but a lot of girls swore that they had been molested by Newts, and this settled the matter for any right-minded American. Later the popular burning of Newts was restricted by being licenced only on Saturdays and only under the supervision of the Fire Department. At that time the Movement against Newt Lynching came into being, led by the Negro Rev. Robert J. Washington; this soon gained about a hundred thousand members, though almost exclusively from among the Negro population. The American press began to claim that this movement was political and subversive; in consequence raids were made on black residential areas and a lot of Negroes were burnt to death while they were praying in their churches for their brothers, the Newts. Hostility to the Negroes reached its peak when, following upon setting fire to the Negro church at Gordonville, Louisiana, the whole town went up in flames. But this belongs only marginally to the history of the Newts.)

similar reflections remained purely academic and produced no practical results, if only because the Newts had never anywhere claimed any civil rights.

Another great discussion, likewise without direct interest or intervention on the part of the Newts, centred on the question of whether Newts could be baptised. The Catholic Church from the very outset consistently held the view that they could not: since the Newts, not being descended from Adam, had not been conceived in original sin, they could not be purged from such sin through the sacrament of baptism. Holy Church did not wish to decide, one way or another, whether the Newts had an immortal soul or any other share in divine grace and salvation; its goodwill towards them could only be expressed by remembering them in a special prayer which would be read on certain days alongside the prayer for the souls in Purgatory and alongside the plea for unbelievers.[17] Matters were not as simple for the Protestant Churches: while conceding to the Newts an intelligence and hence the ability to comprehend Christian teachings, they nevertheless hesitated to make them members of the Church and hence brothers-in-Christ. They therefore confined themselves to publishing (in abridged form) a Holy Scripture for Newts, on waterproof paper, and distributing it in millions of copies. There was also some thought of compiling for the Newts (analogously to Basic English) a kind of Basic Christian, a basic and simplified Christian doctrine; however, efforts along these lines triggered off so many theological disputes that the idea was abandoned.[18] Certain religious sects (especially in America) had no such scruples: they dispatched their missionaries to the Newts to preach to them the True

Among the civil facilities and advantages actually granted to the Newts we might list at least a few: every salamander was registered in the Newt Records at his place of employment; he had to possess an official residence permit; he had to pay capitation tax, actually paid for him by his employer and docked from his food (since Newts did not draw their wages in cash); likewise he had to pay rent in respect of the coast he inhabited, public dues, charges for the construction of the wooden fence, school fees and other public imposts. We simply have to admit quite frankly that in all these respects the Newts were treated like other citizens – which is equal rights of a sort.

[17] Cf. the Holy Father's Encyclical *Mirabilia Dei opera*.

[18] The literature on this subject is so voluminous that a mere bibliography would take up two massive volumes.

Faith and to baptise them in accordance with Holy Writ's
injunction: Go ye therefore and teach all nations. However,
only a handful of missionaries succeeded in penetrating the
wooden fences which divided the salamanders from the
humans: the employers stopped them from getting to the
Newts so they should not needlessly keep them from working.
Occasionally one might come upon a preacher standing at
the tarred fence, among the dogs which would be furiously
barking at their enemies on the far side, fruitlessly but
fanatically proclaiming the Word of God.

As far as is known, monism achieved a somewhat greater
following among the Newts; some of them also believed in
materialism, the gold standard and other scientific doctrines.
One popular philosopher, George Sequenz by name, even
developed a special religious teaching for Newts, its central
and highest article of faith being belief in the Great
Salamander. Admittedly, this faith gained no adherents among
the Newts at all, but it had quite a following among humans,
especially in the big cities, where a huge number of secret
temples of the salamander cult sprang up virtually
overnight.[19] At a later period and almost universally the

[19] Cf. a markedly pornographic brochure among Mr Povondra's papers. This was
an alleged copy of the police records in B——. The details of that 'private printing
for the purpose of scholarly research' cannot be quoted in a decent book. We shall
give here just a few details:

> The temple of the salamander cult on —— street, at number —— , contains
> at its centre a large pool faced with dark-red marble. The water in the pool
> is perfumed with fragrant essences, heated, and illuminated from below by
> ever-changing coloured lights; the rest of the temple is in darkness. To the
> chanting of Newt Litanies there descend into the marble pool the totally
> unclothed male and female Salamander believers, the men from one side, the
> women from the other, all of them members of society; we might mention
> here only Baroness M., the film star S., Ambassador D. and many other well-
> known figures. Suddenly a shaft of blue light illuminates a huge marble block
> towering from the water; on it rests, breathing heavily, a big, old, black Newt,
> known as Mister Salamander. After a moment's silence Mister begins to speak:
> he calls on the believers to abandon themselves fully and wholeheartedly to
> the ritual of the Newt Dance that is about to begin, and to pay homage to
> the Great Salamander. He thereupon rises and starts rocking and twisting
> the upper part of his body. Upon this the male believers, immersed to their
> necks in the water, likewise begin to sway and twist furiously, faster and faster,
> allegedly in order to produce the Sexual Milieu; the female Salamanders
> meanwhile utter a sharp ts-ts-ts and croaking squeals. After this the underwater
> lights go out one by one, and a general orgy is unleashed.

Newts themselves came to accept a different faith, whose origin among them is unknown; this involved adoration of Moloch, whom they visualised as a giant Newt with a human head; they were reported to have enormous submarine idols made of cast iron, manufactured to their orders by Armstrong or Krupp, but no further details ever leaked out of their cultic rituals since they were conducted under water; they were, however, believed to be exceptionally cruel and secret. It would seem that this faith gained ground rapidly because the name Moloch reminded them of the zoological *molche* or the German *Molch*, the terms for Newt.

The preceding chapters will have made it clear that the Newt Problem was initially, and indeed for a considerable time, viewed in the light of whether, and to what extent, the Newts were reasoning and fairly civilised creatures capable of enjoying certain civil rights, even though on the margin of human society and the human order. In other words, it was a domestic issue for each individual state, an issue resolved within the framework of civil law. For a number of years it never occurred to anyone that the Newt Problem might have far-reaching international significance or that it might become necessary to deal with the salamanders not merely as intelligent individual beings but also as a Newt collective or indeed a Newt nation. In point of fact the first step towards such a concept of the Newt Problem came from those somewhat eccentric Christian sects which attempted to baptise the Newts, basing themselves on the scriptural injunction: Go ye therefore and teach all nations. This was the first implication that the Newts were something like a nation.[20] But the first truly international and fundamental acknowledgment of Newt nationhood came in that famous manifesto of the Communist International signed by Comrade Molokov and addressed to 'all

---

We cannot vouch for this account, but it is certain that in all the chief cities of Europe the police, while fiercely tracking down these Salamander sects, had its hands full suppressing the huge social scandals connected with them. We believe, however, that the Great Salamander cult was exceptionally widespread, though for the most part it was practised with less fairyland splendour and, among the poorer sections of the population, even on dry land.

[20] The Catholic prayer mentioned above described them as *Dei creatura de gente Molche* (God's creatures of the Newt nation).

oppressed and revolutionary Newts of the whole world'.[21]
Even though this manifesto did not seem to have any direct
effect on the Newts themselves, it nevertheless produced
considerable reverberations in the international press and was
copiously imitated in the sense that fiery appeals began to rain
down upon the salamanders from the most varied quarters,
calling on them to join this or that ideological, political or social
programme of human society as a massive Newt entity.[22]
    At that point the International Labour Office in Geneva
began to take up the Newt Problem. There two views clashed

[21] The manifesto preserved among Mr Povondra's papers ran as follows:

COMRADE NEWTS!

The capitalist system has found its latest victims. As its tyranny was finally
beginning to crumble against the revolutionary élan of the class-conscious
proletariat, moth-eaten capitalism roped you, Toilers of the Deep, into its
service, enslaving you spiritually by its bourgeois civilisation, subjecting you
to its class laws, depriving you of all liberties and doing everything in its power
to exploit you brutally and with impunity.

(14 lines cut by censor)

Working Newts! The hour is at hand when you will come to realise the whole
burden of the slavery in which you live

(7 lines cut by censor)

and when you will demand your rights as a class and as a nation!

Comrade Newts! The revolutionary proletariat of the whole world extends
its hand to you

(11 lines cut by censor)

with all means at your disposal. Set up works councils, elect your spokesmen,
establish strike funds! Remember that the politically aware working class will
not abandon you in your just struggle and that, hand in hand with you, it
will launch the final attack

(9 lines cut by censor)

Oppressed and revolutionary Newts of all lands, unite! The last battle is at hand!
(Signed) MOLOKOV

[22] In Mr Povondra's collection we only found a few such appeals; Mrs Povondra
presumably burnt the rest. From the surviving material we quote at least a few
headlines:

Newts, cast away your arms! (A pacifist manifesto)

Newts, throw out the Jews! (A German leaflet)

sharply: one recognised the Newts as a new working class and demanded that all social legislation affecting working hours, paid holidays, sickness and old-age insurance, etc., should be extended to them; the opposing view was that the Newts represented a dangerous competition to the human workforce and that Newt labour should quite simply be prohibited. This suggestion was opposed not only by the representatives of the employers but also by the workers' delegates, who pointed out that the Newts were no longer merely an army of workers but also a large and ever growing body of consumers. They demonstrated that employment had recently increased to an unprecedented degree in the metal industry (working tools, machines and metal idols for Newts), in armaments, chemicals (underwater explosives), paper making (textbooks for Newts), cement, timber, synthetic foodstuffs (Salamander Food) and many other branches of industry. The shipping tonnage had risen by 27 per cent over pre-Newt figures, and coal by 18.6

Brother Newts! (An appeal by an anarchist group)

Fellow Newts! (A public appeal by the Sea Scouts)

Friends, Newts! (A public address by the Centre for Aquatic Associations and Breeders of Marine Fauna)

Newts, Friends! (An appeal by the Society for Moral Regeneration)

Citizen Newts (An appeal by the Civic Reform League in Dieppe)

Fellow Newts, join our ranks! (Benevolent Society of Ancient Mariners)

Colleagues, Newts! (Swimming Club Aegir)

Of particular importance (judging by the fact that Mr Povondra had carefully stuck it on some stiff paper) was probably this manifesto which we quote in full:

per cent. Indirectly, as human employment and prosperity increased, turnover rose also in other industries. Most recently the Newts had been placing orders for various parts of machinery according to their own designs; these they themselves assembled below water into pneumatic drills, hammer-drills, submarine engines, printing machinery, underwater transmitters and other equipment of their own design. These products they paid for by an increased work performance: already one-fifth of world production by heavy industry and precision engineering was dependent on Newt orders. Abolish the salamanders and you could close down one-fifth of the factories; instead of the present prosperity you would have millions of unemployed. Naturally enough, the International Labour Office could not disregard these objections; finally, after long negotiations, a compromise solution was reached to the effect that 'the above-mentioned employees of group S (amphibians) may only be employed below or in the water, or on the foreshore up to a maximum of 10 metres from the high water line; that they must not mine coal or extract oil from the seabed; that they must not manufacture paper, textiles or artificial leather from seaweed for consumption on dry land', and so on. These restrictions on Newt production were laid down in a code of nineteen paragraphs which we do not propose to quote in detail if only because, needless to say, no one took any notice of them. But as a generous and truly international solution of the Newt Problem from the economic and social standpoint the above-mentioned code was a meritorious and impressive achievement

Matters did not move so fast with the international recognition of the Newts in the sphere of cultural relations. When the much-quoted article, 'The Geological Composition of the Seabed near the Bahamas', first appeared in the scientific press over the signature of one John Seaman, no one realised that this was in fact the work of an erudite salamander. But when reports and papers in the field of oceanography, geography, hydrobiology, higher mathematics and other exact sciences began to arrive at scientific congresses or at the secretariats of various academies and learned societies, this caused a good deal of embarrassment and indeed resentment, as voiced by the famous Dr Martel: 'That vermin's got anything to teach us?!' The japanese scientist

Dr Onoshita, who was bold enough to quote a Newt study (it was something about the evolution of the yolk sac in the tadpoles of the deep sea fish *Argyropelecus hemigymnus Cocco*) was boycotted by the scientific community and committed harakiri. For academic science it was a point of honour and of status consciousness to ignore any scientific work performed by Newts. The greater was the attention (not to say scandal) caused by the gesture of the *Centre universitaire de Nice*[23] when

[23] Preserved in Mr Povondra's collection we found a journalistic, rather superficial, account of that festive occasion; unfortunately only half of it has survived; the second part has been lost.

Nice, 6 May

The attractive airy building of the Institute for Mediterranean Studies on the Promenade des Anglais is bustling with life today. Two *agents de police* are keeping the pavement clear for the invited guests who cross the red carpet to enter the pleasantly cool amphitheatre. We notice the smiling Mayor of Nice, the Prefect in his top hat, a general in pale blue uniform, gentlemen with the red button of the *Légion d'Honneur*, ladies of a certain age (terracotta predominating as this year's fashionable colour), vice-admirals, journalists, professors and venerable old ladies of all nations, the kind that is always plentiful on the *Côte d'Azur*. Suddenly a slight incident: amidst all those distinguished visitors a strange little creature tries to slip through shyly and unnoticed; from head to toe it is veiled in a kind of black cape or domino, its eyes peer from behind enormous black spectacles, and it is padding hurriedly and uncertainly towards the crowded vestibule. '*Hé, vous,*' cried one of the policemen, '*qu'est-ce que vous cherchez ici?*' But already the frightened arrival is surrounded by university dignitaries, with *cher docteur* here and *cher docteur* there. So that is Dr Charles Mercier, the learned Newt who is giving today's lecture to the flower of the *Côte d'Azur*! Let's quickly slip inside to make sure of a seat in the festively excited auditorium!

Monsieur le Maire, Monsieur Paul Mallory (the great poet), Mme Maria Dimineanu (the delegate of the International Institute for Intellectual Co-operation), the Director of the Institute for Mediterranean Studies and other official personages have taken their seats on the dais. By the side of the dais is the lectern for the lecturer and behind it – well yes, it really is a bath tub. An ordinary bath tub such as you might find in a bathroom. And two officials are now leading that shy creature in the long cape to the dais. There is a burst of slightly embarrassed applause. Dr Charles Mercier bows shyly and looks about him uncertainly for somewhere to sit down. '*Voilà, Monsieur,*' whispers a functionary, pointing to the bath tub. 'That's for you.' Dr Mercier is clearly very embarrassed but does not know how he can refuse this attentive arrangement; he tries to get into the bath as unobtrusively as possible, but he gets tangled up in his long cape and with a noisy splash falls into the water. The gentlemen on the dais get splashed quite a bit but of course behave as if nothing has happened; someone in the audience giggles hysterically but the gentlemen in the front rows turn their heads disapprovingly and hiss pssst! At that moment *Monsieur le Maire et Député* rises to his feet and starts to speak. 'Ladies and gentlemen,' he says, 'I have the honour to welcome Dr Charles

Mercier to our fair city of Nice. Dr Mercier is an outstanding representative of our near neighbours, the denizens of the deep sea.' (Dr Mercier half emerges from his tub and bows deeply.) 'This is the first time in the history of civilisation that the sea and the land are joining hands in scientific collaboration. In the past our intellectual life has come up against an impassable barrier: the world ocean. We could cross it, we could sail our ships on it in all directions, but, ladies and gentlemen, civilisation was unable to penetrate below its surface. That small piece of land on which mankind lives had hitherto been surrounded by a virgin sea, a wild sea; it had been a beautiful frame but also an age-old divide: on one side a rising civilisation and on the other eternal and unchanging nature. That barrier, dear ladies and gentlemen, is now falling. (Applause) We, the children of this great epoch, have been granted the incomparable happiness to be eye-witnesses to the growth of our spiritual homeland, to watch it cross our shoreline, descend into the sea's waves, conquer the deep, and link a modern and civilised ocean to our ancient civilised land. What a fantastic experience! (Bravo!) Ladies and gentlemen, only by the emergence of an oceanic culture, whose eminent representative we have the honour to welcome in our midst today, has our planet become truly and wholly civilised.' (Enthusiastic applause. Dr Mercier rises from his bath and bows.)

'Dear doctor and great scientist' – *Monsieur le Maire et Député* then turned to Dr Mercier who was holding on to the edge of the bath, his gills twitching heavily with emotion – 'you will be able to pass on to your fellow-countrymen and friends on the sea-bed our congratulations, our admiration and our warmest sympathy. Tell them that in you, our marine neighbours, we welcome the vanguard of progress and education, a vanguard that will, step by step, colonise the boundless regions of the sea and establish a new world of culture on the ocean floor. I can see rising within the depths of the ocean a new Athens and a new Rome; I can see flourishing there a new Paris with submarine Louvres and Sorbonnes, with submarine Triumphal Arches and Tombs of Unknown Warriors, with theatres and boulevards. And permit me to utter my most secret thought: I hope that, facing our beloved Nice, there will arise under the blue waves of the Mediterranean a new glorious Nice, *your* Nice, its magnificent submarine roads, parks and promenades forming an ornamental edge to our azure coast. We hope to get to know you better, and we hope you will come to know us better; personally, I am convinced that closer scientific and social contacts, such as we are inaugurating this day under such happy auspices, will lead our nations towards ever closer cultural and political co-operation for the good of all mankind, in the interest of world peace, prosperity and progress.' (Prolonged applause)

Dr Charles Mercier next rose and tried with a few words to thank the Mayor and Deputy for Nice; but for one thing he was too moved and for another his pronunciation was a little strange so that, from his whole speech, I caught only a few laboriously uttered words; unless I am mistaken they included 'deeply honoured', 'cultural relations' and 'Victor Hugo'. After that, evidently very nervous, he hid again in his tub.

The next speaker was Paul Mallory; what he delivered was not an address but a hymnic poem illumined by a profound philosophy. 'I am grateful to Destiny,' he said, 'that I have lived to see the fulfilment and confirmation of one of mankind's most beautiful legends. It is a strange confirmation and fulfilment: instead of a mythical Atlantis that has sunk beneath the waves we are watching, with amazement, a new Atlantis rising from the deep. Dear colleague Mercier, you, who are a poet of spatial geometry, and your learned it invited Dr Charles Mercier, a highly erudite Newt from Toulon harbour, to give a guest lecture (which in fact he delivered with considerable success) on the theory of conic sections in non-Euclidian geometry. That event was attended also by Mme Maria Dimineanu, a delegate representing Geneva organisations; that splendid and generous lady was so taken by the modest behaviour and by the learning of Dr Mercier ('Pauvre petit,' she was said to have remarked, 'il est tellement laid!') that she made it the goal of her tireless life to get the Newts accepted as members of the League of Nations. In vain did statesmen explain to the eloquent and energetic lady that, since they had no state sovereignty of their own and nowhere in the world did they have their own state territory, the salamanders could not be members of the League of Nations. Mme Dimineanu thereupon began to canvas the idea that the Newts should have their own territory somewhere in the world and their own submarine state. That idea, of course, was rather unwelcome if not actually dangerous; in the end, however, a lucky solution was found: a special *Commission for the Study of the Newt Question* would be set up under the League of Nations, with two Newt delegates to be invited to sit on it. At Mme Dimineanu's insistence the first to be so invited was Dr Charles Mercier of Toulon; the other was some Don Mario, an obese and learned Newt from Cuba, a research worker in the field of plankton and neritic epiplankton. This marked the highest international recognition which the Newts had achieved of their existence until then. [24]

> friends, are the first ambassadors of that new world which is rising from the sea – not Aphrodite rising from the foam but Pallas Anadyomene. But far more amazing and infinitely more mysterious is the fact that . . . ' (the rest is missing).

[24] Preserved among Mr Povondra's papers is a rather blurred newspaper photograph showing the two Newt delegates climbing the steps from the Quai du Mont Blanc on the shore of Lake Geneva, to make their way to the sitting of the Commission. It would appear therefore that they were officially accommodated in Lake Geneva itself.

As for the Geneva Commission for the Study of the Newt Question, its important and meritorious work lay chiefly in that it was careful to avoid all controversial political and economic issues. It was permanently in session for a large number of years, with over 500 sittings, at which there was much talk of an internationally unified terminology for the Newts. The fact was that hopeless chaos reigned in that field: alongside the scientific terms Salamandra, Molche, Batrachus and others (terms that they were beginning to regard as rather offensive) a whole string of other titles was proposed. The Newts were to be called Tritons, Neptunids, Tethyds, Nereids, Atlants, Oceanics, Poseidons, Lemurs, Pelagics, Litorales, Bathyds, Abyssides, Hydrions, Zhandemeres

We therefore see the salamanders in strong and steady ascent. Their numbers are already estimated at 7 billion, even though civilisatory progress has dramatically reduced their birth rate (to some twenty to thirty tadpoles per female annually). They have already settled more than 60 per cent of all the world's shores; so far the polar coastlines are uninhabited, though Canadian Newts have begun to colonise the Greenland coast, where they have actually pushed the Eskimos further inland and seized control of fishing and the blubber trade. Hand in hand with the material advancement has gone their civilisatory progress: they have joined the ranks of enlightened nations with compulsory education, and they can boast of hundreds of underwater newspapers appearing in millions of copies, of exemplarily endowed scientific research institutes, and so forth. Obviously, this cultural progress has not always or everywhere taken place without domestic opposition; though we know exceedingly little about the Newts' internal affairs, there are certain indications (for instance the discovery of Newts with their noses or heads bitten off) that for a longish period there reigned a protracted and fierce ideological struggle between the Old Newts and the Young Newts. The Young Newts were evidently in favour of progress without reservations or restrictions; they declared that it was imperative, even under water, to catch up with dry-land culture of all kind, not excepting football, flirtation, fascism and sexual perversions; the Old Newts, on the other hand, clung conservatively to natural Newtism and refused to give up their good old animalic habits and instincts; they certainly rejected all feverish chasing after novelty, regarding it as a decadent phenomenon and a betrayal of inherited Newt ideals. They fulminated also against all foreign influences to which today's misguided youth so blindly succumbed, and they inquired whether such apeing of humans was worthy of proud and self-respecting Newts.[25] We can visualise the

(*Gens de Mer*), Soumarins, etc. The Commission for the Study of the Newt Question was to chose the most suitable name from this list of suggestions, and it was zealously and conscientiously absorbed in that task until the very end of the Newt Age. Admittedly, no final or unanimous conclusion was ever reached.

[25] Mr Povondra's collection also included two or three articles from *Národní Politika* on today's youth; presumably he had included them in this phase of Newt civilisation in error.

coining of such slogans as Back to the Miocene! Down with Humanising Influences! Fight for pure Newtship! And so on. Undoubtedly all the preconditions existed for a deep generation conflict of opinions and for a profound spiritual revolution in the evolution of the salamanders. We regret that we are unable to illustrate this in greater detail; we can only hope that the Newts have benefited from the conflict as much as possible.

So we now find the salamanders on the road to their finest flowering; but the human world, too, is enjoying unprecedented prosperity. New continental coasts are being feverishly constructed, new dry land is emerging from where shallows used to be; artificial air support islands are springing up in the middle of the ocean. Yet all that is nothing compared to the gigantic technical projects for the complete reconstruction of our globe, projects now merely awaiting someone to finance them. Newts are working without respite in the seas everywhere and on the shores of all the continents during the hours of darkness; they appear to be content and do not demand anything for themselves except employment – holes to be drilled into the banks and passages to their dark living quarters. They have their submarine and underground cities, their deep-down metropolises, their Essens and Birminghams on the sea bottom, at a depth of twenty to fifty metres. They have their overcrowded factory districts, their harbours, transport links and agglomerations of millions. In short, they have their own, more or less unknown[26] but, as it seems, technically highly advanced world. Admittedly they have no blast furnaces or smelters of their own, but humans supply

---

[26] A gentleman from Dejvice told Mr Povondra that he had gone for a swim off the beach of Katwijk am Zee. He had swum out a good distance when the lifeguard shouted to him to return. The gentleman in question (a Mr Příhoda, a commission agent) paid no attention and swam further out. The lifeguard thereupon leapt into a boat and paddled after him. 'Oy there,' he said to him; 'you can't bathe here!'

'And why not?' asked Mr Příhoda.

'There are Newts about.'

'I'm not afraid of them,' Mr Příhoda protested.

'They've got some underwater factories here, or something of the sort,' the lifeguard growled. 'Nobody swims here, sir.'

'And why not?'

'The Newts don't like it.'

them with metals in exchange for their labour. They have no explosives of their own, but these too are sold to them by humans. Their energy source is the sea with its high and low tides, with its currents and temperature gradients. Although their turbines were supplied to them by humans, the Newts know how to use them; but what else is civilisation than the ability to make use of things invented by someone else? Even if, for the sake of argument, the Newts have no original ideas of their own they can perfectly well have their own science. True, they have no music or literature of their own but they manage perfectly well without; indeed people are beginning to think that this is marvellously modern of them. So there you are – already humans can learn something from the Newts. And small wonder: what other example are people to follow if not success? Never before in human history has so much been manufactured, constructed or earned as in this great age. Say what you will, the Newts have brought enormous progress to the world, as well as an ideal called Quantity. 'We people of the Newt Age,' is a phrase uttered with justified pride; good heavens, how can you compare us with that outmoded Human Age with its ponderous, finicky and useless fuss that went by the name of culture, the arts, pure science, and what have you! Real, self-assured Newt Age people will no longer waste their time meditating on the Essence of Things; they will be concerned solely with numbers and mass production. The world's entire future lies in a continually increased consumption and production – so we need even more Newts to produce even more and consume even more. The Newts are quite simply Quantity: their epoch-making achievement lies in their huge numbers. Only now can human ingenuity attain its full scope because now it works on a vast scale, at maximum productive capacity and a record economic turnover. In short: this is a great age. So what is still lacking to make this universal contentment and prosperity into a Happy New Age? What is still standing in the way of that dreamed-of Utopia with its technological triumphs and magnificent vistas opening up for man's prosperity and Newt industry, further and further into infinity?

In fact, nothing. For now the Newt Business will be crowned with statesmanlike foresight, to ensure that nothing should come adrift in the machinery of the New Age. In London, a conference of maritime states is being held to elaborate and approve an International Salamander Convention. The high contracting parties agree amongst each other that they will not dispatch their Newts into the territorial waters of other states; that they will not permit their Newts to infringe, in any way whatsoever, the territorial integrity or acknowledged sphere of interests of any other state; that they will not, in any way whatsoever, interfere in the Newt affairs of other maritime states; that in the event of a clash between their and foreign salamanders they will submit to arbitration by the Hague Court; that they will not arm their Newts with any weapons of a calibre in excess of that customary in underwater pistols against sharks (the so-called Šafránek Gun or shark gun); that they will not permit their Newts to enter into any close relations with the salamanders of other sovereign states; that they will not permit their Newts to build new continents or extend their territory without the previous approval of the Permanent Maritime Commission in Geneva, and so on. (There were in all thirty-seven articles.) On the other hand, a British proposal that the maritime powers should undertake not to subject their Newts to compulsory military training was defeated; so was a French proposal that the salamanders should be internationalised and placed under the International Newt Authority for the Regulation of World Waters; so was a German proposal that each Newt should have the emblem of the state whose subject it was branded upon it, as was also another German proposal that each maritime state should be allowed a certain number of Newts on the basis of a numerical ratio. Also defeated was an Italian suggestion that states with a surfeit of salamanders should have new colonisable coasts or seabed plots assigned to them, and a Japanese proposal that the Japanese nation, as a representative of the coloured races, should exercise an international mandate over the Newts (since these were black by nature).[27] Most of these proposals were shelved for discussion at the next conference of maritime powers; for a number of reasons, however, that conference never met.

[27] This proposal was evidently connected with generous political propaganda: thanks to Mr Povondra's zeal as a collector we have a highly significant document on the subject. It states literally:

'With this international instrument,' M. Jules Sauerstoff declared in *Le Temps*, 'the future of the Newts and the peaceful development of mankind are assured for many decades to come. We congratulate the London conference on the successful conclusion of its difficult consultations; we also congratulate the Newts on having been placed, with the statute adopted, under the protection of the International Court at the Hague; they can now calmly and confidently devote themselves to their work and their submarine progress. Let us emphasise again that the depoliticisation of the Newt Problem, as achieved at the London conference, is one of the most important guarantees of world peace. In particular, the disarmament of the salamanders diminishes the likelihood of submarine clashes between individual states. It is a fact that

人造人 米国にて 実見記 経謹 聞

つ最は二種の珱 今著届や怡いが、今紕る部争お仝目す

氏が的夫限全くな怒じ感うにしてやな右いロ」

幸更全なよせ見ら中がを聞無ろめ自分てられ右四四」

それ君全2」

ほせすお運の抵示がもマドーンン君所て痛知ら全福旦向て

五年にうりま「分れそいロッハて中下ケ「ムか」

Ξたよな目下そのじ今竹ロッサム弁目此してかせの有道

布一あれに逆ん反馬強烈で 妻道れ。がせよ明か聞に

企つ人造へニ ……」

– even though numerous frontier and power disputes continue on nearly every continent – world peace is not actually threatened, at least from the maritime side. But even on dry land peace would now seem to be more solidly safeguarded than ever before: the maritime states are fully engaged in constructing new coastlines and are able to extend their territories into the world ocean instead of attempting to rectify their land frontiers. No longer will it be necessary to fight with iron and gas for every inch of ground: the Newts' simple pickaxes and spades will enable every state to build as much territory as it needs. And it is this peaceful Newt work for the peace and prosperity of all nations that the London conference has guaranteed. Never before has the world been closer to perpetual peace and to tranquil though glorious flowering than at this moment. Instead of the Newt Problem, of which we have heard and read so much, we shall, and rightly, speak of the Golden Newt Age.'

3

Mr Povondra Reads the Paper Again

Nothing reveals more clearly the passage of time than our children. Where is that young Frankie whom we left (not so long ago, really) pouring over the left-bank tributaries of the Danube?

'Where the devil is that Frankie again?' Mr Povondra growled, opening up his evening paper.

'You know – same as always,' said Mrs Povondra, bent over her darning.

'Chasing some girl again,' Papa Povondra remarked disapprovingly. 'Damn that boy! Hardly thirty yet and won't stay home a single evening!'

'The socks he wears out,' sighed Mrs Povondra, pulling another hopeless sock over her wooden mushroom. 'What am I to do with this?' she asked, contemplating an extensive hole in the heel, its shape reminiscent of Ceylon. 'Should really throw it away,' she observed critically, but after some lengthy strategic consideration she resolutely stuck her needle into the southern coast of Ceylon.

There was a dignified family silence, so dear to Papa Povondra's heart; only his newspaper rustled, and to it responded a quickly drawn thread.

'Have they got him yet?' Mrs Povondra inquired.

'Got who?'

'That murderer – man who killed that woman.'

'Not worrying about your murderer,' Mr Povondra growled with some distaste. 'It says here that tension has broken out between Japan and China. Now that's a serious matter. Over there it's always a serious matter.'

'I don't believe they'll catch him now,' Mrs Povondra opined.

'Catch who?'

'That murderer. When a fellow kills a woman they hardly ever catch him.'

'Japan doesn't like to see China regulating the Yellow River. That's politics for you. So long as that Yellow River's a nuisance out there, flooding every other moment and causing hunger in China, well that weakens China, see? Lend me those scissors, Mother, I'm cutting it out.'

'Why?'

'Because it says here that 2 million Newts are working on the Yellow River.'

'That's a lot, isn't it?'

'You can say that again! But I bet the Americans are paying for it all. That's why the Mikado would like to employ his own Newts there. – Why, just look at that!'

'What does it say then?'

'It's the *Petit Parisien* saying that France won't put up with it. Too right! I wouldn't put up with it either.'

'What wouldn't you put up with?'

'Italy enlarging the island of Lampedusa. That's a terribly important strategic base, see? From Lampedusa the Italians could threaten Tunis. *Petit Parisien* says that Italy would like to turn that Lampedusa into a full-size naval base. Said to have 60,000 armed Newts there. Makes you think, don't it? Sixty thousand, that's three divisions, Mother. I'm telling you, something's going to happen in that Mediterranean one day. Gimme them, I'm cutting it out.'

Ceylon, meanwhile, was disappearing under Mrs Povondra's industrious fingers: it had now shrunk to the size of Rhodes.

'And England too,' Papa Povondra meditated; 'she's in for trouble too. Someone's been saying in the House of Commons that Great Britain's lagging behind other countries in these underwater constructions. That other colonial powers are feverishly constructing new shorelines and continents, while the British Government, with its conservative mistrust of the Newts – That's the truth, Mother. Those English are terribly conservative. I knew a footmen from the British Legation once and for the love of God he wouldn't let a Czech liver sausage pass his lips. Said they didn't eat that sort of stuff at home and so he wouldn't eat it here either. No wonder other countries are overtaking them.' Mr Povondra shook his head gravely. 'And France is extending her coast at Calais. Now the British papers are raising merry hell that France will be able to fire across the Channel if it gets narrower. That's all they get out of it. They could extend their own coast at Dover and shoot at France.'

'And why must they shoot at all?' asked Mrs Povondra.

'You don't understand these things. These are military considerations. Shouldn't be surprised if the balloon doesn't go up there one day. There or somewhere else. Stands to reason, now what with those Newts the world situation is quite different, Mother. Quite different.'

'You think there'll be a war?' Mrs Povondra sounded worried. 'You know, because of our Frankie. Wouldn't want him to have to go off.'

'War?' Papa Povondra reflected. 'There'll have to be a world war so the states can share out the sea between them. But we'll remain neutral. Somebody's got to be neutral so they can supply arms and the like to the others. That's how it is,' Mr Povondra decided. 'But you womenfolk don't understand.'

Mrs Povondra pressed her lips together and with rapid stitches completed the liquidation of Ceylon from young Frankie's sock.

'And to think,' Papa Povondra spoke up again with barely muted pride, 'that this threatening situation wouldn't have come about without me! If I hadn't taken that captain to see Mr Bondy the whole of history would look different now. Some other doorman mightn't have let him in even, but I said to myself, I'll chance it. And now look at the trouble some countries are in because of it, like England or France! And we don't even know where it all may lead to . . . ' Mr Povondra excitedly puffed at his pipe. 'That's how it is, my girl. Papers are full of those Newts. Here again . . . ' Papa Povondra put down his pipe. 'Here it says that near the town of Kankesanturai in Ceylon the Newts have raided a village. Seems the natives had killed some Newts there first. The police were called out as well as a company of native troops,' Mr Povondra read aloud, 'whereupon a regular exchange of fire developed between Newts and humans. Several soldiers were wounded . . . ' Papa Povondra put down his paper. 'I don't like the look of it, Mother.'

'Why not?' Mrs Povondra was surprised. Carefully and with satisfaction she tapped the area where the island of Ceylon had been with the handles of her scissors. 'Surely there's nothing to it!'

'I don't know,' Papa Povondra burst out and started excitedly to pace the room. 'But I don't like the look of it. No, I don't. An exchange of fire between humans and Newts – no, that shouldn't be.'

'Maybe those Newts were only defending themselves,' Mrs Povondra said soothingly and put the socks away.

'That's just it,' Mr Povondra muttered uneasily. 'Once those brutes start to defend themselves it'll be a sad day. This is the first time they've done it . . . Dammit, I don't like the look of it!' Mr Povondra stopped and hesitated. 'I don't know, but . . . maybe I shouldn't have let that captain in to see Mr Bondy!'

BOOK THREE

War With the Newts

1

The Massacre on the Cocos Islands

On one point Mr Povondra was mistaken: the skirmish at Kankesanturai was not the first clash between humans and Newts. The first recorded conflict occurred several years earlier on the Cocos Islands, in the good old days of pirate raids on the salamanders. But even that was not the earliest incident of its kind: in the Pacific ports there had been a good deal of talk of certain regrettable occurrences when the Newts had put up some sort of active resistance even to the regular S-Trade – but then history does not concern itself with such trifles.

The business on the Cocos or Keeling Islands happened like this. The raiding ship *Montrose* of the well-known Harriman Pacific Trade Company under Captain James Lindley arrived there on its regular hunt for Newts of the so-called Macaroni type. There was a well-known and rich Newt colony in a bay of the Cocos Islands, established at the time by Captain van Toch but, because of its remote situation, was abandoned, as the saying is, to the care of the Good Lord. No one could accuse Captain Lindley of having been in any way negligent, not even in allowing his crew to go ashore unarmed. (The point is that by then the piratical Newt trade had acquired its regularised form. It is true, of course, that in the early days corsair ships and their crews had been armed with machine-guns, and indeed with field guns, not against the salamanders but against unfair competition from other pirates. On Karakelong Island, a landing party from a Harriman steamship had on one occasion clashed with the crew of a Danish ship whose captain had regarded Karakelong as his hunting ground; on that occasion both parties had settled their old scores, and more particularly their prestige and commercial differences by forgetting the Newt hunt and instead opening up at each other with their rifles and Hotchkisses. The Danes had won on land by making a knife charge, but the Harriman steamship had subsequently fired her guns at the Danish ship and succeeded in sinking her with all hands, complete with Captain Niels. That became known as the Karakelong incident. The authorities and governments of the two countries had to intervene at that time, and pirate ships were henceforward forbidden to use heavy guns, machine-guns or hand-grenades. Moreover, the pirate companies divided the so-called free hunting grounds amongst themselves in such a way that each locality was visited by one particular pirate ship only. That gentleman's agreement between the big pirates was actually kept and was respected also by lesser piratical entrepreneurs.) But to return to Captain Lindley. He was acting entirely in the spirit of the customary commercial and naval conventions of his day when he sent his men ashore on the Cocos Islands to hunt for Newts armed only with clubs and oars. Indeed the subsequent inquiry fully exonerated the dead captain.

The landing party which went ashore on the Cocos Islands that moonlit night was commanded by Lieutenant Eddie McCarth, a man with experience of this kind of hunt. It is true that the crowd of Newts he encountered on the shore was unusually large – according to estimates some six or seven hundred strong adult males, whereas he only had sixteen men under his command. But no one can blame him for not abandoning his enterprise, if only because officers and crew of private vessels were customarily paid bonuses based on the number of captured Newts. In their subsequent inquiry the naval authorities found that 'while Lieutenant McCarth must be held responsible for the unfortunate incident, no one would have acted differently in the given circumstances'. The unfortunate young officer actually displayed considerable prudence in not proceeding with the usual gradual encirclement of the Newts – which in view of the numerical ratio could not have been complete anyway – but instead ordering a sudden charge with the objective of cutting the Newts off from the sea, forcing them towards the centre of the island, and stunning them one by one with their clubs and oars. Unfortunately in the course of the charge the line-abreast of the sailors was broken and nearly two hundred salamanders escaped into the sea. Just as the raiding party was belabouring the Newts it had cut off from the sea the sharp cracks of submarine pistols (the shark guns) rang out at their backs: no one had suspected that these *natural* wild Newts of the Keeling Islands had been equipped with anti-shark pistols, and it was never discovered who had in fact supplied these weapons to them.

Michael Kelly, a young sailor who survived the whole catastrophe, related: 'When the firing started we thought that another crew was shooting at us, someone who had also come to hunt for Newts. Lieutenant McCarth immediately turned about and yelled: "What the hell d'you think you're doing, you idiots, this is the *Montrose* crew!" Just then he was hit in the hip but he managed to draw his revolver and started firing. Then he stopped another, in the neck, and fell. So Long Steve picked up an oar and charged the Newts, shouting Montrose! Montrose! The rest of us also yelled Montrose and battered the brutes with our oars as best we could. We left about five of our lot lying there, but the rest of us made it to the water. Long Steve jumped in and started wading out to the boat; but several Newts clung to him and dragged him under. They also drowned Charlie; he screamed to us, "For Christ's sake, boys, don't let them have me," but there was nothing we could do for him. Those bastards fired at our backs. Bodkin turned round and got it in his belly; all he said was, "Not that," and fell. So we tried to get back into the interior of the island: but we'd smashed our oars and clubs against those brutes and we were just running like rabbits. By then there were only four of us left. We were afraid to get too far away from the shore in case we couldn't regain our ship; so we hid behind the rocks and bushes and had to watch the Newts finishing off our mates. They drowned them in the water like kittens, and if someone still tried to swim they bashed his head in with crowbars. It was only then that I noticed I had dislocated my foot and that I couldn't move.'

It appears that Captain James Lindley, who had stayed behind on board the *Montrose,* heard the firing on the island. Whether he thought there had been a clash with the natives, or that some other Newt merchants were ashore, he grabbed the ship's cook and two engine-room men – that was all the crew that was left – got them to load the remaining boat with a machine-gun which he had providentially, if against strict orders, hidden away on his ship and set out to help his crew. He was careful enough not to step on land but brought the boat close in, with the machine-gun ready in its bow, and stood up 'with arms folded'. Let us hand over again to young seaman Kelly.

'We didn't want to call out to the captain because we didn't want the Newts to discover us. Mr Lindley was standing in the boat, arms folded, and called out: "What's going on here?" Then the Newts turned towards him. There were a few hundred of them on the shore, and more and more were swimming in from the sea and encircling the boat. "What's going on here?" the captain asked, and one big Newt then came closer to him and said: "Go back!"

The captain looked at him, for a while he didn't say anything and then he asked: "You're a Newt?"

"We are Newts," said that Newt. "Go back, sir!"

"I want to know what you've done to my men," our Old Man said.

"They shouldn't have attacked us," said the Newt. "Go back to your ship, sir!'

Again the captain was silent for a little while, and then he said quite calmly. "That's it, then. Jenkins, fire!"

And Jenkins, the engine-room man, began to fire his machine-gun at the Newts.'

(In the subsequent inquiry into the whole incident the naval authorities declared literally: 'In that respect Captain James Lindley acted in the manner expected of a British naval man.')

'The Newts were all bunched up,' Kelly's account continued; 'so they were mowed down like corn. A few of them fired their pistols at Mr Lindley but he just stood with his arms folded and didn't even move. Just then a black Newt surfaced from the water behind the boat: he was holding something in one hand like a food tin, with his other hand he ripped something off and dropped it in the water under the boat. Before you could count five a column of water rose up at that spot and there was a muffled but powerful explosion that made the ground rock under our feet.'

(The inquiry officials concluded from Kelly's account that the explosive must have been W-3, an explosive supplied to the Newts working on the fortifications of Singapore for breaking up rocks under the water. But how those charges got from the Newts there to those at the Cocos Islands remained a mystery; some people speculated that they must have been shipped there by people, others believed that even then the Newts must have had some kind of long-distance communications amongst themselves. Public opinion called for a ban on supplying the Newts with such dangerous explosive substances, but the competent authorities declared that it was impossible for the moment to replace W-3, 'a highly effective and comparatively safe' explosive, with any other. And that was the end of the matter.)

'The boat went up in the air ,' Kelly's testimony continued, 'in smithereens. Those Newts who were still alive crowded round the spot. We could not make out if Mr Lindley was still alive, but my three mates – Donovan, Burke and Kennedy – jumped up and raced down to help him, so he shouldn't fall into the hands of the Newts. I tried to run too, but my ankle was dislocated, so I sat down and pulled my foot with both hands to get those joints together again. So I don't know what happened at that moment, but when I looked up Kennedy was lying face down in the sand, and of Donovan and Burke there wasn't a trace – only some swirling under the water.'

Young Kelly then fled further into the island until he found a native village; but the natives acted oddly and did not even want to give him shelter. They were probably scared of the Newts. Seven weeks later a fishing boat found the completely looted and abandoned *Montrose* anchored off the Cocos Islands and rescued Kelly.

A few weeks later His Britannic Majesty's gunboat *Fireball* sailed up to the Cocos Islands and, riding at anchor, awaited darkness. The night was again brilliant with a full moon. The Newts emerged from the sea, sat round in a large circle on the sandy foreshore and began their ceremonial dance. At that moment His Majesty's Ship *Fireball* fired the first shrapnel into their midst. The Newts, those that were not torn to pieces, were stunned for a moment and than began to run towards the sea; at that moment a terrifying salvo from six guns rang out and only a few mutilated salamanders were able to crawl back to the water. Then a second and third salvo cracked out. H M S *Fireball* thereupon stood off half a mile and, moving slowly along the coast, began to fire into the water. This went on for six hours and some 800 rounds were fired. The *Fireball* then sailed away. Even two days afterwards the surface of the sea off the Keeling Islands was still covered with thousands and thousands of dismembered Newts.

The same night the Dutch battleship *Van' Dijck* fired three rounds into a crowd of Newts on the little island of Goenong Api; the Japanese cruiser *Hakodate* sent three shells on to the Newt island of Ailinglaplap; the French gunboat *Béchamel* scattered some dancing Newts on Rawaiwai Island with three salvoes. This was a warning to the Newts. It did not go unheeded: no similar incident (this one was called the 'Keeling killing') ever happened again, and both the regular and the illicit Newt trade was able to flourish undisturbed and as profitably as before.

2

The Clash in Normandy

The clash in Normandy, which took place a little later, was of a different character. There the Newts, employed chiefly at Cherbourg and inhabiting the neighbouring coast, took a tremendous liking to apples. But as their employers did not wish to let them have any on top of their normal Newt food (arguing that this would increase construction costs beyond the fixed budget), the Newts mounted thieving forays into the nearby orchards. The farmers complained to the Préfecture and the Newts were strictly forbidden to roam about the shore beyond the so-called Newt zone. But this did not help: the farmers continued to lose their fruit, and even eggs were said to be disappearing from the hen-coops, and more and more watchdogs were found killed each morning. The farmers thereupon began to guard their orchards themselves, armed with ancient rifles, and shot the poaching Newts. This, of course, would have remained a purely local affair if the Normandy farmers, embittered also by increased taxes and the higher price they had to pay for their ammunition, had not conceived a mortal hatred of the Newts and begun to mount raids on them in complete armed gangs. When the farmers had thus killed considerable numbers of Newts, even where they were working, the hydraulic engineering contractors now complained to the Préfect; the Préfect therefore ordered the confiscation of the farmers' rusty blunderbusses. The farmers, naturally enough, resisted and some unpleasant conflicts occurred with the gendarmerie: the stubborn Normandy farmers were now taking potshots not only at Newts but also at gendarmes. Gendarmerie reinforcements were brought to Normandy and house-to-house searches were made in the villages.

At about that time an exceedingly disagreeable thing happened: in the neighbourhood of Coutance some village youths attacked a Newt who, so they said, was suspiciously creeping up to a chicken-coop; they surrounded him, forced him with his back to the barn wall and began to pelt him with bricks. The wounded salamander swung his arm up and flung on the ground something that resembled an egg; there was an explosion which blew the Newt to pieces, as well as the three boys: eleven-year-old Pierre Cajus, sixteen-year-old Marcel Bérard and fifteen-year-old Louis Kermadec. Another five children were more or less seriously injured. News of the event spread rapidly throughout the region; some seven hundred people came flocking together by bus from far and wide and, armed with shotguns, pitchforks and flails, attacked a Newt colony in the bay of Basse Coutance. About twenty Newts were killed before the gendarmes succeeded in forcing back the infuriated crowd. Sappers summoned from Cherbourg surrounded the bay of Basse Coutance with a barbed wire fence. At night, however, the salamanders emerged from the sea, breached the wire fence with hand-grenades and were evidently about to penetrate inland. Army trucks rushed up a few platoons of infantry armed with machine-guns, and a military cordon was thrown between the Newts and the humans. The farmers, meanwhile, were smashing up local tax offices and police stations and one unpopular tax collector was strung up on a lamp-post with a placard: Down with Newts! The newspapers, especially the German newspapers, spoke of a revolution in Normandy; the government in Paris, however, issued an emphatic denial.

While these bloody clashes between farmers and Newts were spreading along the coast of Calvados, Picardy and the Pas de Calais, the ancient French cruiser *Jules Flambeau* left Cherbourg for the west coast of Normandy; the idea, as was subsequently established, was that her mere presence would have a calming effect both on the local population and on the Newts. The *Jules Flambeau* hove to a mile and a half off Basse Coutance bay; after nightfall her commander, to heighten the effect, ordered coloured flares to be fired. A crowd of people on the shore were watching that splendid spectacle when suddenly they heard a hissing roar and saw a huge column of water rising up by the cruiser's bows. The ship listed over, and simultaneously there was a thunderous explosion. It was obvious that the cruiser was sinking; within a quarter of an hour motorboats were arriving from harbours in the vicinity but no assistance was needed; apart from three men who had been killed by the explosion itself the whole crew managed to save themselves, and the *Jules Flambeau* sank five minutes after her captain, as the last man aboard, had abandoned ship with the memorable remark: 'That's that, then.' An official communiqué issued the same night stated that 'the old cruiser *Jules Flambeau,* due to be scrapped within the next few weeks anyway, ran aground while sailing at night and sank as a result of a boiler explosion'; but the newspapers were not so readily satisfied. While the semi-official press asserted that the ship had struck a German mine of recent manufacture, the opposition and foreign press carried inch-high banner headlines:

FRENCH CRUISER TORPEDOED BY NEWTS
Mysterious Incident off the Normandy Coast
Revolt of the Newts

'We are holding responsible,' the Deputy Barthélemy said in a passionate article in his paper, 'those who armed the animals against humans, those who put bombs in the Newts' paws so they can kill French farmers and innocent children at play, those who supplied those marine monsters with the most modern torpedoes so they can sink the French Navy whenever they choose. I say: we are holding them responsible. Let them be arraigned for murder, let them be called to face a court martial on charges of high treason, let it be discovered what payments they received from armament kings for supplying that marine vermin with weapons against a civilised navy!' And so on. In short, there was general panic, people were rioting in the streets and barricades began to be erected. On the Paris boulevards stood Senegalese riflemen, their weapons piled, and tanks and armoured cars stood by in the suburbs. At that moment M. François Ponceau, the Minister for the Navy, stood up in the Assembly, pale but determined, and declared: The government accepts responsibility for arming the Newts on the French coast with rifles, underwater machine-guns, submarine batteries and torpedo launchers. But while the French Newts only have small-calibre light guns, the German salamanders are equipped with thirty-two-centimetre calibre submarine mortars; while on the French coast there is, on average, one submarine store of hand-grenades, torpedoes and explosives per twenty-four kilometres, there are deep depots of war materials at every twenty kilometres along the Italian coast and at every eighteen kilometres in German waters. France cannot and will not leave her coast unprotected. France cannot dispense with the arming of her Newts. The Minister has already put in hand the most rigorous investigation to determine responsibility for that fatal misunderstanding off the Normandy coast: it would seem that the Newts regarded the coloured flares as a signal for military intervention and were trying to defend themselves. In the meantime both the commander of the *Jules Flambeau* and the Préfect of Cherbourg have been suspended from office; a special commission will establish how hydraulic engineering contractors are treating their Newts; strict supervision will be instituted in this respect in future. The government deeply regrets the loss of human life; the young national heroes Pierre Cajus, Marcel Bérard and Louis Kermadec will be posthumously decorated and buried at public expense, and their parents will receive a gratuitous pension. There will be significant changes in the top command of the French Navy. The government will make the matter a question of confidence by the Assembly as soon as it is in a position to make a more detailed report. The cabinet thereupon announced that it was in permanent session.

The newspapers meanwhile – each according to its political colouring – proposed punitive, extermination, colonising campaigns and crusades against the Newts, a general strike, the resignation of the government, the arrest of all employers of Newts, the arrest of Communist leaders and agitators, and a lot of other similar safety procedures. In view of rumours about a possible closing of coasts and harbours the public feverishly began to lay in stocks of food, and the prices of all goods rose at a vertiginous rate. In industrial cities riots broke out against the price rises; the stock exchange was closed for three days. It was quite simply the tensest and most dangerous situation of the past three or four months. At that moment, however, the Minister of Agriculture, M. Monti, intervened. He arranged for a certain number of railway wagons of apples to be tipped into the sea off the French coast twice a week, needless to say at state expense. This measure had an exceedingly calming effect on the Newts and also satisfied the fruit farmers in Normandy and elsewhere. But M. Monti went even further along the same lines: because for a long time there had been a good deal of trouble with profound and alarming unrest in wine-growing districts – which were suffering from insufficient market demand – he arranged that the state should subsidise the Newts in such a way that every salamander would receive half a litre of white wine daily. At first the Newts were at a loss what to do with the wine because it gave them severe diarrhoea, and so they poured it into the sea; with time, however, they clearly got used to it and it has been observed that since then the French Newts have mated more eagerly though with a lesser fertility than before. Thus the agrarian problem and the Newt affair were solved at a single stroke: the dangerous tension was eased, and when a fresh government crisis arose shortly afterwards in connection with the financial scandal around Mme Töppler, the ingenious and well-tried M. Monti became Minister for the Navy in the new government.

3

The Incident in the Channel

Some time later the Belgian ferryboat *Oudenbourgh* was sailing from Ostend to Ramsgate. Halfway across the Straits of Dover the duty officer noticed 'something happening in the water' half a mile south of her usual course. Because he was unable to make out if somebody was not perhaps drowning he gave orders for the ship to make for the spot where the water was so fiercely churned up. Nearly 200 passengers watched the strange spectacle from the windward side: in some places the water was splashing up in vertical columns, in others something like a black body was flung up with it; over an area about 300 metres across the sea's surface was intensely agitated and seething, and a loud rumble and roar was heard to come from the depth. It was just as if a small volcano was erupting under water. As the *Oudenbourgh* slowly drew near the spot a gigantic precipitous wave suddenly rose up some ten metres from her bows and there was a frightful explosion. The whole ship rose sharply and a shower of near-boiling water descended on her deck; simultaneously a powerful black body smacked down on her foredeck, writhing and screaming in agony: it was a mutilated and scalded Newt. The captain ordered full steam astern to prevent the ship sailing straight into the middle of that exploding inferno but by now explosions were occurring all over the place and the surface was strewn with pieces of dismembered Newts. Eventually the ship was turned about, and the *Oudenbourgh* made off north at full steam. Just then there was a terrifying explosion and a huge column of water and steam, perhaps 100 metres high, shot up some 600 metres astern. The *Oudenbourgh* headed straight for Harwich, radioing warnings in all directions: 'Warning, warning, warning! Great danger of submarine explosions on Ostend–Ramsgate route. Cause unknown. All craft advised to avoid the area!' Meanwhile the rumble and roar continued, almost as if naval exercises were taking place; but because of the spouts of water

and steam there was nothing to be seen. By then torpedo-
boats and destroyers had set out from Dover and Calais at
full steam and squadrons of military aircraft were making for
the spot. However, all they found on arrival was the surface
muddied with yellow slime and covered with dead fish and
mangled Newts.

At first it was thought that some mines had blown up in
the Channel. But when the coasts on both sides of the
Straits were cordoned off by troops, and when the British
Prime Minister (for only the fourth time in world history)
cut short his weekend on Saturday evening to hurry back
to London people began to suspect that this was an affair
of extremely serious international import. The newspapers
carried the most sensational stories, but strangely enough
for once they fell far short of the facts: no one even suspected
that for a few critical days Europe, and with her the whole
world, was hovering on the brink of a warlike conflagration.
It was only some years later, when Sir Thomas Mulberry,
a member of the British Cabinet at the time, lost his
parliamentary seat at the general election and thereupon
published his political memoirs that the public was able to
find out what had actually happened. Except that by then no
one was interested any more.

In essence this was what happened. Both France and
England had begun, each from her own side, to build submarine
Newt fortifications in the English Channel; these would make
it possible, in the event of war, to close the Channel altogether.
Subsequently, of course, each power accused the other of
having started the business; the truth, however, seems to be
that both of them commenced work at the same time, for fear
that their neighbour and ally across the water might get there
first. In short, two colossal concrete fortresses grew up under
the waters of the Straits of Dover, facing each other, equipped
with heavy guns, torpedo launchers, extensive minefields and
in general all the latest achievements of human progress in
the martial arts. On the British side this terrible submarine
fortress was manned by two divisions of heavy Newts and some
30,000 worker Newts; on the French side there were three
divisions of first-rate combat Newts.

It appears that on that critical day a working party of British
Newts encountered some French salamanders on the sea-bed

and that some disagreement arose between them. The French version was that their peacefully working Newts had been attacked by the British Newts who had tried to drive them off; the armed British Newts (it was claimed) had tried to drag some French Newts away with them, and these of course offered resistance. Thereupon the British military salamanders opened up at the French worker Newts with hand-grenades and trench-mortars, forcing the French Newts to resort to the same weapons. The French government felt obliged to demand full satisfaction from His Britannic Majesty's Government as well as the evacuation of the contentious sector of sea-bed; it also required assurances that similar incidents would not be repeated.

The British government, on the other hand, in a special Note to the government of the French Republic, stated that French militarised Newts had invaded the British half of the Channel and begun to lay mines there. The British Newts had drawn their attention to the fact that they were on British working territory; thereupon the French salamanders, armed as they were to the teeth, had responded by throwing hand-grenades, killing a number of British worker Newts. His Majesty's Government much to its regret felt compelled to demand from the government of the French Republic full satisfaction and a guarantee that French military Newts would not in future encroach on the British half of the English Channel.

The French government thereupon declared that it could not tolerate a neighbouring country constructing submarine fortifications in the immediate vicinity of the French coasts. As far as the misunderstanding on the Channel floor was concerned, the government of the Republic proposed that the dispute be submitted, in the spirit of the London Convention, to the adjudication of the International Court at the Hague.

The British government replied that it could not and did not intend to subject the security of the British shores to any external adjudication. As the attacked country it once more emphatically demanded an apology, compensation for the damage caused, and guarantees for the future. Simultaneously the British Mediterranean Fleet, stationed at Malta, set sail at full steam for the west; the Atlantic Fleet received orders to concentrate at Portsmouth and Yarmouth.

The French government ordered the mobilisation of five age classes of its navy.

It seemed that neither country was any longer able to withdraw; after all, it was clear that what was at stake was no more and no less than control of the entire Channel. At that critical moment Sir Thomas Mulberry made a surprising discovery: no worker or combat Newts actually existed (at least *de jure*) on the British side, as a law passed (some time before) under Sir Samuel Mandeville, prohibiting the employment of even a single salamander on the coasts or in the territorial waters of the British Isles, was still in force. Consequently the British government could not officially maintain that French Newts had attacked British Newts; the whole affair therefore shrank to the issue of whether French salamanders, either deliberately or unwittingly, had encroached on the sea-bed of British territorial waters. The authorities of the French Republic promised to 'investigate the matter; the British government did not even suggest submission of the dispute to the International Court at the Hague. The British and French Admiralties subsequently agreed that the submarine fortifications of the two sides should be separated by a neutral strip five kilometres wide – an arrangement which quite extraordinarily strengthened the friendship between the two states.

4

Der Nordmolch

A few years after the establishment of the first Newt colonies in the North Sea and the Baltic the German researcher, Dr Hans Thüring, ascertained that the Baltic Newt – undoubtedly in response to its environment – exhibited a number of divergent physical characteristics. It was said to be somewhat paler, to walk more erect, and to have a cranial index suggesting a longer and narrower skull than that of other Newts. This variety was named *der Nordmolch* or *der Edelmolch* (Andrias Scheuchzeri var. nobilis erecta Thüring).

After that the German press began to show an intense interest in the Baltic Newt. Special importance was attached to the fact that it was just in response to the German environment that this Newt developed into a different and higher racial type, indisputably superior to all other salamanders. With contempt the papers referred to the degenerate Mediterranean Newts, stunted both physically and morally, and to the savage Newts of the tropics, and the altogether low, barbarian and bestial salamanders of other nations. From the Giant Newt to the German Super-Newt was the slogan of the day. After all, was not the prime origin of all modern Newts on German territory? Did their cradle not stand at Oeningen, where the German scientist Dr Johannes Jakob Scheuchzer had discovered their glorious imprint dating back to the Miocene? There cannot therefore be the slightest doubt that the original Andrias Scheuchzeri was born geological ages ago on Germanic soil; subsequently it migrated to other seas and zones and dearly paid for it by its evolutionary descent and degeneration. As soon, however, as it settled once more in its primeval homeland it became what it had originally been: Scheuchzer's noble Nordic Newt, fair, erect and dolichocephalic. Only on German soil, therefore, could the Newts revert to their pure and highest form, as had been found in the Oeningen quarry imprint by the great Johannes Jakob Scheuchzer. Germany therefore needed new and longer coastlines, she needed colonies, she needed oceans, so that new generations of racially pure original German salamanders could develop in German waters everywhere. We need new space for our Newts, the German papers clamoured; and to ensure that this fact was permanently before the German nation's eyes a splendid monument was erected in Berlin to Johannes Jakob Scheuchzer. It showed the great doctor with a fat book in his hand; by his feet, sitting erect, was a noble Nordic Newt, gazing into the distance, towards the infinite coasts of the world ocean.

Needless to say, festive speeches were made at the unveiling of this national monument, and these aroused exceptional interest in the international press. *New German Threat* was the reaction especially in England. Accustomed as we are to this kind of tone, if an official occasion is used for statements to the effect that Germany needs 5,000 kilometres of new sea coasts within the next three years, then we are bound to reply very clearly: All right, try and get them! You'll smash your teeth on the British shores. We are prepared now, and we shall be even better prepared in three years' time. Britain will and must have as many naval units as the two greatest Continental powers together; this ratio is inviolable for all time. If you wish to unleash a mad naval armaments race, so be it; no Briton will permit us to remain behind by as much as a single step.

'We accept the German challenge,' Sir Francis Drake, First Lord of the Admiralty, declared in the Commons on behalf of the government. 'Whosoever lays his hands on any sea will encounter the armour of our ships. Great Britain is strong enough to repel any attack on her headlands or on the coasts of her dominions or colonies. We shall view as such an attack also the construction of new continents, islands, fortifications or air bases in any ocean whose waves wash even the smallest stretch of a British coast. Let this be a final warning to anyone who would try to shift a sea coast by as much as a yard.' Parliament thereupon approved the building of new warships at a preliminary cost of half a billion pounds sterling. It was a truly impressive reply to the construction of the provocative Johannes Jakob Scheuchzer monument. That monument, admittedly, cost only 12,000 Reichmarks.

A reply to these statements came from the brilliant French journalist, the Marquis de Sade, a man usually extremely well informed. Britain's First Lord of the Admiralty (he said) had declared Great Britain to be prepared for all eventualities. Very good. But is the noble lord aware that Germany has in her Baltic Newts a permanent and very well-equipped army already numbering 5 million regular combat Newts who can be employed at a moment's notice in the sea or on shore? Add to them some 17 million Newts in the technical and supply services, ready to operate at any time as a reserve or an army of occupation. Today the Baltic Newt is the best soldier in the world; psychologically perfectly brain-washed, he sees his true and supreme mission in war; he will go into any battle with the enthusiasm of the fanatic, with the cool reasoning of the technician and with the terrifying discipline of a true Prussian Newt.

Is Britain's First Lord of the Admiralty further aware that Germany is feverishly building transport vessels capable of carrying a whole brigade of combat salamanders at a time? Is he aware that she is building hundreds and hundreds of small submarines with an operational range of 3,000 to 5,000 kilometres, crewed solely by Baltic Newts? Is he aware that she is setting up huge underwater fuel tanks in various parts of the ocean? Well, let us ask again: is the British citizen sure that his country is *really* well prepared for all eventualities?

It is not difficult, the Marquis de Sade continued, to visualise the importance of the Newts in any future war: equipped with underwater Big Berthas, mortars and torpedoes for blockading any coasts. God knows, for the first time in world history no one need envy Britain her splendid island situation. But while we are on the subject, is the British Admiralty aware that the Baltic Newts are equipped with a normally very peaceful instrument known as the pneumatic drill? And that this drill can cut ten metres deep into the best Swedish granite in an hour, or to a depth of fifty to sixty metres in English chalk? (This was proved by trial borings secretly conducted by a German technical expedition during the nights of the 11th, 12th and 13th of last month on the English coast between Hythe and Folkestone, right under the nose of the fortifications at Dover.) We would advise our friends across the Channel to work out for themselves how many weeks it would take for Kent or Essex to become riddled with holes below sea level like a chunk of cheese. Hitherto the British islander has been anxiously watching the skies, the only direction from where he thought disaster might come to his flourishing cities, to his Bank of England or to his peaceful cottages, snug under their perpetual green cover of ivy. Let him now press his ear to the ground instead, the ground on which his children are playing: will he not hear, if not today then tomorrow, the grinding sound, the crunching progress, inch by inch, of the tireless and terrible cutting head of the Newts' drills, boring holes for as yet unheard-of explosive charges? No longer the war in the air but a war under water and underground is the latest marvel of our age. We heard some self-assured words from the captain's bridge of proud Albion: yes, she still is a mighty ship riding the waves and ruling them; yet one day these waves might close over a ship blown to smithereens and sinking to the depths of the sea. Would it not be wiser to oppose this danger in time? Three years from now it will be too late!

This warning by the brilliant French commentator caused tremendous excitement in England. In spite of all denials people in the most diverse parts of England heard the crunch of the Newts' drills underground. German official quarters, of course, emphatically repudiated and refuted the article quoted, describing it as sheer incitement and enemy propaganda from start to finish; simultaneously, however, major combined exercises were taking place in the Baltic between the German Navy, land forces and combat salamanders. As part of these exercises a Newt sapper platoon, before the eyes of foreign military attachés, blew up a strip of undermined sand dunes near Rügenwalde, an area of six square kilometres. It was said to have been a magnificent spectacle when, with a dreadful rumbling, the earth rose up 'like a cracked ice-floe', to break up a moment later into a gigantic wall of smoke, sand and boulders. The sky grew dark, almost as though it were night, and the raised sand fell over a radius of nearly a hundred kilometres, indeed after a few days it fell as a sandy rain as far away as Warsaw. After that magnificent explosion so much freely suspended fine sand and dust remained in the earth's atmosphere that throughout Europe the sunsets were exceptionally beautiful right to the end of the year – blood-red and fiery as never before.

The sea which flooded the shattered stretch of coast was later named the Scheuchzer-See and became the goal of countless school outings and excursions of German children who sang the popular Newt anthem: *Solche Erfolche erreichen nur deutsche Molche.*

5

Wolf Meynert Writes His Great Work

Perhaps it was those magnificent and tragic sunsets that inspired the Koenigsberg recluse philosopher Wolf Meynert to write his monumental *Untergang der Menschheit* (Decline of Mankind). We can vividly picture him pacing the seashore, bare-headed in a flowing cloak, staring with fascinated eyes at that flood of fire and blood filling more than half the sky. 'Yes,' he whispers in ecstasy, 'yes, the time has come to write the epilogue to the history of mankind!' And so he sat down and wrote it.

The tragedy of the human race is being played out, Wolf Meynert began. Let us not be blinded by feverish enterprise or technological prosperity; these are but the fever patches on the cheeks of an organism already marked by death. Never has mankind experienced a greater upsurge to its life than today; yet find me one person who is happy, show me one class that is content, or one nation that does not feel threatened in its existence. Amidst all the gifts of civilisation, in Croesus-like wealth of spiritual and material values, we are all increasingly gripped by an irresistible sense of uncertainty, anxiety and malaise. And Wolf Meynert relentlessly analysed the spiritual condition of the world today, that mixture of fear and hate, of mistrust and megalomania, of cynicism and despondency: in one word, despair, Wolf Meynert concluded briefly. Typical terminal symptoms. Moral agony.

The question is: is or was man ever capable of happiness? Man certainly, as indeed every living creature − but not mankind. Man's whole tragedy lies in the fact that he was forced to become mankind, or that he became mankind too late when he had already been irreparably differentiated into nations, races, faiths, estates and classes, into rich and poor, educated and uneducated, into rulers and oppressed. Herd together

same as newts

horses, wolves, sheep and cats, foxes and deer, bears and goats; shut them into one enclosure and compel them to live together in that nonsensical crowd which you call the social order, and to observe common rules of life; it will be an unhappy, dissatisfied, fatally divided herd, in which not one of God's creatures will feel at home. This is a more or less accurate picture of the great and hopelessly heterogeneous herd that is called mankind. Nations, estates, or classes cannot in the long run co-exist without crowding in on each other and getting in each other's way to the point when it becomes unbearable. They can either live forever separated from each other – this was possible while the world was still big enough for them – or against each other, locked in a life-and-death struggle. For biological human entities, such as race, nation or class, the only natural road to homogeneity and undisturbed happiness is: to establish room for themselves and exterminate all others. And this is precisely what the human race failed to do in time. Today it is too late. We have made ourselves too many doctrines and obligations to protect 'the others' instead of getting rid of them; we have thought up a moral code, human rights, treaties, laws, equality, humanity and heaven knows what else; we have created the fiction of mankind which embraces both us and 'the others' in a notional higher entity. What a fatal error! We have placed the moral law above the biological law. We have violated the great natural prerequisite of all community existence: that only a homogeneous society can be a happy society. That attainable happiness we have sacrificed to a great but impossible dream: to create *one* mankind and *one* order out of all people, nations, classes and strata. It was a piece of magnanimous stupidity. It was, in its way, man's only respectable attempt to rise above himself. But for that extreme idealism the human race is now paying by its inevitable disintegration.

The process whereby man attempts to organise himself into mankind is as old as civilisation itself, as old as the first laws and the first communities; if now, after many thousands of years, we have reached a stage when the gulf between races, nations, classes and ideologies has become as wide and as deep as it is today, then we can no longer shut our eyes to the fact that our unfortunate historical endeavour to create from the totality of individuals some kind of mankind has finally and tragically failed. Actually we are beginning to realise it; hence those attempts and plans to unite human society in a different way, by making room for *one* nation, *one* class or *one* faith. But who can tell how deeply we are already infected with the incurable disease of differentiation? Sooner or later each supposedly homogeneous entity will inevitably again break up into a heterogeneous collection of different interests, parties and estates, and so on, which will either destroy each other or again suffer by living together. There is no way out. We are moving in a vicious circle; but evolution will not forever go round in circles. Nature itself has seen to this by making room in the world for the Newts.

It is no accident, Wolf Meynert reflected, that the Newts have vitally asserted themselves at the very time when the chronic disease of mankind, of that badly accreted and forever disintegrating macro-organism, is entering upon its agony. Insignificant deviations apart, the Newts present themselves as a single huge and homogeneous whole: they have not so far developed any greatly differentiated tribes, languages, nations, states, faiths, classes or castes; they have neither masters nor servants, neither freemen nor serfs, neither rich nor poor; admittedly there are differences among them due to the division of labour, but in itself they represent a homogeneous, uniform and, as it were, consistent mass, biologically equally primitive in all its parts, equally poorly endowed by nature, equally subjugated and living at the same low level of existence. The most abject Negro or Eskimo has an incomparably higher standard of living, enjoying infinitely richer material and cultural assets than these billions of civilised Newts. Yet there is nothing to suggest that the Newts suffer by it. On the contrary. We must surely see that they do not on the whole require any of those things which man needs to find relief and solace from his metaphysical terror and existential *angst*. They manage without philosophy, without life after death and without art; they do not know what imagination is, or humour, or mysticism, or play or dreams; they are absolute existential realists. They are as far removed from us humans as are ants or herrings; these they differ from merely in having adapted to a different living environment, namely human civilisation. They have settled in it as dogs have settled in human habitations; they cannot live without that environment but they do not cease to be what they are:

a very primitive and little differentiated animal group. It is sufficient to them to live and multiply; they can even be happy because they are not disturbed by any sense of inequality among them. They are, quite simply, homogeneous. Which is why, one day, indeed *any* day in the future, they may achieve without difficulty what mankind has failed to accomplish, their worldwide community, in short: universal Newtdom. That day will mark the end of the thousand-year-old agony of the human race. There will not be enough room on our planet for two trends, each trying to rule the whole world. One of them will have to yield. We already know which one that will be.

Today about 20 billion civilised Newts are living on the entire globe, or about ten times the number of humans; biological necessity as well as historical logic demand that the Newts, being subjugated, will have to liberate themselves; that, being homogeneous, they will have to unite; and that, thereby becoming the greatest power the world has ever seen, they will *have to* take over dominion over it. Do you believe they are foolish enough to spare man then? Do you believe they will repeat his historical mistake of subjecting defeated nations and classes instead of exterminating them? The mistake that out of selfishness man created ever new conflicts between people so that, out of magnanimity and idealism, he could then try to bridge them? No, Wolf Meynert exclaimed, the Newts will not commit *that* historical nonsense, if only because they will take heed of my book! They will be the inheritors of the whole of human civilisation; all that we have done and that we have attempted in our endeavours to rule the world will drop into their laps. But they would be defeating themselves if together with that heritage they attempted to take us over as well. They must rid themselves of man if they are to preserve their own homogeneity. Unless they do this we shall sooner or later introduce amongst them our own dual destructive proclivity: to create differences and to tolerate them. But we need have no fear of that: today no creature that will continue the history of mankind will repeat its suicidal madness.

There is no doubt that the Newt world will be happier than the human world was; it will be unified, homogeneous and governed by the same spirit. Newt will not differ from Newt in language, opinions, faith or demands on life. There will be among them neither cultural nor class divisions, but only the division of labour. There will be no masters and no slaves, for they will serve the Great Newt'Entity which will be their god, their ruler, their employer and their spiritual guide. There will be but one nation and but one standard. It will be a better and a more perfect world than ours was. It will be the only possibly Happy New World. Very well then, let us make room for it; there is nothing that expiring mankind can do now other than to accelerate its own demise – in tragic beauty, unless it is too late even for that.

We have here presented Wolf Meynert's views in the most accessible form possible; we are aware that, as a result, they lose a lot of their effectiveness and profundity which so fascinated the whole of Europe in their day, and especially the young who accepted the belief in the decline and impending end of mankind with such enthusiasm. True, the Reich government banned the teachings of the Great Pessimist because of certain political consequences and Wolf Meynert had to seek asylum in Switzerland; nevertheless, the entire educated world received Meynert's theory of the decline of mankind with satisfaction. The book (632 pages of it) was published in all world languages and many millions of copies were widely read also among the Newts.

6

A Warning from X

Perhaps it was also a result of Meynert's book that the literary
and artistic avant-garde at the centres of culture proclaimed
the slogan: After us the salamanders! The future belongs to
the Newts. The Newts are the cultural revolution. No matter
that they have no art of their own: at least they are not weighed
down by idiotic ideals, dry-as-dust traditions and all that
bombastic, boring, pedantic old rubbish that went by the name
of poetry, music, architecture, philosophy, and culture
generally – senile words that turn our stomachs. Fortunate
indeed that they have not yet succumbed to regurgitating
man's outmoded art; we shall create a new art for them! We
young ones will blaze a trail for worldwide salamandrism: we
want to be the first Newts, we are the salamanders of
tomorrow! Thus a young poetic movement came into being,
the salamandrian movement, and a new Tritonic (tri-tonic)
music, and pelagic painting, which drew its inspiration from
the plastic world of jellyfish, sea anemones and corals.
Moreover, the shore-regulating work of the Newts was seen
as a new source of beauty and monumentality. We are sick
and tired of nature, the cry went up; let us have smooth
concrete banks instead of the old rugged cliffs! Romanticism
is dead; the continents of the future will be bounded by clean
straight lines and reshaped into spherical triangles and rhombs;
the old geological world must be replaced by a geometric one.
In short, here was something new again, something futuristic,
new spiritual sensations and new cultural manifestos; those
who omitted to climb on the bandwagon of the coming
salamandrianism early on realised bitterly that they had missed
their chance and so took their revenge by proclaiming the pure
humanism, the return to man and to nature, and other
reactionary slogans. In Vienna a concert of Tritonic music
was booed out, in Paris at the Salon of the Independents an
unidentified culprit had slashed a pelagic painting called

Capriccio en bleu – in short, salamandrianism had begun its victorious and irresistible advance. Naturally there was no lack of reactionary voices who opposed the 'Newt mania', as they called it. The most fundamental in that respect was an anonymous English pamphlet published under the title *A Warning from X*. This brochure achieved considerable popularity but the identity of its author was never revealed; many people believed him to be a high dignitary of the Church, bearing in mind that in English X is an abbreviation for Christ.

In his first chapter the author attempted some statistics on the Newts, while at the same time apologising for the unreliability of his figures. Even the estimated total of all salamanders fluctuates at this moment between seven and twenty times the total human population of the world. Equally uncertain is our information on the number of factories, oil wells, algae plantations, eel farms, utilised water power and other natural resources owned by the Newts under water; we do not even have approximate data on the productive capacity of Newt industries; least of all do we have any information on the state of Newt armaments. We know, of course, that the salamanders are dependent on humans for their consumption of metals, machine parts, explosives and numerous chemicals; but, for one thing, all states keep the nature and the quantities of the arms they supply to the Newts strictly secret, and, for another, we know surprisingly little about what the Newts down in the depth of the sea actually manufacture from the semi-finished goods and the raw materials they buy from humans. It is certain that the salamanders do not want us to know these things; too many divers lowered to the sea-bed have perished in recent years, either by drowning or by asphyxiation, for their deaths to have been purely accidental. And this is truly an alarming situation both from an industrial and a military point of view.

It is, of course, difficult to imagine, X continued in subsequent paragraphs, what the Newts could or might wish to take from man. They cannot live on dry land, and we cannot on the whole prevent them from living the way they want under water. Their habitat and ours are precisely and permanently separated from each other. It is true, no doubt, that we require certain labour performances from them, but then we very largely feed them and supply them with raw materials and commodities which but for us they would not have at all, such as metals. But even though there are no practical grounds for any antagonism between us and the Newts, there exists, I would suggest, a metaphysical revulsion: surface creatures are confronted by creatures of the deep (abyssal creatures); creatures of the night are opposing the creatures of day; the dark watery pools against the bright dry earth. The demarcation line between water and land is somehow sharper than it used to be: *our* land is lapped by *their* water. We could survive perfectly well and forever in separate spheres, merely exchanging certain services and products – yet it is difficult to avoid the uneasy feeling that this is probably impossible. Why? I cannot give you definite reasons, but the feeling is there; it is something like a premonition that one day the watery world itself will turn against the dry land to settle the question of who rules whom.

I have to admit to a rather irrational anxiety, X continued, but I should feel a lot easier if the Newts came out with some demands on mankind. At least then one could negotiate with them, one might conclude various arrangements, agreements and compromises with them – but their silence is terrifying. I fear their incomprehensible reserve. They might, for example, demand certain political advantages for themselves: to be perfectly frank, Newt legislation everywhere is somewhat obsolete and no longer worthy of creatures as civilised or numerically as strong as they are. It would be proper to redefine afresh the rights and duties of the Newts, in a manner more favourable to them; one might consider some measure of autonomy for the salamanders; it would be only equitable to improve their working conditions and to recompense them more appropriately for their work. In many respects it would thus be possible to improve their lot *if only they would request it*. We could then make a number of concessions to them and bind them to us by compensatory agreements; at least we should be gaining a number of years. But the Newts do not request anything; they merely increase their productive performance and their orders; the time has come to ask ourselves where both these trends will stop. There used to be talk of a yellow peril, a black or a red peril – but those at least were humans and we have a more or less clear idea of

what humans can want. Yet even though at present we have
no inkling of what mankind will one day be forced to defend
itself against, one thing is clear already: that if the Newts will
be on one side, then the *whole* of mankind will be on the other.

Men against the Newts! It is high time the issue was put
this way. After all, to be perfectly honest, a normal person
instinctively hates the salamanders, he is nauseated by them
– and afraid of them. Something like a chilling shadow of
fear is descending on mankind everywhere. What else is that
frenetic indulgence, that insatiable thirst for amusement and
pleasure, that orgiastic licence that has seized present-day
humanity? There has not been such moral decadence since
the days when barbarian invasion was about to fall upon the
Roman Empire. This is not just the fruit of unprecedented
material prosperity but a desperate drowning of the voice of
fear of disintegration and annihilation. One last cup before
we meet our end! What shame, what delirium! It seems that
God in his awful mercy is allowing nations and classes first
to deteriorate as they rush to their ruin. Do you wish to read
the fiery *Mene-tekel* written up above mankind's great feast?
Just look at the luminous inscriptions which throughout the
night shine on the walls of our dissolute and profligate cities!
In that respect we humans are already approaching the Newts:
we live more by night than by day.

If only those salamanders weren't so terribly mediocre, X
rather unhappily blurted out. Yes, they are more or less
educated – but that makes them even more blinkered because
they have acquired from human civilisation only that which
is mediocre and utilitarian in it, mechanical and repeatable.
They stand beside mankind as the famulus Wagner stands
beside Faustus: their learning comes from the same books as
that of the human Faustuses but with the difference that to
them they are sufficient and that they are not gnawed by any
doubt. The most terrible thing is that they have multiplied
that half-educated, brainless and smug type of civilised
mediocrity on a vast scale, in millions and billions of identical
specimens. But no, I am wrong: the most terrible thing is that
they are so successful. They have learned how to use machines
and numbers, and it became obvious that that was enough
for them to become masters of their world. They have omitted
from human civilisation everything that was aimless, playful,

fantastic or ancient; as a result they have omitted everything that was human in it and adopted solely its practical, technical and utilitarian side. And that pitiful caricature of human civilisation is doing splendidly: it is building technological miracles, renewing our ancient planet, and eventually fascinating mankind itself. From his disciple and servant Faustus will learn the secret of success and of mediocrity. Either mankind will face up to the Newts in a history-making life-and-death conflict or it will be irrevocably salamandrised. For my part, X concluded sadly, I would rather see the former.

Well, take heed of X's warning, the unknown author continued. It is still possible to shake off that cold and slimy grip in which we are all held. We must rid ourselves of the salamanders. There are too many of them already; they are well armed and capable of turning on us war material of whose overall strength we know virtually nothing. But a more terrible danger to us than their numbers and strength is their successful, and indeed triumphal, inferiority. I do not know which we should fear more: their human civilisation or their insidious, cold and bestial cruelty; but the two together represent something unimaginably terrifying and almost diabolical. In the name of culture, in the name of Christianity and humanity we must free ourselves from the Newts. And here the anonymous apostle exclaimed:

You fools, stop feeding the Newts! Stop employing them, dispense with their services, let them emigrate to wherever they can feed themselves like other marine creatures! Nature itself will deal with their excessive numbers: if only man, human civilisation and human history will at last stop *working for the salamanders*!

And stop supplying the Newts with arms, put an end to supplying them with metals and high explosives, stop sending them machines and human manufactures! You would not supply teeth to tigers or venom to snakes; you would not light fires under a volcano or breach flood-protection dams. Let an embargo be imposed on supplies to all the oceans, let the Newts be put outside the law, let them be accursed and excluded from our world, *let a Union of Nations against Newts be set up!*

Let all mankind be ready to defend its existence weapon in hand; let a world conference of all civilised countries be convened on the initiative of the League of Nations, the King

of Sweden or the Pope of Rome, to form a World Union or
at least a Club of all Christian nations against the salamanders!
This is the fateful moment when, faced with the terrible pressure of the Newt danger and human responsibility, we may
succeed in achieving what the world war with its countless victims failed to achieve – the creation of a United States of the
World. May God grant it! If *that* were achieved then the Newts
would not have come in vain but would have been the instrument of God.

This eloquent pamphlet produced a lively echo among broad
circles of the public. Elderly ladies agreed chiefly with the point
that an unprecedented decline of morals had set in. Business
columnists in the daily press, on the other hand, pointed out
that it was impossible to restrict deliveries to the Newts since
this would cause a huge drop in production and a serious
depression in numerous branches of human industry. Agriculture, too, relied heavily on vast orders of maize, potatoes and
other crops for Newt feeding stuffs; any reduction in the number of salamanders would result in a serious decline in the foodstuffs market and reduce farmers to the brink of ruin. The
workers' trade unions suspected Mr X of being a reactionary
and announced that they would not tolerate any restrictions on
the export of goods destined for the Newts; no sooner had the
working people achieved full employment and performance
bonuses than Mr X wanted to take the bread out of their
mouths; the working class sided with the Newts and repudiated
any attempt to reduce their living standards and to surrender
them pauperised and defenceless to the mercy of capitalism. As
for the Union of Nations against Newts, all responsible political
bodies objected that this would be unnecessary; after all, there
already was the League of Nations and the London
Convention under which the maritime states had undertaken
not to supply heavy armaments to their Newts. Naturally one
could not very well expect any state to disarm unless it had
a guarantee that another maritime power was not secretly
arming its Newts and thereby increasing its military potential
at the expense of its neighbours. Nor could any state or
continent compel its Newts to emigrate elsewhere because this
would increase not only the industrial and agricultural markets
of other states and continents but also their military strength;

and this would be most undesirable. And there were many more such objections of a kind that any reasonable person would have to agree with.

Nevertheless, the pamphlet, *A Warning from X*, could not fail to leave a deep impression. Nearly everywhere a populist anti-Newt movement was gaining ground, and Associations for the Liquidation of Newts, Anti-Salamander Clubs, Committees for the Defence of Mankind and many other similar organisations were set up. The Newt delegates were insulted in Geneva on their way to the twelve-hundred-and-thirteenth meeting of the Commission for the Study of the Newt Question. The close-boarded fences along the seashores had threatening slogans painted on them, such as Death to Newts, Down with Salamanders, and the like. Many Newts were stoned to death; no salamander dared raise its head out of the water in daylight. In spite of that there were no protest manifestations or acts of revenge from *their* side. They were simply invisible, at least during the day; and people who peeped over the Newt fences saw only the infinite and indifferently murmuring sea. 'Look at those bastards,' people were saying spitefully; 'won't even show their faces!'

And into that oppressive silence erupted the so-called *Louisiana Earthquake*.

7

The Louisiana Earthquake

That day – it was 11 November at one o'clock in the morning – a sharp earth tremor was felt in New Orleans; several shanties in the Negro quarter collapsed; people ran out into the streets in panic but the tremors did not recur; there was only a violent squall, a brief howling cyclone, which smashed windows and lifted roofs in the narrow Negro streets; a few dozen people were killed; then a heavy rain of mud descended.

While the New Orleans fire brigades drove out to the worst hit streets, the telegraphs chattered with incoming messages from Morgan City, Plaquemine, Baton Rouge and Lafayette: SOS! Send rescue parties! Half the place swept away by earthquake and cyclone; Mississippi dykes in danger of collapsing. Send immediately earthwork teams, ambulances and all men capable of work! – From Fort Livingston came only the laconic inquiry: Hi, are you in the shit too? – then came a signal from Lafayette: Attention, attention! Worst hit spot New Iberia. Communications appear severed between New Iberia and Morgan City. Help needed there! – A moment later Morgan City came through on the telephone: Have lost contact with New Iberia. Highway and railroad presumed cut. Send ships and aircraft to Vermilion Bay! We are OK for supplies. Have about thirty dead and 100 injured. – Presently a telegram came from Baton Rouge: New Iberia reported worst hit. Send assistance to New Iberia. We only need workmen, but fast; our dykes now cracking. Doing all we can. – A little later: Hello, hello, Shreveport, Natchitoches, Alexandria sending relief trains to New Iberia. Hello, hello, Memphis, Winona, Jackson sending trains via New Orleans. All cars carrying people direction Baton Rouge dam. – Hello, Pascagoula calling. Have several dead. Do you need help?

By then fire trucks, ambulances and rescue trains were on their way to Morgan City – Patterson – Franklin. After 4 a.m. came the first detailed report: Track between Franklin and New Iberia, seven kilometres west of Franklin, cut by water; appears that earthquake opened up deep fissure running into Vermilion Bay which has become flooded by sea. As far as has been possible to establish so far, the fissure runs from Vermilion Bay in an east-north-easterly direction, near Franklin it turns north, running into Grand Lake, extending thence further north to a line Plaquemine–Lafayette, where it ends in a small ancient lake; a second arm of the fissure connects Grand Lake to the west with Lake Napoleonville. Total length of subsidence about eighty kilometres, width two to eleven kilometres. Epicentre of earthquake was evidently here. By amazing good fortune fissure avoided all major settlements. Even so, loss of life considerable. In Franklin sixty centimetres of mud rained down, in Patterson forty-five centimetres. People from Atchafalaya Bay state that during tremor sea receded by about three kilometres, thereupon came hurtling back towards shore with wave thirty metres high. Fears that many people killed on shore. Still no contact with New Iberia.

Train with the Natchitoches party meanwhile approaching New Iberia from west; first reports, routed via Lafayette and Baton Rouge, frightful. Some kilometres short of New Iberia train was halted because track buried in mud. Refugees relate that about two kilometres east of the city a mud volcano appeared and instantly threw up masses of thin cold mud; New Iberia, they say, has disappeared under deluge of mud. Further progress in darkness and continuing rain exceedingly difficult. Still no contact with New Iberia.

Simultaneously a message came in from Baton Rouge:

SEVERAL THOUSAND MEN NOW WORKING ON MISSISSIPPI DYKES STOP   IF ONLY IT STOPPED RAINING   STOP   WE   NEED   PICKS   SHOVELS TRUCKS PEOPLE STOP   ARE SENDING HELP TO PLAQUEMINE: WATER RUNNING OVER THE TOP OF THEIR BOOTS POOR BASTARDS.

Telegram from Fort Jackson:

AT HALF PAST ONE A.M. SEA WAVE SWEPT AWAY THIRTY HOUSES NO IDEA WHAT IT WAS ABOUT SEVENTY PEOPLE WASHED AWAY HAVE

ONLY JUST FIXED TRANSMITTER POST OFFICE ALSO BASHED ABOUT HELLO CABLE IMMEDIATELY WHAT THE DAMN THING WAS FRED DALTON TELEGRAPHIST HELLO INFORM MINNIE LACOSTE THAT I AM OK ONLY BROKEN WRIST AND CLOTHES WASHED AWAY MAIN THING TRANSMITTER OK AGAIN FRED.

The most concise message came from Port Eads:

SEVERAL KILLED BURYWOOD ALL SWEPT OUT TO SEA.

Meanwhile – it was now about eight in the morning – the first planes sent out to the stricken areas were returning. The entire coast from Port Arthur (Texas) to Mobile (Alabama) was reported to have been flooded by a tidal wave during the night; there were wrecked or damaged houses everywhere. South-eastern Louisiana (from the Lake Charles – Alexandria–Natchez highway) and southern Mississippi (up to the line Jackson–Hattiesburg–Pascagoula) were covered with mud. A new inlet had opened up from Vermilion Bay approximately three to ten kilometres wide, running inland like a long zigzag fjord almost as far as Plaquemine. New Iberia seemed to have been badly affected but a lot of people could be seen shovelling away the mud that was covering houses and roads. It had been impossible to land. The heaviest loss of life was probably on the coast. Off Point au Fer a steamship was sinking, presumed to be Mexican. Near Chandeleur Islands the sea was covered with wreckage. The rain was easing throughout the region. Visibility good.

The first special editions of the New Orleans papers came out soon after four in the morning; as the day wore on later editions carried further details; by eight o'clock the papers had photographs of the stricken area and maps of the new inlet of the sea. At half past eight they published an interview on the causes of the Louisiana earthquake with Dr Wilbur R. Brownell, a leading seismologist from Memphis University. It was too soon for any definitive conclusions, the scientist stated, but it would seem that the tremors were unconnected with the volcanic activity still occurring in the Central

American volcanic belt situated opposite the affected area. Today's earthquake seemed instead to be of tectonic origin, i.e. it had been caused by the pressure of mountain masses – the Rocky Mountains and Sierra Madre on the one side and the Appalachian range on the other – on the extensive depression of the Gulf of Mexico of which the wide plain of the Mississippi delta was a continuation. The fissure now running out of Vermilion Bay was but a new and relatively insignificant rift, a minor episode in the geological downward movement that had created the Gulf of Mexico and the Caribbean Sea with the arc of the Greater and Lesser Antilles, that remnant of an ancient continuous mountain range. There was no doubt that the Central American subsidence would continue, bringing new tremors, faults and fissures. It could not be ruled out that the Vermilion fissure was a mere prelude to a revival of tectonic activity centred on the Gulf of Mexico. In that event we might witness enormous geological catastrophes with almost one-fifth of the United States sinking below the sea. On the other hand, if that were to happen, we could expect, with a high degree of probability, that the sea-floor in the neighbourhood of the Antilles would begin to rise instead, or even further to the east where ancient legend spoke of a drowned Atlantis.

Nevertheless, the eminent scientist continued reassuringly, there was no reason to take seriously any fears of imminent volcanic activity in the affected area; the supposed craters ejecting mud were nothing but eruptions of swamp gases associated with the Vermilion fissure. It would not be surprising if huge underground gas bubbles existed in the Mississippi alluvium: these might explode on contact with the air and throw up hundreds of tons of water and mud. Naturally, Dr W. R. Brownell repeated, a definitive explanation would have to await further developments.

While Brownell's prognostications of geological catastrophes were running through the rotary presses, the Governor of the state of Louisiana received from Fort Jackson a telegram with the following text:

REGRET LOSS OF HUMAN LIVES STOP WE TRIED TO AVOID YOUR CITIES BUT DID NOT EXPECT REBOUND AND IMPACT OF TIDAL

WAVE AFTER EXPLOSION STOP HAVE
ASCERTAINED THREE HUNDRED AND FORTY-
SIX FATAL HUMAN CASUALTIES ALONG ENTIRE
COAST STOP   ACCEPT DEEP SYMPATHY STOP
CHIEF SALAMANDER STOP HELLO HELLO THIS
IS FRED DALTON CALLING FROM FORT
JACKSON POST OFFICE THREE NEWTS HAVE
JUST LEFT HERE: ARRIVED AT POST OFFICE
TEN MINUTES AGO HANDED IN TELEGRAM
WHILE AIMING PISTOLS AT ME BUT HAVE
GONE NOW HIDEOUS CREATURES PAID UP AND
RUSHED INTO WATER CHASED BY DOCTOR'S
DOG SHOULDN'T BE ALLOWED TO WALK
ABOUT TOWN OTHERWISE NO FURTHER NEWS
GIVE MY LOVE AND KISSES TO MINNIE
LACOSTE FRED DALTON TELEGRAPHIST

For a long while the Governor of the state of Louisiana
shook his head over that telegram. Some joker, that Fred
Dalton, he said to himself at last. Better not put it in the
papers.

8

The Chief Salamander Presents His Demands

Three days after the Louisiana earthquake a new geological disaster was reported, this time from China. With a massive thunderous earth tremor the coast in Kingsu province had burst open north of Nanking, about halfway between the Yangtse estuary and the ancient bed of the Hwang-ho. The sea had rushed into the breach and linked up with the big lakes Pan-jün and Hung-tsu between the cities of Hwaingan and Fugjang. It seemed that as a result of the earthquake the Yangtse had shifted its river-bed below Nanking, flowing instead towards Lake Tai and on to Hangchow. No estimate, even approximate, could yet be made of the loss of life. Hundreds of thousands were fleeing into the northern and southern provinces. Japanese warships had been ordered to make for the stricken coast.

Although the scale of the earthquake in Kiangsu greatly exceeded the disaster in Louisiana it received little attention on the whole: the world was accustomed to catastrophes in China and, so it seemed, the odd million lives did not matter greatly there. Besides, it was scientifically obvious that this was a mere tectonic earthquake, associated with a deep ocean trench near the Riukiu and Philippine archipelagos. Three days later, however, European seismographs registered renewed tremors with an epicentre somewhere near the Cape Verde Islands. More detailed reports stated that a severe earthquake had hit the Senegambian coast south of St Luis. A deep subsidence had occurred between the towns of Lampul and Mboro; this was flooded by the sea which penetrated as far as Meringhen and the Dimara wadis. According to eye-witness accounts a column of fire and steam had burst from the ground, accompanied by a frightful rumble, flinging sand and stones over a wide radius; after that the sea was heard rushing into the opened rift. Loss of life was not heavy.

This third earthquake caused something akin to panic. IS VOLCANIC ACTIVITY REVIVING ON EARTH? the newspapers asked. EARTH'S CRUST BEGINNING TO CRACK, reported the evening papers. The experts suggested that the 'Senegambian rift' might have been caused by the eruption of a volcanic vein associated with the Pico volcano on Fogo Island in the Cape Verde archipelago; that volcano had last erupted in 1847 and had since been regarded as extinct. The West African earthquake, therefore, had nothing in common with the seismic phenomena in Louisiana or Kiangsu, which had evidently been of a tectonic character. People, however, did not seem to care greatly whether it was as a result of tectonic or volcanic causes that the earth was cracking. The fact was that churches everywhere were crowded with people who had come to pray. In some parts even the churches had to be kept open at night.

About one o'clock in the morning – that was on 20 November – radio hams throughout most of Europe observed heavy interference on their receivers, just as if some new, unusually powerful transmitter had gone into operation. They found it on a wavelength of 203; there was a rushing noise as though from machinery or the waves of the sea. From that protracted unending hum suddenly came a terrible croaking voice (they all described it in similar terms: hollow, quacking, as if artificial, and simultaneously enormously magnified by a loudspeaker), and that froglike voice shouted excitedly: 'Hello, hello, hello! the Chief Salamander speaking. Hello, the Chief Salamander speaking. Stop all broadcasting, you men! Stop your broadcasting! Hello, the Chief Salamander speaking!' Then another strangely hollow voice asked: 'Ready?' 'Ready.' Next came a click as if a circuit was being switched, and again another unnaturally squawky voice called: 'Attention! Attention! Attention!' 'Hello!' 'Now!'

And now a croaky, weary, but nevertheless commanding voice broke the nocturnal silence: 'Hello, you humans! Louisiana calling. Kiangsu calling. Senegambia calling. We regret the loss of human lives. We do not wish to inflict unnecessary losses on you. We only want you to evacuate the seashores in the places we shall notify you of from time to time. If you conform you will avoid regrettable accidents. Next time we shall give you at least a fortnight's advance warning

of the areas where we will enlarge our sea. So far we merely
have been conducting technical experiments. Your high
explosives have worked well. Thank you.

'Hello, you people! No need for alarm. We have no hostile
intentions towards you. We only need more water, more
coasts, more shallows to live in. There are too many of us.
There's no longer enough room for us on your coasts. That's
why we have to dismantle your continents. We shall turn them
all into bays and islands. In this way the overall length of the
world's shorelines can be increased by a factor of five. We
shall construct new shallows. We cannot live in the deep ocean.
We shall need your continents as in-fill material. We have
nothing against you but there are too many of us. For the
time being you can move inland. You can move up into the
mountains. The mountains will be demolished last.

'You wanted us. You spread us all over the globe. Now
you've got us. We want to be on good terms with you. You
will supply us with steel for our drills and picks. You will
supply us with high explosives. You will supply us with
torpedoes. You will work for us. Without you we cannot
remove the old continents. Hello, you people. On behalf of
the Newts of all the world the Chief Salamander offers you
co-operation. You will work with us on the demolition of your
world. We thank you.'

The weary croaky voice fell silent and a protracted hum
was heard as of machinery or the sea. 'Hello, hello, you
people,' the squawky voice spoke up again; 'and now you'll
hear a programme of light music from your gramophone
records. We start with 'The March of the Tritons' from the
film spectacular *Poseidon*.

The newspapers, of course, described this nocturnal broadcast
as a 'crude joke in poor taste' by some pirate transmitter.
Nevertheless, millions of people sat by their radio receivers
the following night, waiting to hear whether that frightening,
fanatic, squawky voice would speak again. It came on the air
at exactly one o'clock to the accompaniment of a loud splashing
and rushing noise. 'Good evening, you people,' it squeaked
cheerfully. 'To start with we shall play for you a recording
of the Salamander Dance from your operetta *Galathea*.' When
the penetrating and shameless music was over the same

frightful yet somehow joyful squawky voice returned. 'Hello, you people! A moment ago the British gunboat *Erebus* which tried to destroy our transmitter station on the Atlantic Ocean was sunk by a torpedo. The crew were drowned. Hello, we are calling the British government: stand by your loudspeakers. The ship *Amenhotep*, home port Port Said, refused to hand over to us at our port of Makallah the high explosives we had ordered. She claimed to have received orders to stop all further shipments of explosives. The ship, of course, was sunk. We advise the British government to revoke that order by tomorrow morning; otherwise the ships *Winnipeg*, *Manitoba*, *Ontario* and *Quebec*, all of them en route from Canada to Liverpool with cargoes of grain, will be sunk. Hello, we are calling the French government: stand by your loudspeakers. Recall the cruisers now sailing towards Senegambia. We still need to widen the newly formed inlet there. The Chief Salamander has instructed me to convey to both governments his unshakable wish to establish with them the most friendly relations. This is the end of the news. We shall now broadcast a recording of your song ''Salamandria, valse érotique''.'

The following afternoon the ships *Winnipeg*, *Manitoba*, *Ontario* and *Quebec* were sunk south-west of Mizen Head. A wave of horror swept over the world. In the evening the BBC announced that His Majesty's Government had issued an order prohibiting the supply to the Newts of any kind of foodstuffs, chemicals, equipment, weapons or metals. At one o'clock at night an excited voice squawked on the radio: 'Hello, hello, hello, the Chief Salamander speaking! Hello, the Chief Salamander is about to speak!' And then came that weary, croaky, angry voice: 'Hello, you people! Hello, you people! Hello, you people! Do you think we shall allow ourselves to be starved out? Stop your nonsense at once! Any action you take will rebound on you! In the name of all Newts everywhere I am addressing Great Britain. From now on we are imposing a total blockade of the British Isles with the exception of the Irish Free State. I am closing the English Channel. I am closing the Suez Canal. I am closing the Straits of Gibraltar to all shipping. All British ports are closed. All British ships in whatever sea they may be will be torpedoed. Hello, I am addressing Germany. I am increasing my order for high explosives tenfold. To be delivered immediately to the Skagerak main depot. Hello, I am addressing France. Speed up deliveries of the ordered torpedoes to submarine forts C-3, BFF and Ouest-5. Hello, you people! I am warning you. If you restrict deliveries of foodstuffs to us I shall commandeer them myself from your ships. I am warning you again.' The weary voice sank to a husky, scarcely comprehensible croak. 'Hello, hello, I am addressing Italy. Prepare to evacuate the region Venice–Padua–Udine. This is my final warning, you people. We've had enough of your nonsense.' There followed a lengthy pause, with a background rushing as of a black and cold sea. Then the cheerful, squawky voice was back again: 'And now, again from one of your recordings, we shall play that latest success, ''The Triton Trot''.'

9

The Vaduz Conference

It was an odd sort of war, if indeed it can be called a war since there was no Newt state nor any recognised Newt government against which war might be formally declared. The first country that found itself in a state of war with the salamanders was Great Britain. During the very first hours the Newts sank virtually all her ships anchored in ports anywhere; there was no way of offering resistance. Only vessels on the high seas were relatively safe for the moment, especially if they were cruising over the deeper ocean areas; thus that section of the British Navy was saved which broke through the blockade of Malta and concentrated above the Ionian Deep. But even these units were soon tracked down by small Newt submarines and sunk one by one. Within the first six weeks Britain lost four-fifths of all her tonnage.

Not for the first time in history did John Bull reveal his famous tenacity. His Majesty's Government did not negotiate with the Newts nor did it revoke its embargo on supplies. 'A British gentleman,' the Prime Minister declared, speaking for the whole nation, 'will protect animals but he does not negotiate with them.' Within a few weeks there was a desperate shortage of food in the British Isles. Only children received a small slice of bread and a few spoonfuls of tea or milk daily; the British people bore it all with exemplary fortitude, even though they sank so low as to eat all their racehorses. The Prince of Wales with his own hands ploughed the first furrow on the links of the Royal Golf Club, for carrots to be raised for the London orphanages. The tennis courts at Wimbledon were planted with potatoes, the racecourse at Ascot was sown to wheat. 'We shall make any sacrifices, even the heaviest,' the leader of the Conservative Party assured Parliament, 'but we will not surrender British honour.'

Because the blockade of the British sea coasts was complete, Britain was left with but one way of importing supplies and maintaining contact with the colonies, and that was by air. 'We must have 100,000 aircraft,' the Air Minister announced, and anyone possessing hands and feet placed themselves in the service of that slogan. Feverish preparations were made to ensure a daily output of 1,000 aircraft; but that was where the governments of the other European states intervened with sharp protests against a violation of the balance in the air; the British government had to desist from its air programme and undertake not to build more than 20,000 aircraft, and that only over a period of five years. So there was no alternative to continuing to go hungry or to paying horrendous prices for foodstuffs supplied by the aircraft of other countries; a pound loaf cost ten shillings, a brace of rats one guinea, a tin of caviare twenty-five pounds. This was a great time for continental trade, industry and agriculture. As the navy had been eliminated from the start, military operations against the Newts were conducted on land and from the air. The land forces fired their guns and machine-guns into the water, without, however, seeming to inflict any significant losses on the salamanders. Aerial bombardment of the sea was a little more successful. The Newts retaliated by shelling the British ports with their underwater guns, reducing them to heaps of rubble. They also shelled London from the Thames Estuary, whereupon army command made an attempt to poison the salamanders with bacteria, crude oil and caustic substances poured into the Thames and into certain bays of the sea. To this the Newts replied by releasing a screen of poison gas over one hundred and twenty kilometres of British coastline. It was only a demonstration but it sufficed: for the first time in history the British government was obliged to request other powers to intervene, referring to the prohibition of gas warfare.

The following night the croaky, angry and heavy voice of the Chief Salamander again came on the air: 'Hello, you people! Britain had better stop her nonsense! If you poison our water we will poison your air. We are only using your own weapons. We are no barbarians. We don't want to make war on humans. We don't want anything except our right to live. We are offering you peace. You will supply us with your manufactures and you will sell us your continents. We are willing to pay a fair price for them. We are offering you nothing but peace. We are offering you gold for your lands.

Hello, I am addressing Great Britain. Notify me of your price for the southern part of Lincolnshire along the Wash. You have three days to consider it. For that period I am suspending all hostilities except the blockade.' At that moment the underwater artillery barrage fell silent. So did the guns on shore. It was a strange, almost frightening, silence. The British government announced in Parliament that it did not intend to negotiate with the Newts. The population along the Wash and the Lynn Deep were warned of the probability of a major Newt attack, advised to evacuate their homes and move inland; however, the trains, cars and buses supplied for the purpose removed only the children and a few of the women. All the men stayed put; they simply could not believe that an Englishman could lose his land. A minute before the expiry of the three-day armistice the first shot rang out: this was a shot fired by a British gun of the Loyal North Lancashire Regiment to the accompaniment of its regimental march, 'The Red Rose'. An instant later came a colossal explosion. The mouth of the river Nene sank all the way up to Wisbech and was flooded by the sea from the Wash. The famous ruins of Wisbech Abbey vanished under the waves, as did Holland Castle, the George and Dragon inn, together with other memorable buildings.

The next day the British government, in reply to a Commons question, stated that, from a military point of view, everything possible had been done to protect the British coast; however, further and much more extensive attacks on British territory could not be ruled out. Nevertheless, His Majesty's Government could not negotiate with an enemy who waged war on civilians and women. (Hear, hear.) What was at stake was no longer the fate of Britain but that of the whole civilised world. Britain was ready to consider international guarantees to limit these terrible and barbarian attacks, which represented a menace to mankind itself.

A few weeks subsequently a world conference of states met in Vaduz.

It was held in Vaduz because there was no danger from the Newts in the High Alps and also because the majority of wealthy and socially important people from coastal regions had already settled there. The conference, as was universally conceded, got down very briskly to the resolution of all topical international issues. In the first place, all countries (except Switzerland, Abyssinia, Afghanistan, Bolivia and other land-locked states) refused as a matter of principle to recognise the Newts as a sovereign belligerent power, mainly because if they did so their own salamanders might regard themselves as members of such a Newt state. It could not be ruled out that a Newt state, if recognised, might attempt to exercise sovereignty over all waters and coasts inhabited by Newts. For that reason it was both legally and practically impossible to declare war on the salamanders or to bring any international pressure to bear on them; each state was entitled only to take action against *its own* Newts; it was, in fact, a purely domestic matter. For that reason there could be no question of any collective diplomatic or military action against the Newts. The only international aid that could be given to states attacked by the salamanders was the granting of foreign loans for their successful defence.

Britain thereupon submitted a proposal that all states should at least undertake not to supply weapons or explosives to the Newts. After mature deliberation the proposal was turned down, mainly because such an undertaking was already contained in the London Convention but also, secondly, because a country could not be prevented from supplying to its own Newts technical equipment 'solely for their own requirements' and arms for the defence of their own coasts; thirdly, because maritime countries were 'naturally interested in maintaining good relations with the denizens of the sea' and therefore considered it desirable 'to refrain at this moment from any measures which the Newts might regard as discriminatory'. Nevertheless, all states were prepared to vouchsafe that they would supply weapons and high explosives also to the states attacked by the Newts.

In confidential discussion a Columbian proposal was adopted to the effect that at least unofficial talks should be initiated with the Newts. The Chief Salamander would be invited to send his plenipotentiaries to the conference. The British representative strongly objected to this, refusing to sit at the same table as the Newts; in the end, however, he agreed to absent himself by taking a trip to the Engadine for reasons of health. That night all maritime countries broadcast in their official codes an invitation to His Excellency the Chief Salamander to nominate his representatives and send them to Vaduz. His reply was a croaking 'Yes; this time we'll still come to you; next time your delegates will come into the water to see me.' This was followed by a brief official announcement: 'The authorised representatives of the Newts will arrive at Buchs by the Orient Express in the evening of the day after tomorrow.'

All preparations for the arrival of the Newts were made with the greatest possible haste; the most luxurious bathrooms were got ready in Vaduz and a special train brought in tank-wagons of sea-water for the delegates' bath-tubs. On the platform at Buchs in the evening there would only be a so-called unofficial welcome; only the secretaries of the delegations would be present, together with the representatives of the local authorities and about two hundred journalists, photographers and film cameramen. At precisely 6.25 p.m. the Orient Express pulled into the station. From the saloon car three elegant tall gentlemen stepped out on to the red carpet, followed by a number of perfectly groomed secretaries, evidently men of the world, with heavy briefcases. 'And where are the Newts?' someone asked in a low voice. Two or three official personages advanced a little uncertainly towards the three gentlemen; but already the first of them said under his breath and in a low voice: 'We are the Newt delegation. I am Professor Van Dott from the Hague. Maître Rosso Castelli, an attorney from Paris. Doctor Manoel Carvalho, an attorney from Lisbon.' The gentlemen bowed and made their introductions. 'So you aren't Newts,' the French secretary breathed. 'Of course not,' said Dr Rosso Castelli. 'We are their lawyers. I am sorry – these gentlemen here are probably wanting to film the scene.' So the smiling Newt delegation was eagerly filmed and photographed. The Legation secretaries present also showed their satisfaction. Very sensible and decent of those salamanders to send humans to represent them. It's always easier to talk to humans. Most importantly, a certain amount of unpleasant social embarrassment is avoided.

That very night the first meeting was held with the Newt delegation. On the agenda was the question of how peace could most speedily be restored between the Newts and Great

Britain. Professor Van Dott requested permission to speak. It was incontestable, he said, that the Newts had been attacked by Great Britain: the British gunboat *Erebus* had attacked the Newts' transmitter boat on the open sea; the British Admiralty had violated business relations with the Newts by preventing the ship *Amenhotep* from unloading a cargo of explosives which had been ordered; thirdly, by its embargo on all deliveries the British government had initiated a blockade of the salamanders. The Newts had not been able to complain about these hostile actions either at the Hague, since the London Convention did not grant to the Newts the right to lodge complaints, or in Geneva, since they were not members of the League of Nations. Hence they had no alternative but to resort to self-defence. Nevertheless, the Chief Salamander was willing to suspend all hostilities, but only on these conditions: (1) Great Britain will apologise to the Newts for the above-mentioned wrongs; (2) she will revoke all bans on deliveries to the Newts; (3) as reparation she will cede to the salamanders, without compensation, the low-lying river lands of the Punjab, where the Newts could establish new coasts and marine bays. – The chairman of the conference thereupon announced that he would report these conditions to his esteemed colleague, the representative of Great Britain, who happened to be absent at that moment; he could not, however, disguise his fear that these terms would scarcely be found acceptable. Nevertheless, it seemed reasonable to hope that they could be seen as a basis for further discussions.

The next item on the agenda was a complaint by France in the matter of the Senegambian coast which the Newts had blown up, thereby interfering with French colonial rule. The famous Paris attorney Dr Julien Rosso Castelli, representing the Newts, asked for the floor. 'Prove it,' he said. The world's greatest experts in the field of seismography had given it as their opinion that the earthquake in Senegambia had been of volcanic origin and associated with the ancient volcanic activity of the Pico volcano on Fogo Island. 'Here,' exclaimed Dr Rosso Castelli, bringing his palm down with a smack on his file, 'is their expert scientific opinion. If you possess proof that the Senegambian earthquake was due to my clients' activities, please gentlemen, I am waiting to see it.'

The Belgian delegate, Creux: 'Your Chief Salamander himself announced that the Newts had done it!'

Professor Van Dott: 'His statement was unofficial.'

Maître Rosso Castelli: 'We are instructed to deny his statement just referred to. I demand that the technical experts be heard on whether it is possible to create artificially a sixty-seven kilometre rift in the earth's crust. I suggest that they should give us a practical demonstration on the same scale. In the absence of any such proof, gentlemen, we shall speak of volcanic activity. Nevertheless, the Chief Salamander is willing to purchase from the French government the marine inlet which has formed in the Senegambian rift and which is suitable for the establishment of a Newt colony. We are authorised to agree a price with the French government.'

Minister Deval, the French delegate: 'If we are to view this as compensation for the damage caused, we might talk about it.'

Maître Rosso Castelli. 'Very well. The Newt government, however, demands that the purchasing contract include also the Landes region from the Gironde estuary to Bayonne, an area of 6,720 square kilometres. In other words, the Newt government is willing to purchase from France this part of her southern French soil.'

Minister Deval (a native of Bayonne and Deputy for Bayonne): 'So that your Newts can turn a piece of France into the sea-bed? Never! Never!'

Dr Rosso Castelli: 'France will come to regret those words, sir. Today we were still offering a purchasing price.'

The meeting was thereupon suspended.

At the next sitting the subject under discussion was a major international package offered to the Newts: instead of their unacceptable destruction of old, densely populated continents they should construct new coasts and islands for themselves; in that event ample credits would be offered to them, and the new continents and islands would be recognised as their independent and sovereign state territory.

Dr Manoel Carvalho, the great Lisbon lawyer, expressed his thanks for this offer which he would convey to the Newt government. But any child would understand that the construction of new continents was far more laborious and costly than demolishing existing land. His clients needed new coasts and bays within the shortest possible time; to them this was a matter of life and death. Mankind would be wise to accept the generous offer of the Chief Salamander who, at this moment, was still willing to purchase the world from mankind rather than seize it by force. His clients had discovered a process for extracting the gold contained in sea-water; in consequence they had available to them virtually unlimited financial means; they were in a position to offer a good, indeed an excellent, price for the human world. You may be sure, he continued, that in the course of time the value of the world will decline, especially if, as might be expected, further volcanic or tectonic disasters were to occur, far more extensive than the ones we have so far witnessed; as a result of them, moreover, the surface of the continents was being diminished. Today the world may still be sold with its full present dimensions; once only the ruins of mountains remain above the water's surface, no one is going to give you a brass farthing for it! 'True, I stand here as the representative and legal adviser of the Newts,' Dr Carvalho exclaimed, 'and I must protect *their* interests: but I am a man like you, gentlemen, and the good of the human race is as close to my heart as it is to yours. That is why I advise you, nay, implore you: sell your continents while there is time! You may sell them in their entirety or in lots of individual countries. The Chief Salamander, whose magnanimous and modern thinking is by now universally known, undertakes that in all future necessary alterations to the earth's surface he will, as far as possible, spare human life; flooding will be conducted in easy stages and in such a way that no panic or unnecessary catastrophes are created. We are empowered to embark on negotiations, either with this revered world conference as a whole or with individual countries. The presence of such outstanding lawyers as Professor Van Dott or Maître Julien Rosso Castelli should be a guarantee to you that, alongside the just interests of our clients, the Newts, we shall, hand in hand with you, defend what is most dear to all of us: human culture and the good of mankind as a whole.'

In a somewhat depressed atmosphere another proposal was put on the agenda: that Central China be yielded to the salamanders for inundation. In return the Newts would undertake to guarantee in perpetuity the coasts of the European states and their colonies.

Dr Rosso Castelli: 'In perpetuity is a trifle on the long side. Shall we say for twenty years?'

Professor Van Dott: 'Central China is a trifle on the small side. Shall we say the provinces of Nganhuei, Honan, Kiangsu, Chi-li and Föng-tien?'

The Japanese representative protested against the cession of Föng-tien province which was situated within the Japanese sphere of interest. The Chinese delegate was given the floor, but unfortunately nobody understood what he was saying. There was growing unrest in the conference room; the time by now was one o'clock at night.

At that moment the secretary of the Italian delegation entered the room and whispered something into the ear of the Italian representative, Count Tosti. Count Tosti turned pale, rose to his feet and, ignoring the fact that the Chinese delegate, Dr Ti, was still speaking, exclaimed hoarsely: 'Mr Chairman, I request a hearing. News has just been received that the Newts have flooded part of our province of Venice in the direction of Portogruaro.'

A terrible silence fell, with only the Chinese delegate continuing to speak.

'But the Chief Salamander warned you ages ago, didn't he?' Dr Carvalho grunted.

Professor Van Dott fidgeted impatiently and raised his hand. 'Mr Chairman, perhaps we could return to the matter under discussion. We are talking about Föng-tien province. We are authorised to offer the Japanese government compensation for it in gold. There is also the question of how much the states with an interest in this matter would pay our clients for removing China altogether.'

At that moment the night-time hams were listening to the Newt radio. 'You have been listening to a recording of the Barcarole from "The Tales of Hofmann",' the announcer squeaked. 'Hello, hello, we are now switching over to the region of Venice, Italy.'

And then all that was to be heard was a dark and boundless rushing sound as of rising waters.

10

Mr Povondra Takes
It Upon Himself

Who would have said that so much water and so many years had
passed under the bridge! Even our Mr Povondra is no longer
the doorman at the G. H. Bondy residence; he is now what you
might call a venerable old gentleman, peacefully enjoying the
fruits of his long and conscientious life in the form of a small
pension. But how far will a few hundreds go with these
horrendous wartime prices? A good job that a chap can now and
again catch a fish or two: there he would sit in his boat, rod in
hand, gazing – all that water flowing past in just a single day,
and where did it all come from? Sometimes he would hook a dace
and sometimes a perch; there were somehow or other more fish
about, probably because the rivers were so much shorter. Not
a bad fish, actually, perch; true, most of it was bones but the flesh
tasted a little like almonds. And Mother certainly knew how to
do them. Mr Povondra, of course, did not know that the fire on
which his wife cooked those perch was usually lit with those
newspaper cuttings which he used to collect and sort. To tell the
truth, Mr Povondra gave up collecting when he retired; instead
he got himself an aquarium where, along with little golden carp
he kept small newts and salamanders; he would look at them for
hours on end as they lay there motionless or crawled out on the
bank of stones he had built for them; then he would shake his
head and say: 'Who'd have thought it of them, Mother!' But
a man can't just sit and stare; that's why Mr Povondra took up
fishing. And why not, men must always have something to do,
Mother Povondra thought indulgently. Better that than if he
went to the pub to argue politics!

Yes, a lot, a great lot of water had passed under the bridge.
Even Frankie is no longer a schoolboy swatting his geography,
nor even a young man wearing out his socks chasing after

worldly vanities. He too is a man of mature years; thank God he's a junior clerk at the post office – so his conscientious study of geography was, after all, good for something. He's beginning to be sensible, Mr Povondra thought to himself as he let his boat drift a little below the Legionnaire's Bridge. He'll come and see me today; he's off on Sundays. I'll pick him up in the boat and we'll row up to the point of Archer's Island; the fish bite better there. And Frankie will tell me what's new in the papers. And then we'll go home, to Vyšehrad, and our daughter-in-law will bring the two children . . . For a little while Mr Povondra indulged in the peaceful happiness of being a grandfather. Why, little Mary will start school next year, he thought happily; and little Frankie, his grandson, already weighed thirty kilos! Mr Povondra had a strong and profound feeling that everything was part of vast and well-ordered world.

And over there by the water's edge his son was already waiting, waving to him. Mr Povondra rowed his boat to the bank. 'So you're here at last,' he said reprovingly. 'Watch out you don't fall in!'

'Are they biting?' the son inquired.

'Not too well,' the old gentleman grumbled. 'Go a bit upstream, shall we?'

It was a pleasant Sunday afternoon; it was not yet the hour when those lunatics and loafers rush home from their football and similar forms of madness. Prague was empty and quiet; the few people who were strolling along the embankment or over the bridge were in no hurry: they were walking in a decent and dignified manner. They were superior, sensible people who did not jostle in crowds or jeer at fishermen on the river. Papa Povondra again had that good and deep sensation of order.

'What news in the papers?' he asked with paternal severity.

'Nothing much, dad,' the son replied. 'All it says here is that those Newts have worked their way up to Dresden.'

'Well, then the Germans are in the shit,' the old gentleman decided. 'D'you know, Frankie, those Germans, they were an odd sort of nation. Educated but odd. I knew a German once, he was a driver at a factory; terribly rude man he was, that German. But kept his vehicle in order, I'll say that for him. So Germany too has disappeared from the map of the world,' Mr Povondra reflected. 'And the hullaballoo it used to make! Really dreadful: it was the army first and last, nothing but soldiering. But even the Germans aren't a match for the Newts. Believe me, I know those Newts. Remember me showing them to you when you were a little boy?'

'Look out, dad,' the son said. 'You've got a nibble.'

'It's only a minnow,' the old gentleman grumbled and moved his rod. So it's Germany's turn now, he mused. Well, one's no longer surprised at anything. The fuss that was made some years ago when the Newts inundated a country! Even if it was only Mesopotamia or China the papers were full of it. But by now no one's getting excited any more, Mr Povondra reflected sadly, blinking over his rod once or twice. One gets used to anything, and that's a fact. It's not happening here, so why worry? If only things weren't so dear! Take the price they're charging for coffee nowadays; well, of course, Brazil has also disappeared under the water. Bound to affect shop prices when part of the world's drowned!

Mr Povondra's float was bobbing on the gentle ripples. All those territories the Newts had flooded with the sea, the old gentleman reflected. There was Egypt, and India, and China – why, they even had a go at Russia, and what a huge country that used to be! When you think that the Black Sea now extended all the way up to the Arctic Circle – my, all that lot of water! There's no denying it: they've bitten off quite a chunk of our continents! A good job it took them so long . . .

'You say,' the old gentleman spoke up, 'those Newts have got to Dresden?'

'Sixteen kilometres from Dresden. That means nearly the whole of Saxony is under water.'

'I went there once with Mr Bondy,' Papa Povondra recalled. 'Used to be a tremendously rich country, Frankie, but to say you ate well there – no you couldn't say that. Otherwise a very decent lot, better than the Prussians. No comparison really.'

'But Prussia's gone too.'

'I'm not surprised,' the old gentleman snapped. 'I can't stand the Prussians. But the French will be all right now with Germany going down the drain. They'll heave a sigh of relief, they will.'

'Not for long, dad,' Frankie objected. 'It said in the paper recently that a good one-third of France is already drowned.' 'Yes,' the old gentleman sighed. 'We used to have a Frenchman, at Mr Bondy's I mean, a footman. Jean his name was. Always after the women, really disgusting it was. You know, you're punished for it in the end, all that frivolity.'

'But ten kilometres outside Paris they defeated the Newts, or so it said,' Frankie reported. 'Apparently they had mined the area and blew it all up. Routed two Newt army corps, it said.'

'Well, yes, the French are good soldiers,' Mr Povondra observed expertly. 'That Jean would stand no nonsense either. Don't know where he got his strength from. Reeked like a barber's shop but when he was in a scrap he certainly knew how to fight. But two Newt army corps, that's not enough. Come to think of it,' the old gentleman mused, 'people were better at fighting people. And it didn't take so long. With these Newts here the war's been going on for twelve years and still there's nothing; it's all preparation of more favourable positions . . . Now when I was a youngster a battle was a battle. You had 3 million men on one side and three million on the other,' the old gentleman gestured until the boat rocked, 'and then, hell, they charged each other . . . This here isn't a proper war at all,' Papa Povondra was getting angry. 'It's all concrete barriers, but a proper bayonet charge – what a hope!'

'But, dad, men and Newts can't get at each other,' Povondra junior tried to justify the modern method of warfare. 'You can't make a bayonet charge into the water, can you now?'

'That's just it,' Mr Povondra grunted contemptuously. 'They can't get at each other. But you set men against men, and you'd be surprised what they can do! But what does your lot know about war!'

'So long as it doesn't come here,' young Frankie said a little unexpectedly. 'You know, when a man has children . . .'

'What do you mean, here?' the old gentleman burst out somehow irritably. 'You mean here, to Prague?'

'Well, into Bohemia, yes,' Povondra junior said worriedly. 'I keep thinking that if the Newts have already got to Dresden . . .'

'Don't be silly,' Mr Povondra rebuked him. 'How could they get here? Across our mountains?'

'Perhaps along the Elbe – and then up the Vltava.'

Papa Povondra snorted angrily. 'Don't talk nonsense – along the Elbe? That would only get them as far as Podmoklí and no further. Why, it's all rocks there. I've been there. No fear, the Newts won't get through to us, we're all right. And the Swiss are all right too. That's the great advantage of not having a sea coast, you know. Anyone with a coast is in trouble nowadays.'

'But with the sea coming up all the way to Dresden . . .'

'That's where the Germans are,' the old gentleman declared dismissively. 'That's their lookout. But the Newts can't get through to us, stands to reason. They'd first have to remove those rocks – and can you imagine the work that would be?'

'Work,' Povondra junior objected gloomily, 'is something they're rather good at. Remember that in Guatemala they managed to submerge a whole mountain range.'

'That's different,' the old gentleman declared very resolutely. 'Don't talk so silly, Frankie! That was in Guatemala and not here. Things are different here.'

Povondra junior sighed. 'If you say so, dad. But when you consider that those brutes have already drowned about a fifth of the continents . . .'

'By the sea, you fool, but nowhere else. You don't understand politics. The states by the sea are at war with them but we aren't. We are a neutral country and that's why they can't touch us. That's the long and the short of it. And stop talking or I won't catch anything.'

Silence reigned over the water. The trees on Archer's Island were already casting long delicate shadows on the surface of the Vltava. From the bridge came the tinkle of the trams, and along the embankment strolled nursemaids with prams and conservatively clad people in their Sunday best.

'Dad,' young Povondra breathed in an almost childish voice.

'What is it?'

'Isn't that a catfish?'

'Where?'

From the river, immediately in front of the National Theatre, a large black head was showing above the water, slowly advancing upstream.

'Is it a catfish?' Povondra junior repeated.

The old gentleman dropped his rod. 'That?' he jerked out, pointing a shaking finger. 'That?'

The black head disappeared under the water.

'That was no catfish, Frankie,' the old gentleman said in what did not seem like his normal voice. 'We're going home. This is the end.'

'What end?'

'A Newt. So they're here already. We're going home,' he repeated, pulling his fishing rod apart with uncertain hands. 'So this is the end.'

'You're shaking all over,' Frankie said in alarm. 'Aren't you feeling well?'

'We're going home,' the old gentleman babbled excitedly, his chin chattering pitifully. 'I'm feeling cold. That's just what we needed! You realise, this is the end. So they've got here already. Christ, it's cold. I'd like to go home.'

Povondra junior looked at him searchingly and grabbed the oars. 'I'll take you back, dad,' he said, also in a voice not quite his own, and with vigorous strokes aimed the boat at the island. 'Just leave it, I'll tie her up.'

'Why is it suddenly so cold?' the old gentleman wondered, his teeth chattering.

'I'll give you a hand, dad. Come along now,' the younger man said soothingly and took his arm. 'I think you caught a chill on the water. That was only a bit of wood.'

The old gentleman was trembling like a leaf. 'A bit of wood, eh? Wood, my foot. I know a Newt when I see one, better than most people. Let me go!'

Povondra junior did what he had never before done in his life: he waved down a taxi. 'To Vyšehrad,' he said and pushed his father inside. 'I'll take you home, dad. It's getting late.'

'Yes, it is late,' Papa Povondra stammered. 'Too late. This is the end, Frankie. That was no bit of wood. It's them!'

Povondra junior practically had to carry his father up the steps. 'Get his bed ready, Mum,' he hurriedly whispered in the door. 'Got to get dad into bed, he's sick.'

And now Papa Povondra was lying on his featherbed; his nose was sticking out strangely from his face and his lips were mouthing and mumbling something incomprehensible; how old he was looking. Now he had calmed down a little . . .

'Are you feeling better, dad?'

At the foot of the bed Mother Povondra stood sniffing and crying into her apron; their daughter-in-law was lighting a fire in the stove, and the children, little Frankie and Mary, were staring at their granddad with wide frightened eyes, as if they did not recognise him.

'Don't you want the doctor, dad?'

Papa Povondra looked at the children and whispered something; and suddenly tears began to stream from his eyes.

'Do you want anything, dad?'

'It was me, it was me,' the old gentleman whispered. 'I want you to know that it was all my fault. If I hadn't let that captain in to see Mr Bondy none of this would ever have happened . . .'

'But nothing has happened, dad,' Povondra junior said soothingly.

'You don't understand,' the old gentleman wheezed. 'This is the end, you know. The end of the world. Now the sea's going to come here too, now that the Newts have got here. It's all my doing; I shouldn't have let that captain in . . . People should know who's to blame for it all.'

'Nonsense,' the son said harshly. 'Don't let this idea go to your head. Everybody did it. The states did it, finance did it . . . They all wanted to have as many Newts as possible. They all wanted to make money out of them. We sent them armaments too and all sorts of things . . . We are all responsible for it.'

Papa Povondra fidgeted restlessly: 'Oceans covered everything once, and they'll do so again. This is the end of the world. A gentleman told me once that where Prague is now was sea-bed at one time. I think the Newts were the cause of it even then. D'you know, I shouldn't have let that captain in. Something was telling me, don't do it - but then I thought maybe that captain would give me a tip . . . And he never did, you know. For no purpose at all I've wrecked the whole world . . .' The old gentleman was swallowing something like tears. 'I know, I know very well that this is the end for us. I know it was my fault . . .'

'Wouldn't you like some tea, granddad?' the younger Mrs Povondra asked compassionately.

'All I'd like,' the old gentleman sighed, 'all I'd like is for these children to forgive me.'

11

The Author Talks to Himself

'You're going to leave it there like that?' the author's inner voice piped up at this point.

'What do you mean?' the writer asked a little uncertainly.

'You're letting Mr Povondra die like this?'

'Well,' the author defended himself; 'I don't like doing it but . . . After all, Mr Povondra has reached a ripe old age; let's say he's quite a bit over seventy . . .'

'And you're leaving him in this mental agony? You won't even tell him, granddad, things aren't quite as bad really; the world isn't going to perish from the Newts; mankind will be saved, and you'll live to see it? Can't you please do something for him?'

'All right, I'll send the doctor to him,' suggested the author. 'The old gentleman's probably got a nervous fever; at his age, of course, this can easily lead to pneumonia but maybe, God willing, he'll pull through; perhaps he'll live to dandle little Mary on his knee and question her on what she learned at school . . . The joys of old age, why yes; let the old gentleman have the joys of old age!'

'Some joys,' the inner voice jeered. 'He'll clasp that child to him in his old arms, frightened that she too might one day have to flee from the rushing waters which will inexorably drown the whole world; he'll knit his bushy eyebrows in terror and whisper: I did all that, Mary dear, I did all that . . . Listen, do you *really* want to let all mankind perish?'

The author frowned. 'Don't ask me what I want. Do you suppose *I* am making the continents crumble into dust, do you suppose *I* wanted this kind of ending? It is simply the logic of events; how can I interfere with it? I did what I could; I warned people in good time; that X, that was partly me. I preached: don't give the Newts weapons or high explosives, stop that hideous trade in salamanders, and so on – you know what happened. Everybody always had a thousand perfectly sound economic and political arguments why this wasn't possible. I'm not a politician nor an economist; how could I convince them? So what's to be done? The world will probably disintegrate and become inundated – but at least it will do so for universally accepted political and economic reasons, at least it will do so with the aid of science, engineering and public opinion, with the application of all human ingenuity! No cosmic catastrophe – just national, power-political, economic and other reasons. What can you do against that?'

The inner voice was silent for a while. 'And aren't you sorry for mankind?'

'Hold it, not so fast! No one's saying the whole of mankind has to perish. The Newts only need more coasts on which to live and lay their eggs. Let's say that instead of compact continents they'll shape the dry land into long spaghetti, so they'll have the maximum coastlines. Let's say that some people will survive on those strips of dry land, all right? And that they'll make metals and other manufactures for the salamanders. After all, the Newts can't work with fire themselves, see?'

'So men will serve the Newts.'

'That's right, if you want to call it that. They'll simply work in their factories as they are doing now. They'll just have different masters. When all's said and done, it mightn't be all that different . . .'

'And you're not sorry for mankind?'

'For God's sake leave me alone! What can I do? It's what people wanted; they all wanted to have Newts, commerce wanted them, and industry and engineering, the statesman wanted them and the military gentlemen did. Even young Povondra said so: we are all responsible for it. Of course, I am sorry for mankind! But I was most sorry for it when I watched it rushing headlong to its own ruin. It's enough to make you want to scream, looking back at it now. Scream and raise your hands as a man might when he sees a train running on to the wrong track. Too late to stop it. The Newts will go on multiplying, they'll go on reducing the old continents piece by piece . . . Don't you remember how Wolf Meynert proved that man must make room for the Newts, and only the salamanders will establish a happy, uniform and homogeneous world . . .'

'For Christ's sake, Wolf Meynert! Wolf Meynert's an intellectual. Have you ever known anything too horrible, too murderous or too nonsensical for an intellectual not to want to seize on it for the purpose of regenerating the world? Leave it at that. Do you know what little Mary is doing at this moment?'

'Little Mary? I suppose she's playing in Vyšehrad. You must be quiet, she's been told, granddad's sleeping. She doesn't know what to do and is terribly bored . . .'

'So what's she doing?'

'I've no idea. Probably trying to touch the tip of her nose with the tip of her tongue.'

'There you are. And you'd let something like a new Flood overcome her?'

'Stop it now! D'you think I can work miracles? What must be will be. Let everything take its inexorable course! There's some kind of consolation even in this: that whatever is happening follows its own inevitability and its own law.'

'Wouldn't it be possible to stop the Newts somehow?'

'It wouldn't. There are too many of them. Room's got to be made for them.'

'Couldn't they be made to die out somehow? Maybe by some new disease or through degeneration . . .'

'Too facile, old chap. Why should Nature put right what man has messed up? There you are, even you don't believe any longer that men will help themselves. In the end you'd like to rely on mankind being saved by someone or something! Let me ask you this; do you know who *even now*, with one-fifth of Europe inundated, is supplying the Newts with high explosives and torpedoes and drills? Do you know who is feverishly working in laboratories night and day to discover even more efficient machines and substances to blow up the world? Do you know who is lending money to the Newts, who is financing this End of the World, this whole new Flood?'

'I do. Every factory in the world. Every bank. Every country.'

'So there you are. If it was merely a case of Newts against people something might perhaps be done; but people against people – that's something you cannot stop.'

'Hold on – people against people! That gives me an idea. Perhaps in the end we might get Newts against Newts.'

'Newts against Newts? How do you mean?'

'For instance . . . once the salamanders have become too numerous they might squabble amongst themselves for some little piece of coast, for some bay or something; next they'll be fighting together for bigger and better coasts; and in the end they'll have to fight for world coasts – don't you think? Newts against Newts! How's that? Wouldn't *that* be the logic of history?'

'Oh no, that won't do. Surely Newts can't fight Newts. That would go against nature. Surely the Newts are one genus.'

'So are men one genus, old chap. And, as you've seen, it doesn't stop them. One genus, and look at all the things they're fighting over! No longer over somewhere to live, but for power, for prestige, for influence, for glory, for markets and heaven knows what else! So why shouldn't salamanders fight amongst themselves, for instance for prestige?'

'But why should they do so? What would they get out of it?'

'Nothing, except possibly that one lot would temporarily have more coasts and more power than another lot. And after a while it would be reversed.'

'And why should one lot have more power than another? Surely they are all equal, they are all Newts; they all have the same skeleton, they are equally ugly and equally mediocre. So why should they kill each other off? In the name of what would they be fighting each other?'

'Just leave them alone; something's bound to crop up. How's this: one lot's living on the western coast and another on the eastern: they could fight each other under the banner of West against East. Here you have the European salamanders and down there the African; it would be unnatural if sooner or later the ones didn't want to be something more than the others! So they'll want to prove it to them in the name of civilisation, or expansion, or I don't know what: some ideological or political reasons will always be able to be found to make the Newts of one coast slit the throats of the Newts of another. The salamanders have the same civilisation as us, old chap; they won't be short of power-political, economic, legal, cultural or other arguments.'

'And they've got weapons. Don't forget that they're superbly armed.'

'Oh yes, they've got heaps of arms. So there you are. Just think: aren't they bound to learn from man how history is made?'

'Wait a minute, wait a minute!' (The author has leapt to his feet and has begun to pace his study.) 'You're right: it would be unnatural for them not to learn from man! I'm beginning to see it. You need only look at the map of the world . . . damn, where is that map of the world?'

'I can see it.'

'Right then. Here's your Atlantic with the Mediterranean and the North Sea. Over here we've got Europe and over there is America . . . So here is the cradle of culture and modern civilisation. Somewhere here the ancient Atlantis lies drowned . . .'

'And now the Newts are drowning a new Atlantis for us.'

'That's just it. And here you have the Pacific and the Indian Ocean. The ancient, mysterious Orient, old chap. The cradle of mankind, it is said. Somewhere here, east of Africa, the mythical Lemuria lies beneath the waves. Here is Sumatra, and a little to the west of it . . .'

'. . . the tiny island of Tana Masa. The cradle of the Newts.'

'That's it. And there King Salamander reigns, the spiritual head of the salamanders. Here Captain van Toch's tapa-boys are still found, the original semi-savage Pacific Newts. In short, *their* Orient, see? That whole area is now called Lemuria, whereas that other region, the civilised, Europeanised and Americanised, modern and technologically advanced region is Atlantis. There the dictator is the Chief Salamander, a great conqueror, engineer and soldier, the Genghis Khan of the Newts, the destroyer of continents. A terrific personality, old chap.'

('Listen, is he *really* a Newt?')

('No. The Chief Salamander is a human. His real name is Andreas Schultze and during the World War he was a sergeant-major somewhere.')

('That explains it!')

('Well, yes. So now you've got it.') All right, then: here's Atlantis and here is Lemuria. This division has geographical, administrative, cultural reasons . . .'

'. . . and national ones. Don't forget the national reasons. The Lemurian salamanders speak pidgin English while the Atlantian ones speak Basic English.'

'Very well. In the course of time the Atlantians work their way through the Suez Canal into the Indian Ocean . . .'

'Naturally. The classic road to the East.'

'Correct. On the other hand, the Lemurian Newts are pushing past the Cape of Good Hope to the west coast of Africa. Because they're claiming that *all* Africa belongs to the Lemurians.'

'Naturally.'

'Their slogan is Lemuria for the Lemurians, foreigners out, and so on. A gulf of mistrust and ancient enmity opens between Atlantians and Lemurians. Enmity of life and death.'

'In other words, they become nations.'

'Right. The Atlantians despise the Lemurians and call them dirty savages. The Lemurians for their part hate the Atlantian Newts and regard them as imperialists, western devils and violators of ancient, pure and original Newtdom. The Chief Salamander demands concessions on the Lemurian coasts, allegedly in the interests of trade and civilisation. The venerable old King Salamander, however reluctantly, has to give in; he is simply less well armed. In Tigris Bay, not far from where Baghdad stood, the balloon goes up: native Lemurians raid an Atlantian concession and kill two Atlantian officers, allegedly for some nationalistic insult. As a result . . .'

'. . . war breaks out. Naturally.'

'Yes, a world war of Newts against Newts.'

'In the name of Culture and Justice.'

'And in the name of Genuine Newtdom. In the name of National Glory and Greatness. The slogan is: it's them or us. The Lemurians, armed with Malayan krises and Yogi daggers, mercilessly slit the throats of the Atlantian invaders; in return the more advanced Atlantians, with their European education, release poisonous chemicals and cultures of lethal bacteria into the Lemurian seas – and so successfully that all the world oceans are infested. The sea is infected with an artificial culture of gill pest. And that, old chap, is the end. The Newts become extinct.'

'All of them?'

'Every one of them. They'll be an extinct race. All that's left of them is that ancient Oeningen imprint of Andrias Scheuchzeri.'

'And what about the humans?'

'The humans? Oh yes, the humans. Well, they gradually start coming down from the mountains to the shores of what remains of the continents, but the ocean will stink for a long time yet from the decomposition of the Newts. The continents will slowly grow in size again with fluvial deposits, the sea will gradually retreat inch by inch, and everything will be almost as it used to be. A new legend will arise of a Great Flood sent by God upon a sinful humanity. And there will be stories of drowned mythical lands said to have been the cradle of human culture; there will perhaps be legends about some country called England or France or Germany . . .'

'And then?'

'. . . I don't know how it goes on.'

Other Books by Karel Čapek
Available from Catbird Press